MURDER
ON THE
SALSETTE

Also by Conrad Allen

MURDER

ON THE

SALSETTE

Conrad Allen

ST. MARTIN'S MINOTAUR 🅼 NEW YORK

www.minotaurbooks.com

Library of Congress Cataloging-in-Publication Data

Allen, Conrad, 1940–
    Murder on the Salsette / Conrad Allen.—1st ed.
        p.   cm.
    ISBN 0-312-30793-4
    EAN 978-0312-30793-6
    1. Dillman, George Porter (Fictitious character)—Fiction.   2. Masefield, Genevieve (Fictitious character)—Fiction.   3. Private investigators—Fiction. 4. Ocean travel—Fiction.   I. Title.

PR6063.I3 175M898 2005
823'.914—dc22

                                                              2004057030
First Edition: April 2005

10 9 8 7 6 5 4 3 2 1

This one is for Judith.
Bon voyage!

MURDER
ON THE
SALSETTE

ONE

Bombay was truly a meeting place of nations. As he stood in the harbor and gazed around, George Porter Dillman saw faces of many differing hues and heard voices in a confusing variety of languages. He had never been in such a cosmopolitan environment before. Bombay was not only the gateway to India, it was a large, populous, vibrant, utterly fascinating city in its own right. Unlike many ports, which were simply modes of access to a country or an island, it was a place where the traveler was encouraged to stay, to explore, and to marvel. During his short time there, Dillman had certainly marveled at its sights and relished its unique atmosphere.

Situated on a peninsula some eleven miles long, the city occupied a site that formed a natural breakwater, enclosing the bay. Docks and wharves abounded, all of them swarming with people. Apart from its cordial hospitality, Dillman's abiding memories of Bombay would be its baking heat, its pungent odors, and its deafening noise.

1

Picking his way through the crowd, it seemed to him that the harbor was the hottest, smelliest, and most earsplitting part of the city. It was also one of the busiest. Not only were the wharves teeming with bodies, the water itself was packed with craft of all sizes and shapes. Steamships and tugboats were very much in a minority, surrounded by a veritable forest of masts as ketches, barges, schooners, trawlers, cutters, yawls, sloops, dhows, and other sailing vessels jostled for position.

Having worked in the family business of designing and building oceangoing yachts, Dillman was delighted to see so much canvas still in use. He paused to enjoy the scene before moving on. In his white linen suit and his straw hat, he was a striking figure, tall, lithe, and elegant, obviously at ease in foreign surroundings and unperturbed by the hectic bustle all around him. The man who fell in beside him was far less relaxed. Mopping his brow with a spotted handkerchief, he was short, florid, and running to fat. Though he was close to Dillman's age—in his early thirties—he looked much older and walked with a stoop.

"I do hope it's cooler onboard the ship," he observed.

"I'm sure that it will be," replied Dillman.

"Ah, you're an American," said the other, hearing the Bostonian accent. "I thought you were one of us."

"In some senses, I am. My family comes from English stock."

"You'll never persuade me that that's the same thing as being born and brought up in the Home Counties. America is a different planet. So is India, for that matter. Can't wait to get back to civilization."

"India's civilization is much older than yours," noted Dillman.

"Perhaps that's what's wrong with it." He offered a sweaty palm. "Nevin is the name. Dudley Nevin."

"Pleased to meet you," said Dillman, shaking his hand. "My name is George Dillman."

"What brings you to Bombay, Mr. Dillman?"

"Curiosity. I stopped off on the way back from Australia."

"You're leaving just in time," said Nevin. "When the monsoon season gets under way, India is well nigh unbearable. Not that it's tolerable at the best of times, mark you. I loathe the country."

"Then why come to India in the first place?"

"I *work* here."

"In Bombay?"

"No, in Delhi. I had to travel all the way here in one of those giant frying pans they call trains. It was murder, Mr. Dillman," he complained. "There were times when I felt like one of those men in the fiery furnace. What were their names?"

"Shadrach, Meschach, and Abednego."

"Those are the chaps."

"Yet they survived the ordeal," Dillman reminded him. "Even when the furnace was heated to seven times its normal temperature, they came out unscathed. Just like you, Mr. Nevin."

"I don't feel unscathed."

"What do you do in Delhi?"

"Pray for my contract of employment to come to an end."

"Are you in business?"

"The Civil Service."

"Why take the job if you dislike the country?"

"Because I didn't know that I *would* dislike it so much until I got here," said Nevin. "I was beguiled by Kipling. He made India sound so interesting. I thought that coming here would be a big adventure."

"I'm sorry it's disappointed you. My time here has been delightful."

"How long have you stayed?"

"Only a week."

"Try sticking it out for a year," moaned Nevin. "Then you'd

get some idea of how bad it can be. This climate is torture for Europeans."

Dillman gave a wry smile. "I'm an American, remember."

"I was forgetting."

Nevin was a tense, unhappy, irritable man but Dillman sensed that he would improve on acquaintance. He looked forward to meeting the Englishman when the latter was not under such obvious pressure. They had now joined the queue that snaked toward the gangway and Dillman took the opportunity to appraise the vessel on which they were about to sail. Named after one of the islands off Bombay harbor, the *Salsette* had the reputation of being the most beautiful ship owned by the P & O—the Peninsular and Oriental Steam Navigation Company. George Dillman could see why.

With her two yellow funnels and two masts in perfect proportion, the *Salsette* was an arresting sight. She had a long, sleek, white-painted hull that reminded Dillman of a yacht, and the large golden cockerel at her masthead signified that she was the fastest ship in the fleet. Designed for the express mail and passenger shuttle between Bombay and Aden, she was trim and refined, accommodating a hundred first-class passengers and a hundred and twenty second-class, but having limited cargo space. Dillman had once worked for Cunard, sailing a number of times on each of its acknowledged "pretty sisters," the *Caronia* and the *Carmania*, yet he was forced to admit that the *Salsette* was an even more attractive example of marine architecture. It was not just her smaller size—her tonnage was less than a third that of the Cunard liners—it was to do with her intrinsic design. Moored in her berth, she had undeniable charm.

Dillman was still admiring her when Nevin spoke to him again.

"Why are you going to Aden?" he asked.

"To pick up a ship to London," replied Dillman.

"Lucky old you!"

"Aren't you going home to England, Mr. Nevin?"

"If only I were!" sighed the other. "No, I don't have enough time. I'm visiting a cousin who has a diplomatic posting in Aden. Anything to get away from India for a while."

"If you hate it so much, why do you stay?"

"Three main reasons. One, I'm contracted to work in Delhi. Two, I left England under something of a cloud so I might not be entirely welcome there. Three—most important of all—my father."

"How does he come into it?"

"Old soldier. Served most of his time in India and loved it. He more or less bullied me into coming here. Said it would make a man of me."

"Yet you didn't join the army."

"Heavens, no! Far too dangerous."

"Things are fairly stable here now, aren't they?"

"Don't you believe it, Mr. Dillman," warned Nevin. "This country is brimming with resentment against us. Ungrateful lot, if you ask me. Can't they see what we've done for them?" he asked with a touch of indignation. "Granted, we may not be on the verge of another mutiny but there are hotheads everywhere, stirring up trouble. It was only a couple of years ago that someone organized mass picketing of the liquor shops here in Bombay."

"Why? To reduce government excise revenue?"

"Yes. And it gave them the chance to flex their muscles. It's the same in Punjab, Madras, and elsewhere. Too many extremists, wanting to give us a bloody nose."

"Nobody likes being ruled by a distant foreign power."

Nevin laughed. "I might have known an American would take their side," he said good-humoredly. "Because you threw off your colonial shackles, you encourage others to do the same. I think I've found you out, sir. You're a rabble-rouser."

"I confess it," said Dillman, amused by the notion.

"But you take my point, don't you? If there *is* trouble, I don't want to be drafted in as part of the army to quell it with force. I don't have my father's blood lust." He became reflective. "Mark you, I wouldn't have minded the other side to military life."

"The other side?"

"The luxury, Mr. Dillman. All that leisure time to play polo or drink as much as you wanted at the club. And you have to do so little for yourself. When my father was only a lieutenant," he recalled, "he had twelve servants at his beck and call. Imagine that."

"I'm not sure that I'd care to," said Dillman. "It breeds laziness."

"It epitomizes the superiority of the British nation."

"That's not how I see it, Mr. Nevin."

"Ah, yes," said Nevin with a chuckle. "You Americans believe all that nonsense about equality. You don't acknowledge that one people can be superior to another. If you lived in India as long as I have, you'd soon change your tune."

"I very much doubt that."

They were on edge of the gangway now. Dillman put down his suitcase so that he could take his ticket from his pocket. Nevin did likewise. Dabbing at his brow with the handkerchief, he gave his companion a shrewd glance.

"Traveling alone, I suppose?" he said.

"Yes," answered Dillman. "Quite alone."

"In that case, I hope that we'll see more of each other."

"So do I."

"I'll promise to be in a more amenable mood next time."

"Being on Indian soil obviously upsets you."

"That's why I'm so anxious to get away from it, Mr. Dillman."

"You said earlier that you left England under a cloud."

"That's right. Blotted my copybook."

"In what way?"

"That would be telling," said Nevin with a sly grin. "I think I'd need to know you a lot better before I'd even consider letting you in on the secret."

Genevieve Masefield had befriended them in the customs shed. It wasn't merely the sound of English voices that drew her to them, it was the fact that one of the ladies was in a Bath chair. Genevieve was struck by the bravery needed to travel halfway across the world in open defiance of a physical handicap. She was even more impressed when she heard what their itinerary had been. Constance Simcoe rattled off the names.

"Jaipur, Delhi, Simla, Amritsar, Lahore," she said. "It was so much cooler up in the hills. We kept on the move yet we feel we've only scratched the surface of India."

"You're so courageous," said Genevieve.

"Not really, Miss Masefield. We're very nosey, that's all."

"You make me feel so provincial."

"Didn't you say you'd just come back from Australia?"

"Well, yes," agreed Genevieve.

"Then you're a seasoned traveler."

"I only saw Perth, really. I didn't have the time or the inclination to explore a country in the way that you've done."

"We did have some assistance," explained Tabitha Simcoe, pushing her mother along in the Bath chair while porters carried the luggage in their wake. "Uncle Harold lives in Bombay. He was our guide for the first part of the tour."

"About time my brother did something useful," opined Constance.

"Mother!"

7

"Harold was never the most helpful person. I love him dearly, of course, but he can be very selfish and inconsiderate."

"He was a saint," argued Tabitha. "After all that he did for us, it's unkind of you to say anything different. Really, Mother! What will Miss Masefield think of us?"

"I think that you're an example to us all," said Genevieve.

Constance smiled serenely. "The best way to see India is from a Bath chair," she remarked. "You can drink it slowly in as you roll along."

"Only if someone is kind enough to push you, Mrs. Simcoe."

"That's where Tabby comes in."

"I try," her daughter said loyally.

The family likeness was not strong. Constance Simcoe was a thin, angular, wasted woman in her late fifties with a haggard face that was cunningly hidden by wisps of hair that had been trained around its periphery. Her voice suggested breeding, her clothing hinted at wealth. Her manner had a kind of imperious jocularity to it. Tabitha, by contrast, was a tall, full-bodied, handsome woman in her twenties with the resigned look of someone who had given up all hope of marriage in order to look after her mother. Like Genevieve, both of them wore wide-brimmed straw hats to ward off the hot sun, though thick clouds were now gathering to block out its rays. When they came out of the customs shed, Constance Simcoe held a small bottle to her nose and inhaled.

"I need something to take away the stink," she said, slipping the bottle back into her purse. "It's the one thing about Indian cities that I find a little repulsive. They do reek somewhat. We sprinkled gallons of lavender water on our clothing, didn't we, Tabby?"

"Yes, Mother."

"But even that didn't always do the trick."

"No, Mother."

"Attention to hygiene is not what it should be."

"This is India," said Tabitha. "It's not like Cheltenham."

"You don't need to tell me that," grumbled her mother, rolling her eyes in disapproval. "In Cheltenham—thank God—you wouldn't find men relieving themselves against the nearest wall. It's a most disagreeable habit."

"Is that where you live?" said Genevieve. "In Cheltenham?"

"Yes, Miss Masefield. It's the center of our universe. And you?"

"London."

"Are you looking forward to going home?"

"Very much so. I'm looking forward to the voyage, as well."

"So are we. One meets such interesting people."

Genevieve did not realize that a compliment had just been paid to her. She was too busy looking up at the ship that awaited them at the pier. The *Salsette* was much smaller than Genevieve had anticipated but her lines and proportions had an instant appeal for her. Silhouetted against a sky that was slowly darkening, the bright colors of the vessel stood out even more. Tabitha noticed the involuntary smile that lit up Genevieve's face.

"Have you sailed on the *Salsette* before?" she wondered.

"No," replied Genevieve.

"We did. Such a joy to look at, isn't she?"

"But not such a joy to sail in," added her mother. "The *Salsette* rolled too much for my liking. I'd prefer a much larger vessel like the *Marmora.*"

"I sailed on her to Australia," said Genevieve.

"How did you find the voyage?"

"I had no complaints whatsoever, Mrs. Simcoe."

"Nor did we when the *Marmora* took us to Egypt last year. Ah," she went on with an air of satisfaction, as she saw two figures descending on her. "I've been spotted."

Clad in smart uniforms, the two stewards had come to help

her onto the ship. One of them took over the task of pushing the Bath chair while the other asked the passengers ahead to stand aside and let them through. Whisked along with the others, Genevieve found herself jumping the queue. When they reached the gangplank, the two men lifted the Bath chair and carried it between them, taking care to keep it on an even keel. Tabitha took advantage of her brief moment alone with Genevieve to confide something to her.

"We're not really brave," she said timidly. "To be honest, there were times when I was so frightened that I wished we were back in Cheltenham. No, Miss Masefield, *you're* the only person who's shown true bravery."

Genevieve was surprised. "Me?" she said.

"You've done something that I'd never dare to do."

"Have I, Miss Simcoe?"

"You went on a long voyage on your own," said Tabitha wistfully. "The very thought of it terrifies me. Look at you. You're a beautiful young woman yet you had no qualms about sailing all the way to Australia and back. That takes real courage."

Max Cannadine was a portly Englishman in his early forties with a pleasant face and short dark hair that was bisected by a center parting. As purser on the *Salsette,* he had a wide range of responsibilities. One of them was to welcome Dillman aboard and he did so with alacrity, pumping the American's arm and beaming at him.

"Delighted to have you with us, Mr. Dillman," he said.

"Thank you, Mr. Cannadine."

"Your reputation goes before you."

"Is that good or bad?"

"Excellent. You're a credit to P and O. And from what I hear, you had a wonderful record of success when you worked for Cunard, as well. I can sleep easily in my bunk, knowing that we have such a brilliant detective onboard."

"There are two of us," Dillman said modestly. "Genevieve Masefield deserves just as much praise as I do. We work as a team. Without her, I'd not be nearly so effective."

"I'm anxious to meet the lady."

"Genevieve will be along in due course."

They were in the purser's office, a small but impeccably tidy room with a desk, a few upright chairs, a couple of filing cabinets, and prints of other P and O vessels on the walls. As soon as he had unpacked in his cabin, Dillman had sought out the purser. His first impression was that Cannadine would be friendly and cooperative.

"I'm only sorry that we can't offer you something to test your mettle," said the purser, waving his visitor to a chair. "Very little happens on the *Salsette,* I'm afraid."

"You must have some petty crime."

"An occasional pickpocket, maybe. Yes, and the odd cardsharp. Nothing to offer you and your partner a challenge worthy of you. There isn't really the time for anyone to do any dastardly deeds. On average, it takes us only four days to reach Aden."

"Murder can take less than four seconds, Mr. Cannadine."

"Nothing like that ever occurs on the *Salsette.*"

"I hope that it never does."

"It's always been such a lucky ship. At least, I've always found it so. The passengers provide the interest, of course, but we're also a mail shuttle, connecting with the Australian steamers that dock at Aden every other week." The purser grinned. "You might call us a nautical version of the Pony Express."

"A sort of Sea Horse, you mean?"

Cannadine laughed. "Fair comment!"

"Don't worry about us," said Dillman. "Genevieve and I will just fade into the background. Having so few passengers will make our job considerably easier. We had well over two thousand on the *Lusitania*."

"How on earth did you keep an eye on that lot?"

"Nervously."

The purser laughed again, then he picked up some papers from his desk and handed them to Dillman. "Passenger lists," he explained. "Just to let you know who everyone is and where their cabins are. Nobody famous onboard this time. We've carried royalty in the past."

"What about drugs?"

"What about them?"

"Well, even during my short visit to Bombay, I saw how much opium and *bhang* were being smoked. Has anyone ever tried to smuggle it out in appreciable quantities?"

"Not that I know of, Mr. Dillman."

"It must be a temptation. It would be a lucrative trade."

"Lucrative but despicable," said Cannadine, seriously, "I'd hate to think that the *Salsette* is helping to line the pockets of any drug smugglers. But then," he went on, relaxing, "there's no danger of that on this trip. We have you and Miss Masefield as our guard dogs."

"We'll keep a close eye on everyone, Mr. Cannadine."

"Good." The purser rubbed his hands together. "I'm sure that it's going to be a trouble-free voyage from start to finish. Aren't you?"

Before Dillman could reply, an answer came from above. After a loud rumble of thunder, there was a sudden flash of lightning that illumined the office for a split second. An electric storm was at hand.

"Oh dear!" said Cannadine. "I think I spoke too soon."

TWO

Genevieve Masefield had never seen anything like it. The storm came so quickly and unexpectedly that it took her completely unawares. She was unpacking her trunk when she heard the boom of thunder and saw the flash of lightning at the porthole of her cabin. Within seconds, the heavens opened and rain fell with a speed and violence that shocked her. Scouring the ship, it sent everyone running for cover. It drummed on the hull, pounded on the deck, danced on the lifeboats, and made a series of rapid pinging sounds on the funnels, turning the *Salsette* into a gigantic musical instrument. Genevieve thought that a hose had been turned on the glass in her porthole. Thunder rolled again and there was another flash of lightning, even more vivid than the first, before the rain seemed to increase its velocity.

She was grateful that she was already aboard. Several passengers were still making their way along the pier, caught in the downpour and soaked to the skin, their summer-wear no protection against the ferocity of the storm. Hunched up, and protesting noisily, they scampered toward the gangway through the impromptu pools of water that had already formed on the ground. Heavy rain might bring relief from the oppressive heat but it also spread confusion and drenched its victims. Genevieve tried in vain to carry on hanging up her dresses in the wardrobe. The fury of the storm kept distracting her.

Though it lasted a mere ten minutes, it seemed like an age to Genevieve before the deluge slowly began to ease off. The noise softened, the sky brightened, and her porthole was no longer under attack by gushing water. She began to relax, consoling herself with the thought that at least the torrent had hit them while they were still in Bombay harbor. Had they been caught in open sea, the effect would have been even more dramatic. In the course of her travels, Genevieve had endured many squalls in midocean but she had always been forewarned about those. None had unsettled her as much as this stormy farewell to India.

When the rain finally stopped, she was able to unpack the last few items. The cabin was small but well-appointed and it would offer her both comfort and privacy on the short voyage to Aden. The only problem was that she would be sleeping in it alone. There was a tapping on the door that Genevieve recognized as the signal from her partner. She opened the door to admit George Dillman. Embracing her warmly, he kissed her on the lips.

"Settling in?" he asked.

"I was until that thunderstorm broke out."

"Yes, it was rather spectacular, wasn't it?"

"I was quite scared, George."

"Of a little drop of rain? No need to be."

"It's easy to say that," she said, "but it took me by surprise."

"We've been building up to it for days, Genevieve. If we stayed on for the monsoon season, you'd see much more rain than that."

"Then I'm glad we're leaving."

"Are you?" he said with mock disappointment. "I hoped that you'd have fond memories of Bombay. I certainly do."

"And so do I," she promised, slipping her arms around his neck to kiss him. "It was blissful, George. You know that."

"Unforgettable."

The visit to Bombay had been a rare break in their duties. They had seized on the opportunity of a week there in order to sample some of the delights of India and to enjoy a delayed honeymoon. Having worked together closely for some time, they had been married by the captain aboard the *Marmora* on a trip to Australia. Assignments on other P & O vessels had forced them to postpone the celebrations until now, but the long wait had been very worthwhile.

"I do wish we could share a cabin," she said.

"It's too dangerous."

"But we're husband and wife now."

"*We* know that, darling," he told her, "but it's important that nobody else does. It would limit us a great deal. There are places we can go as individuals that we'd never reach as a couple."

"It seems so strange—pretending to be single again."

"Strange but necessary. Besides, you won't have to keep up the pretense indefinitely. Who knows? You may hear a familiar knock on your door one of these nights."

"It will probably be the steward, bringing me a cup of cocoa."

"A steward who answers to the name of George Porter Dillman."

She laughed. "Does that mean I have to tip you?"

"We'll see." He glanced around her cabin and gave a nod of approval. "Almost identical to mine," he said. "I'm at the far end of the corridor, by the way. Number forty-two."

"I prefer you in here."

"I prefer it, as well, but we'll have to ration ourselves. To all intents and purposes, we're traveling independently. Even the purser doesn't realize that we're married."

"Have you met him yet?"

"Yes," replied Dillman. "His name is Max Cannadine. I took to him at once. He's one of those nice, helpful, efficient characters that P and O always manages to find. Make yourself known to him when you have a moment."

"I will, George. Did you meet anyone else?"

"Only a fellow called Dudley Nevin. He's a disgruntled civil servant who wishes he'd never come anywhere near India. He's sneaking off to Aden to visit a cousin."

"How can anyone be disgruntled with India?" she asked with a shrug. "It's such a beautiful country."

"Not if you're sitting behind a desk all day long."

"But it has a sense of mystery. You can almost feel it."

"I fancy that Mr. Nevin has an air of mystery about him, as well," he decided. "A man with hidden depths. I intend to plumb some of them. We've arranged to have dinner together."

"I've agreed to dine with the Simcoes."

"Who are they?"

"Constance and Tabitha Simcoe," she said. "They're a mother and daughter who've been touring northern India. I take my hat off to them."

"Why?"

"Mrs. Simcoe is disabled. She has to go everywhere in a Bath chair. Think of the sorts of problems that that must create. Yet they didn't let it deter them at all."

"What are they like?"

"Very pleasant and very English. They come from Cheltenham."

"I daresay I'll bump into them in due course."

"You'll have no difficulty picking them out, George."

"Not if one of them is in a Bath chair. Besides," he went on, taking something from his inside pocket, "they'll be part of a small but solid English contingent we have aboard." He handed her some papers. "This is the passenger list that the purser gave me. We have almost every nation under the sun on the *Salsette*."

"Even some Americans?" she teased.

"Yes, there's enough of us to make our presence felt. But we also have French, Italians, Dutch, Germans, Chinese, a lone Irishman, Scandinavians, and Portuguese—in addition to a fair number of Indians and Arabs, that is."

"You've obviously done your homework."

"I like to know who my fellow passengers are, Genevieve."

"Anyone who needs careful watching?"

"The lady in cabin number eleven."

"But that's *my* cabin," she said.

He grinned. "Then I'll have to watch you very carefully, won't I?"

Dillman enfolded her lovingly in his arms once again.

Paulo Morelli made sure that nobody was looking before he took a comb from his pocket. Standing in front of the gilt-framed mirror, he slicked his hair back neatly then showed his teeth in a dazzling smile. A steward in first class, Morelli was a slim, swarthy, handsome young man of middle height who took immense pride in his appearance. He was using the comb on his mustache when the purser came down the corridor. Max Cannadine smiled tolerantly.

"Preening yourself yet again, Paulo?" he taunted.

"I like to look nice for my passengers," said the other, putting the comb away. "It is—how you say it—an article of faith with me."

"The only thing you're interested in is impressing the ladies."

"Why not, Mr. Cannadine? Every man needs a hobby."

"You're not paid to enjoy your hobby."

"All that I do is to look at them."

"Keep yourself pure in thought, word, and deed."

Morelli flashed a grin. "I'm an Italian—not a monk."

"You're a steward aboard the *Salsette*," warned the purser, "and that's all that matters. We want no more hanky-panky, Paulo."

"What do you mean?"

"You know very well what I mean, so don't look so innocent. More than one female passenger has had cause to complain about you in the past. The kindest thing said was that you were over-attentive."

"I try to be friendly, that is all."

"There are barriers," stressed Cannadine. "Strict barriers between passengers and crew members. Overstep those barriers and you'll be in hot water. Do you understand?"

"Yes, sir."

"Remember your wife back in Genoa."

"I do, sir. All the time."

"Then don't be tempted again."

"It was not my fault on the voyage from Aden," protested the steward. "That Spanish lady—it was she who chased me. She only complain because I turn her down. I have to, Mr. Cannadine. I'm a married man." He put a hand to his heart. "And I know my duty."

"See that you do it."

The purser was very fond of Paulo Morelli. With all his faults, the Italian was a conscientious steward who worked hard and sent most of his wages dutifully home to his wife. What Cannadine liked about him was his resolute cheerfulness. Morelli skipped happily through life. No matter how bad a situation, or how oner-ous his tasks, he always managed to retain his sense of fun. It was a tonic to have him aboard.

"Where were you when the storm broke out?" asked Cannadine.

Morelli gave an impish grin. "Hiding under my bunk."

"You should be used to that kind of thing by now."

"The others, they say it is a bad omen."

"That's just foolish superstition."

"We do not want bad weather on the voyage."

"We'll take what we can get, Paulo. When we set sail from Bombay, we're in God's hands. All things considered, He looks after us pretty well."

"That's why I pray before we set sail."

"And what do you pray for?"

"Lots of pretty ladies to look after."

The purser smiled. "Control yourself, man."

"I'm only human, sir."

"Far too human. However," said Cannadine, "talking of looking after someone, did the chief steward have a word with you?"

"What about?"

"A passenger called Mrs. Simcoe."

"Ah, yes. The lady in the chair with wheels."

"She may need help from time to time, especially when she wants to go out on deck. I suggested that you'd be the ideal person to keep an eye on her. Don't let me down, Paulo."

"I'd never do that, Mr. Cannadine."

"Introduce yourself to Mrs. Simcoe and her daughter."

"Oh, I will," said Morelli, "and to the lady in number eleven."

"Number eleven?"

"I saw her come aboard. She is the most beautiful *signorina* on the whole ship even though she is English. It is a pity that *she* does not have a chair with wheels—or I would push her around the deck all day long."

"Who on earth are you talking about, man?"

"Miss Masefield," said the other. "Miss Genevieve Masefield."

By the time that the *Salsette* was ready to set sail, the burning sun had obliterated most of the vestiges of the storm. The deck was bone-dry, the funnels no longer dribbled with moisture and the puddles that had formed in the tarpaulins covering the lifeboats were quickly evaporating. It was almost as if the downpour had never happened. Reassured by the clear sky, most passengers ventured out to take a last look at Bombay as they departed. Genevieve Masefield was among them. No sooner did she appear on the main deck than she saw Tabitha Simcoe beckoning her across to the rail.

"I was hoping to see you here, Miss Masefield," said Tabitha.

"I wouldn't have missed it. I always enjoy this moment."

"So do I. It's such an emotional experience. There's the nostalgia of leaving somewhere you've loved and the excitement of sailing across an ocean in a foreign clime."

"Did your mother not wish to join you?"

"Oh, she did, but she felt too weary. I left her in the cabin to have a nap. Mother tires easily," she confided. "In public, of course, she always manages to keep up appearances but she's not a strong woman."

"All the more reason to admire her for undertaking such a trip. Yes," added Genevieve, "and all the more reason to praise you as well."

"Me?"

"You're the one who shoulders the responsibility, Miss Simcoe. It must be very hard on you at times."

"Not at all," said Tabitha, nobly. "She's my mother."

Genevieve was pleased to meet her alone. Without Mrs. Simcoe, her daughter was a different woman. Tabitha was more animated, more confident, more curious about what was going on around her. In the most ladylike way, she was even taking note of some of the young men on deck. The person who interested her most, however, was Genevieve.

"I'm so glad that we met you, Miss Masefield," she said, squeezing Genevieve's hand. "I just *know* that we're going to be friends."

"In that case, you can stop being so formal with me. Foreign travel ought to release us from social conventions. Please call me Genevieve."

"Thank you. I will. Oh, and you must call me Tabby."

"Not Tabitha?"

"I'm Tabby to people who are close to me. But you're wrong about social conventions disappearing when we're abroad," she went on. "Wait until you meet Major and Mrs. Kinnersley. They're sticklers for decorum. To be honest, they're the only people we've encountered that we found it impossible to like."

"Why was that, Tabby?"

"They were ghastly."

"Unable to shake off their reserve, you mean?"

"No, Genevieve. They were just so thoroughly unpleasant. Mrs. Kinnersley is the worst. She's the most dreadful snob. And she treats that poor girl abominably."

"Their daughter?"

"Hardly," said Tabitha. "I'd be amazed if Mrs. Kinnersley had any children—let alone any maternal instincts. No, this is a young Indian servant who travels with them. I feel sorry for the girl. I'd hate to be at the mercy of a woman like that."

"Colonial life does give people airs and graces."

"Mrs. Kinnersely was *born* with them." Hearing the sharpness in her voice, Tabitha became apologetic. "Look, I shouldn't be harsh on her after so short an acquaintance. Please forgive me for being a trifle outspoken. Perhaps we just caught them on a bad day."

"What was your mother's opinion?"

"Exactly the same as mine, Genevieve. Except that Mother expressed it rather more trenchantly."

Genevieve was amused. "I can imagine."

The ship's engines had been throbbing away while they spoke and they now took on a more powerful beat. After a loud blast on her hooter, the *Salsette* pulled gently away from the pier, cheered from below by the army of relatives, friends, and those who worked at the harbor. Even though she knew nobody whatsoever in the crowd, Genevieve waved as enthusiastically as anyone. Pleased to be going at last, her happiness was tempered with sadness that they were leaving a city where she and her husband had been able to be themselves for a change. Now that they were at work once more, they had to wear their masks.

"What will you remember most about India?" asked Tabitha.

"The kindness of the people."

"Yes, Genevieve, it made me feel so guilty."

"About what?"

"The way we've treated them. India is supposed to be the jewel in the crown of the British Empire, and we've all benefited from that. But where are the benefits for the Indian people themselves? Most of them live in abject poverty," said Tabitha, grimacing. "The slums of Bombay are beyond belief. They made my stomach turn."

"Yet the people don't complain," observed Genevieve. "That's what is so remarkable about them. They have the gift of acceptance."

"That's not a gift, it's a defect. They deserve better."

"I agree with you, Tabby."

"And they're entitled to have it."

Once again, Tabitha heard a passion in her voice that she regretted and she apologized at once. Genevieve waved away her protest.

"You were right in what you said. We *should* feel guilty."

"I spoke out of turn."

"Only to me," said Genevieve, "and that's what friends are for."

"Yes," agreed Tabitha, hugging her impulsively. "Oh, Genevieve, I can't tell you how wonderful it is to have someone with whom I can be honest. This voyage is going to be a delight for me."

Genevieve felt mildly alarmed. Much as she liked Tabitha, she did not want to be monopolized by her for the next four days or she would be unable to do her job properly. It was important to widen her social circle, to get to know as many people as she could. Tabitha, she feared, wanted a more exclusive relationship with her. The other woman confirmed it by her next remark. Holding Genevieve by the shoulders, she gazed at her with a mixture of admiration and yearning.

"You're the person I've always wanted to be," she confessed.

When the ship set sail, George Dillman was part of the crowd on the promenade deck, enjoying the occasion but taking a close look at the other passengers while he was doing so. Dudley Nevin was there, talking to an elderly woman with a parasol, and so was a Norwegian couple with whom he had exchanged a few words in the customs shed. Other faces imprinted themselves on his memory. Dillman wondered where the trouble would arise. Even when there were little over two hundred passengers aboard, the law of averages would come into play. Someone would probably be out to make money by stealing it, cheating at cards or extracting it from their victims by means of a confidence trick. Dillman had to remain alert.

As the cheers of the crowd began to die away, the short, red-faced, round-shouldered man beside him turned to look up at Dillman. His eyes twitched as he spoke.

"That was quite a send-off, wasn't it?" he commented.

"Yes," said Dillman, realizing that he was talking to a fellow American. "Though I'm not entirely sure if they were sorry to see us go or glad to get rid of us." He offered his hand. "George Dillman."

"Boston, Massachusetts," guessed the other, shaking his hand warmly. "Judging by your accent, that is. My name is Wilbur Rollins. New York City and proud of it."

"You've every right to be. It's a fine place."

"You're a long way from Boston, my friend."

"I always wanted to see the world before I settled down."

"I'm trying to do it the other way around," admitted Rollins. "I made all the big decisions first—a wife, a family, a career—then had the urge to travel when I turned fifty."

"On your own?"

The other man sighed. "My wife died two years ago, I'm afraid, and the children have families of their own now. Time to spread my wings."

"I hope it's been a memorable experience."

"Quite magical, Mr. Dillman. And all grist to my mill."

"Your mill?"

"I'm a writer," explained Rollins. "One day, everything I've seen and done will end up between the pages of a book. I've made copious notes at every stage of my journey."

Rollins was an engaging companion, intelligent, well-informed, and full of amusing anecdotes. Once Dillman got used to the nervous twitch around the man's eyes, he was drawn to him. In turn, the New Yorker obviously felt as if he had made a real friend. While many of the passengers dispersed to their cabins, the two men remained talking on deck. They were over a mile out of the harbor when something caught their attention. Rollins was astonished.

"Look at that!" he exclaimed. "Do you see what I see?"

"Very well," said Dillman.

"Why on earth are they doing that *there*?"

Dillman was as baffled as he was. What they were staring at was a large cargo ship that was anchored well away from the harbor while the coal in its holds was being discharged into lighters. In addition to the crew, hundreds of people were visible on the deck, coolies, women, and children. Coal was being unloaded by the most primitive and laborious method. Using shovels shaped like Dutch hoes, the coolies were filling small flat baskets then handing them along a human chain to be emptied down chutes into the lighters.

"How much coal would they have aboard?" wondered Rollins.

"Five thousand tons at least, I'd say."

"It will take them an eternity to unload all that."

"Yes," said Dillman. "They're not even using the steam winches and derricks. Everything's being done manually by a shore gang, just as in the old days."

"But *why*? That's what I want to know."

"It saves docking charges, for a start. My guess is that the agent in charge of the stevedoring arrangements has worked out some kind of deal that gives him and the ship's owners a tidy profit. The only people who won't come out of this well are the coolies."

"And their families," said Rollins, taking a pad and pencil from his pocket. "Why bring all those women? They're not just wives. I can see a few grandmothers, as well." He began to write something in his notepad. "It's almost as if they *live* on the ship."

"That's effectively what they will do until the holds are emptied."

"And then?"

"Well," said Dillman, "presumably they'll want to take fresh cargo onboard. Bagged rice and baled cotton, most likely. I suspect that they'll move to the dock to pick that up. The crew will want to come ashore to see the sights of Bombay."

"*This* is one of the most extraordinary sights I've seen here," said Rollins, scribbling rapidly, "and it will certainly be mentioned in the book I'm working on at the moment."

"Why—what's it called?"

"*Women at Sea.*"

Popular with the passengers, Paulo Morelli only aroused envy among his colleagues. His good looks and his Latin charm won him compliments from the ladies and—they suspected—even more personal marks of favor at times. Stewards were forbidden to fraternize with the passengers and it was a rule that was rigidly enforced, yet Morelli somehow managed to get around it—or, at least, he gave the impression of doing so. Part of his success was due to the zest he brought to his job, performing even the most boring and repetitious tasks with smiling eagerness. A first meeting with new passengers, he believed, was crucial. If a relationship got off to a good start, he had something to build on.

Accordingly, he worked his way along the cabins that had been assigned to him for the voyage, tapping on each door, introducing himself to the occupants and asking if there was anything they required. When he came to the cabin belonging to Constance and Tabitha Simcoe, he recalled what the purser had told him. He was to take special care of the older woman. Morelli had no qualms about doing that. He had seen her come aboard in her Bath chair and knew that she was traveling with an attractive daughter. In devoting himself to the mother, he told himself, he could ingratiate himself with the younger woman.

Finding the nearest mirror, he checked his appearance and smoothed down his mustache with a forefinger. Then he crossed to the door and used his knuckles to rap on it.

"This is your steward!" he called.

There was no answer. After waiting for a few moments, he knocked harder, but still got no response and assumed that the two ladies were still on deck. Instead of meeting them, he decided, he would take a quick look into their cabin. Morelli had a good eye and a quick brain. A glance into someone's wardrobe could tell him a great deal about them and he had made some intriguing discoveries that way. Making sure that nobody was about, he used his key to open the door and stepped swiftly inside.

Morelli gasped in surprise and came to a dead halt. The cabin was occupied, after all, but not by someone who was able to let him in. Sprawled on the floor, lying face down, was Constance Simcoe.

"Dio mio!" he exclaimed. "What happened?"

THREE

When the ship was clear of the harbor, Genevieve Masefield decided to leave the main deck and call on the purser. She was forced to wait for a short time while Max Cannadine was trying, with great patience, to calm down an irate female passenger. Unable to get her own way, the woman, plump, middle-aged, and raven-haired, eventually stalked off and Genevieve was able to introduce herself. Cannadine shook her hand gratefully.

"It's such a relief to meet someone who hasn't come to complain," he said. "That Portuguese lady was the third in a row who's not happy with her cabin. Because she spoke very little English and because I only know few words of Portuguese, it was a rather fraught conversation."

"Well, I haven't come to demand a change of cabin, Mr. Cannadine."

"That's music to my ear."

"The facilities seem excellent to me."

"The *Salsette* was built for speed and comfort."

"I'm sure that it will be an enjoyable voyage," said Genevieve. "You've met my partner, I understand?"

"Yes, Mr. Dillman and I had a brief chat. As I told him, we never have any serious problems onboard. You and he should have a quiet time of it."

"That will make a pleasant change."

"Each of you has a cabin in first class, but I assume that you'll divide your duties. Who will look after the second-class passengers?"

"Both of us," she said. "Once we've found our way around, we'll take it in turns to drift into the public rooms in second class to see what's going on. George is an absolute master at blending in. Did you know that he used to work as an actor?"

"No," replied Cannadine, "but the news doesn't surprise me. He has all the right attributes for the stage. But then," he went on with a smile of frank admiration, "so do you, Miss Masefield."

"I've never been attracted to work in the theater."

"That's a pity. I'd certainly pay to watch you."

"Then you're going to be disappointed, Mr. Cannadine. I don't court attention. I prefer to stay in the shadows and look on. That's why I enjoy my work so much. It's like being a spectator at a play—I sit there and watch a drama unfold."

"Until something untoward happens."

"That's always a possibility, I fear."

"But then, if a crime is involved, you have the ability to interrupt proceedings. That must give you a lot of satisfaction."

"Oh, it does, believe me."

Like her partner, Genevieve found the purser to be affable and observant. Though he moaned about complaints from passengers, he did so without rancor and she was sure that he could handle any emergency with calm efficiency. Cannadine exuded the quiet confidence of a man who loved his job and endeavored to do it properly.

"I hear that Mr. Dillman used to be a Pinkerton agent," he said.

"That's correct. They trained him well."

"Has he been able to pass on some of the tricks of the trade?"

"Yes," said Genevieve. "George has taught me everything. He also pointed out that my greatest asset is my appearance."

Cannadine beamed. "I'd happily endorse that judgment."

"What he meant was that I deflect suspicion. Nobody who meets me for the first time suspects for a moment that I might be employed as a ship's detective. People are off guard. They tend to confide in me."

"They confide in me, as well," said the purser, ruefully, "but all that I get to hear are their reproaches. The engines are too noisy, the ship rolls too much, the food is not to their taste, the service is tardy, and so on." He gave a dry laugh. "I even had a Frenchman in here earlier who complained that he'd been caught on the pier by that storm."

"P and O is not responsible for the weather."

"He seemed to think it was." There was a tap on his door. "One moment, please," he called. "Another brickbat, no doubt," he said to Genevieve. "It's always like this at the start of a voyage."

"Then I won't get in your way any longer. I just wanted to make contact so that you knew who I was."

"Thank you." He opened the door for her. "It's a pleasure to have you aboard, Miss Masefield."

"Good-bye."

Paulo Morelli was waiting outside, his expression serious. When he saw Genevieve, however, he brightened at once and grinned broadly.

"Ah, you have met the lady," he said. "Do you agree with what I told you, Mr. Cannadine?"

"What do you want, Paulo?" asked the purser.

"I came to report something, sir. You tell me to keep the eye on that lady in the chair with wheels."

"So?"

"She is not well," said Morelli. "When I go to her cabin, Mrs. Simcoe is lying on the floor."

"Poor woman!" said Genevieve, alarmed. "I met her earlier. What's wrong with Mrs. Simcoe?"

Morelli shrugged. "I not know," he said. "But I call the doctor. He is with her now—and so is her daughter, Tibby."

"Tabby."

"Yes, that was the name her mother call her—Tabby. I think you should know about this, sir."

"Thank you, Paulo," said Cannadine. "You did the right thing."

"Maybe the heat, it was too much for her."

"Let's hope that's all it was."

"I'd better go and see how she is," said Genevieve with concern. "Mrs. Simcoe doesn't enjoy good health, alas. Do excuse me."

Morelli stood aside so that she could walk briskly down the corridor. With a sly smile, he nudged the purser.

"Do you see what I mean, Mr. Cannadine? She is gorgeous."

"Keep your mind on your work, Paulo."

"That is unusual for an English lady," said Morelli. "They look nice but they are always so cold and—how do you say it—aloaf?"

"Aloof," corrected Cannadine. "It means cool, distant, detached."

"Miss Masefield is none of those things."

"It's not your place to pass comments about the passengers."

"With this lady," said the Italian, eyes sparkling, "I cannot help it. I only wish that it was *her* that I find on the floor of her cabin. I would love to offer the first aid to Miss Genevieve Masefield."

George Dillman was strolling around the main deck when he first noticed him. Tall, frail, elderly, and with a long white beard, the Sikh wore the traditional turban and attire of his religion. In one hand, he was holding a newspaper. A small crowd had gathered around him. Dillman saw how much respect the Indian passengers were showing the old man, but two members of the crew were more skeptical. One of them, an officer in his smart uniform, gave a laugh of disbelief.

"That's nonsense," he said. "Nobody can foretell the future."

"I can," declared the old man. "I have strange powers."

"Yes—to extract money out of the pockets of gullible fools. I've seen you mystics before, in the market. You're nothing but clever tricksters."

"That is unkind of you, sir. I do have special gifts."

"Prove it."

"What is the point? You will only mock."

"I won't mock," said Dillman, struck by the old man's dignified bearing. "I'd never have believed that anyone could charm snakes with a pipe until I actually saw a man doing it in Bombay."

The mystic smiled. "Thank you, my friend. But it may be easier to charm a snake than to convince these two gentlemen that I am what I claim to be. They are too suspicious of me."

"Not at all," said the officer, pleasantly. "We simply need proof."

"Then I will give it to you—at a price."

"You see? I knew that there'd be money involved."

"One rupee, that is all."

"I'd say you're getting a bargain," said Dillman to the officer. "One rupee is not much to risk. I'll act as stakeholder, if you like."

The man was dubious. "Let's hear more about this proof first."

"As you wish," said the mystic. "I will demonstrate my powers." He held up his newspaper. "I will take one sheet of this and place it on the deck. You and I will both stand on it, side by side."

"And then you'll make us float into the air. Is that it?"

"No, sir. I will give you a chance to earn your rupee. You will have the rest of the newspaper, rolled up in your hand. All that you have to do is to hit me with it and the money is yours."

"That's ridiculous. I'm bound to win."

"Then you must accept my wager."

"You really want me to clip you with the newspaper?"

"I want you to try, sir," said the old man, "but I will use the power of my mind to stop you. I will give you the proof that you demand."

Dillman sensed that the Sikh would somehow win the bet, though he had no idea how. There was a weird, mystical air about the old man and Dillman loved his clear, gentle, measured voice with its Welsh lilt.

"It sounds like an easy way to earn a rupee," he opined. "It's a pity the stake is not higher."

"Yes," agreed the officer. "Is there any chance of increasing it?"

"Of course," said the Sikh. "Name your price."

"Ten rupees."

"Give them to our American friend here."

Both men handed the coins to Dillman. The old man then tore one sheet out of the newspaper and gave the rest of it to his challenger. Rolling it up, and egged on by his companion, the officer got ready to strike but it was not as simple as he had imagined. The Sikh led them all across to a steel bulkhead with a riveted door set into it. Bending down, he slid half of the sheet of newspaper under the door.

"Now, sir," he said to the officer. "You stand on the piece on the other side of the door and try to hit me."

The watching Indians clapped their hands in approval and, to his credit, the officer took his defeat with good grace. He burst out laughing.

"I deserved that," he said. "I was beaten by the power of the mind."

"Would you like another demonstration?" asked the mystic.

"No, no. I'd only lose again. Take the money. You earned it."

Still laughing, he walked away with his friend. Dillman was highly amused. He handed over the twenty rupees to the old man.

"I was wondering how you were going to do it," he admitted.

"Thank you for your help," said the mystic. "My name is Guljar Singh, by the way. I live in Bombay."

The detective shook his hand. "George Dillman," he said.

"What you saw was only a trick, Mr. Dillman. I would not have you think that is all I have to offer. I really am a fortune-teller who can see into the future."

"So am I, Mr. Singh. The moment that officer took your bait, I could foretell that he would lose his money."

Singh chuckled. "You should have placed your own bet."

"I prefer to be an independent witness."

"Then you can witness something else, my friend. I tell you this in confidence," he went on, taking a step closer and lowering his voice. "From the moment I stepped onto this ship, I was afraid."

"Of what?" asked Dillman.

There was no immediate answer. Staring in front of him, Guljar Singh seemed go off into a kind of trance. His eyes grew wide and milky, his mouth opened, and he began to mumble softly. It was a full minute before he was able to focus on Dillman again.

"Something terrible will happen on the *Salsette*," he predicted. "I do not know what it is or when it will come, but it is hanging over us. Beware, Mr. Dillman. We have trouble ahead."

"No, Mother," said Tabitha Simcoe. "You must not even think of it."

"It's my decision and I stick by it," affirmed Constance.

"Why not have dinner served in here?"

"I agree with your daughter, Mrs. Simcoe," said Genevieve. "After your fall earlier, you need rest. I think it would be a mistake to put yourself under any strain."

"What strain is there in sitting at a table in congenial company? If I stay here, Miss Masefield, I'll be bored to death." Constance Simcoe used her walking stick to pull herself upright. "I'm fine now."

"Dr. McNeil said that you should take it easy," urged Tabitha.

"Ha! What do doctors know? If I'd listened to them, I'd have been bedridden for the last ten years. I'm fine now. Besides, I'm starting to feel hungry."

Genevieve had called at their cabin to find the older woman in a combative mood. Constance Simcoe was making light of the incident. She conceded that she had occasional bouts of vertigo and sometimes passed out, but she was not going to let that interfere with the pleasures of the voyage. Genevieve was impressed by her powers of recovery. Propped up on her walking stick, Constance was still rather flushed but she had regained all of her old spirit.

"Do you remember what happened?" asked Genevieve.

"More or less," replied Constance. "I was sitting in the chair and wanted to get something from the wardrobe. When I hauled myself up, I had a sudden dizzy spell and fell down. The next thing I knew, this young steward was bending over me and jabbering in Italian."

"Just as well that he found you when he did."

"I'm relieved that you didn't hurt yourself," Tabitha said anxiously. "You might have hit your head on the table or even broken a bone."

"Stop worrying, Tabitha," scolded her mother. "I'm much tougher than I look. You should know that by now."

"I blame myself for this. I shouldn't have left you alone for so long."

"Fiddlesticks! You wanted to see the ship set sail."

"I thought you were taking a nap," said Genevieve.

"I was. I dozed off in the chair. When I woke up, I needed a clean handkerchief so I got up—then fell flat on my face." She gave a throaty laugh. "After I've taken those pills the doctor gave me, I'll be prancing around the deck like a two-year-old."

Tabitha turned to Genevieve. "Whatever am I to do with her?"

"Perhaps your mother *should* join us in the dining saloon," said Genevieve, revising her opinion. "If she feels well enough, that is."

"I'm as fit as a fiddle," announced Constance, hobbling a few steps with the aid of her stick to prove it. "I didn't come on this trip to stay cooped up in a cabin. I want to *meet* people."

"If you insist, Mother," sighed Tabitha.

"I do—on one condition."

"What's that?"

"We don't sit next to that abominable Mrs. Kinnersley. A frightful woman." She turned to Genevieve. "Did Tabby mention her to you?"

"Yes," said Genevieve. "I heard about Major and Mrs. Kinnersley."

"The sort of people who give the English a bad name."

"I'll make sure I steer clear of them."

"Do that, Miss Masefield. The major was bad enough, boasting about his regiment and the number of servants he had to fetch and carry, but his wife was even worse. When I told her that we lived in Cheltenham, do you know what she said?"

"No, Mrs. Simcoe."

"Cheltenham was dull and old-fashioned. She said that it lacked any real style. To live in Cheltenham, she claimed, was to be buried up to the neck in all that was second-rate."

"I can see that she was not trying to endear herself to you."

"Endear herself?" snapped Constance. "That old bat? The only way that Mrs. Kinnersley could endear herself to me is by jumping overboard with a ton weight in her arms."

"Ah, there you are, Mr. Dillman," said Dudley Nevin, waving cheerily to him. "Have you met Major and Mrs. Kinnersley yet?"

"I've not had that pleasure," said Dillman, politely.

Formal introductions were made and handshakes exchanged. Major Romford Kinnersley was a tall, thin, straight-backed man in his fifties with a stern face and a protruding Adam's apple. His wife, by contrast, was a short, fleshy woman whose glinting green eyes failed to offset the plainness of her features. From the way that they had reacted to the sound of his accent, Dillman could see that they had no fondness for the American nation.

"Where do you hail from, Mr. Dillman?" asked the major.

"Boston, Massachusetts," said Dillman.

"Oh, yes. The notorious Tea Party."

"The city does have other claims to fame."

"To fame or to infamy?"

"Treat this fellow with care," warned Nevin in jest. "Mr. Dillman is a demagogue. A born rabble-rouser."

"Really?" said the major. "In first class?"

"Whom *will* they let in next?" added his wife, haughtily.

"Mr. Nevin is having a joke at my expense," said Dillman. "I'm quite harmless, I assure you. I haven't led a rebellion for years now."

The four of them were standing outside the dining saloon. On the first evening afloat, dress was optional but both Nevin and Major Kinnersley had opted for white tie and tails. Matilda Kinnersley was wearing a black evening gown with a large golden brooch pinned to one shoulder. An ivory fan hung from her wrist. Even though he was immaculate, she looked askance at the lounge suit that Dillman had chosen, making him feel as if he had committed a major social solecism.

"Shall we find a seat?" suggested Nevin.

"Yes," muttered the major. "Why not, old chap?"

They were not the ideal dinner companions but Dillman could not escape them now. Within a minute, he found himself sitting next to Dudley Nevin and opposite the Kinnersleys. By comparison with its counterparts on the *Lusitania* and the *Mauretania*— the premier Cunard vessels on which Dillman had sailed—the first-class dining saloon was small and rather subdued, but its design was attractive and its decoration exquisite. It also had an intimacy that the larger ships lacked. The detective was not permitted to take in his surroundings for long. Matilda Kinnersley began her interrogation immediately.

"What are you doing in this part of the world, Mrs. Dillman?"

"Broadening my mind," he replied.

"Do you have any family?"

"I come from a long line of marine architects, Mrs. Kinnersley. We design and construct large yachts. I'm an apostle of sailing ships."

"How quaint!"

"There's nothing to beat the experience of crossing the Atlantic under sail," said Dillman. "I did it for the first time when I was only ten."

"Things have moved on, fortunately," noted the major, clearing his throat. "Steamships have transformed our life for the better. Steam trains as well, mark you." He allowed himself a proud smile. "British inventions, of course."

"Nobody denies that, Major."

"I wish that someone would invent a way to keep the railway carriages cool in hot weather," said Nevin, testily. "I was roasted alive on the trip from Delhi."

"One gets used to the heat in time," said Kinnersley.

"It's a matter of self-control," added his wife. "Isn't it, my dear?"

"Yes, Matilda. Self-control and adaptability—two sterling English virtues. We can't have these people thinking we're upset by their climate. Dash it all," he continued, smacking the table for emphasis, "if *they* can cope with it, then so can we."

"Where are you stationed?" said Dillman.

"Simla."

"Isn't it cooler there, Major?"

"Temperatures can still soar."

"Wearing those thick uniforms must make the problem far worse."

"Can't dispense with those," the other man said gruffly. "We have to remind the local population who we are."

"I thought that a lot of your troops were Indian sepoys."

"Too many of them, Mr. Dillman. That's how the mutiny started. Because we recruited them, we trusted the fellows. And what did they do in return? They turned on us."

"My father was killed at Cawnpore," announced Mrs. Kinnersley.

"Along with so many other British heroes, I fear."

"How does that make you feel about India?" asked Dillman.

"I have no feelings, sir. I merely do my duty."

"So do I," said Nevin, "but it doesn't stop me from cursing this country every day. I've grown to detest everything about it. But I know that our American friend takes a different view."

"I found Bombay such an exciting city," said Dillman.

"Exciting to leave behind."

"No, Mr. Nevin. Exciting to visit again, as I'll surely do one day."

Mrs. Kinnersley was crisp. "In one of your sailing ships?"

"Ideally."

"What a bizarre notion!"

"I felt an affinity for the country, Mrs. Kinnersley," said Dillman. "Even though my stay was only brief, I was at home in India."

"Watch out, everyone!" cautioned Nevin with a grin. "Give him the chance and he'll turn native on us."

Mrs. Kinnersley shot Dillman a well-bred look of scorn while her husband reached for the menu. The major was deep in contemplation of the fare on offer before he spoke.

"Let's change the subject, shall we?" he ordered.

Genevieve was full of admiration for the way that it was done. Because P & O knew in advance that they had a disabled passenger, they made sure that Constance Simcoe's cabin was on the same deck as the dining saloon. It meant that she could be wheeled there in her Bath chair by the willing Paulo Morelli, and was able, with her daughter, to take her seat before any of the other passengers arrived. The Bath chair was removed. By the time Genevieve joined them at their table, the two women were happily ensconced opposite Wilbur Rollins. After being introduced to the American, Genevieve sat beside him.

Rollins was wearing a smart navy blue suit and the ladies had chosen evening gowns. In her emerald green silk dress, and with some carefully selected jewelry, Genevieve was easily the most attractive of the women. Constance Simcoe wore a ruby-colored gown with puffed sleeves, and with taffeta flowers sewn across the neckline. Tabitha's wardrobe had yielded a pale blue dress that showed off her figure to advantage, and, like her mother, she had a pearl necklace. Genevieve noticed how she had gone back into her shell again. On deck, Tabitha had been much more relaxed. With her mother—on duty, so to speak—she was stiff and watchful.

It was not long before they discovered the purpose of Wilbur Rollins's visit to India. Genevieve was intrigued to hear that he was a writer but Constance Simcoe raised her eyebrows in astonishment.

"*Women at Sea?*" she said.

"Yes, Mrs. Simcoe," he replied. "It's a fascinating subject."

"I didn't know there were such things as female sailors."

"Oh, yes. There were many of them in olden days. The person who lured me here—if I may put it that way—was Hannah Snell."

"Who was she?" wondered Tabitha.

"A formidable woman in eighteenth-century London," he explained. "Dressed as a man, she spent four and half years as a marine. Amongst other things, she sailed to India and fought in the Siege of Pondicherry. I went there earlier this month as part of my research."

"Did nobody suspect that she was a woman?" asked Genevieve.

"Apparently not, Miss Masefield. Hannah became quite famous in the 1750s. When she told her story to the newspapers, they gave her a lot of publicity, so she began to appear on stage at the New Wells, a theater close to the Tower of London."

"How extraordinary!"

"Is that all that she was?" said Constance. "A kind of freak?"

"Far from it," replied Rollins, warming to his subject. "She was a very brave woman. Think of the hardships she must have endured aboard. There was no Suez Canal in those days. They would have had to sail around the Cape of Good Hope and that was a fearsome ordeal."

"Why on earth did she do it?"

"Out of a spirit of adventure, Mrs. Simcoe. It was the same with Mary Anne Talbot, another eighteenth-century lady."

"There's nothing ladylike about being a sailor."

"That's why she had to disguise herself as a man," said Rollins. "She started very young as a drummer boy in the army under Captain Bowen. When the regiment was shipped to St. Domingo, Mary Anne Talbot deserted and joined a French privateer."

"Think of the risks she must have run," said Tabitha.

"She must have had nerves of steel. Her ship was captured by Admiral Howe's fleet and she became a cabin boy on the *Brunswick,* a British vessel, that soon saw action against the French. Mary Anne was wounded by musket balls."

"Was that the end of her naval career?" asked Genevieve.

"Oh, no. She joined the *Vesuvius,* a bomb ketch that patrolled the French coast. Along with the rest of the crew, the poor woman was taken prisoner by the French and held for eighteen months in Dunkirk. On her release, Mary Anne signed on as a steward on a merchant ship."

"You're making all this up," accused Constance.

"Mother!" reprimanded Tabitha.

"Well, it all sounds so fanciful."

"Mr. Rollins has obviously researched his subject carefully."

"I have," he confirmed, hurt by the suggestion that he was inventing the stories. "I was a college professor for twenty years before I became a full-time writer. I follow strict academic principles."

"I'm sure that you do," said Tabitha, trying to mollify him.

"What happened to Mary Anne Talbot in the end?" said Genevieve.

"She came back to England on the *Ariel,* the merchant ship, and signed off. Then the strangest thing happened," he went on with a chuckle. "Mary Anne was drinking in a London tavern near the river when a press gang suddenly burst in. The only way that she could escape being forced to join the navy was to reveal that she was a woman. And that brought her career afloat to an end— at the age of nineteen!"

Constance snorted. "Thank heaven she was no daughter of mine!"

"I rather admire her," confessed Tabitha.

"Don't be silly, Tabby. What *is* there to admire?"

"Her courage, for a start."

"And her resilience," noted Genevieve. "Mary Anne had one setback after another yet she somehow kept going. Thank you, Mr. Rollins. This has been a revelation to me. The only women at sea I've heard of before were the ones who became pirates."

"Women pirates!" said Constance with polite derision. "Now, that is something I simply refuse to believe."

"Then you've never come across Mary Read and Anne Bonney," said Rollins, wagging a finger. "They were true buccaneers, Mrs. Simcoe—every bit as ruthless and bloodthirsty as the men. Yes," he added, glancing around the room. "I know that it's hard to credit when you look at all the charming ladies here this evening, but women are capable of committing the most appalling crimes."

While the rest of the passengers were enjoying a delicious meal and making new acquaintances, the thief slipped into the cabin and subjected it to a swift search. The visit was productive. When the lid of a hatbox was removed, something glinted at the bottom of it. Pocketing the haul, the thief opened the door, checked that nobody was in the corridor, then left. The whole thing had taken less than two minutes.

FOUR

As the meal progressed and the wine flowed, Major Romford Kinnersley became steadily more expansive and even offered a few anecdotes from his military career, but his wife remained cold and humorless. Dillman sensed a deep bitterness in the woman, concealed for the most part behind her supercilious manner, but showing itself from time to time in her gratuitous barbed remarks. Food and drink were of such high quality that Dudley Nevin had liberal quantities of both. Mellowing as dinner wore on, he forgot all about his hatred of India and started to quote Kipling's poems. When the meal was over, Matilda Kinnersley pleaded tiredness and excused herself from the table, leaving the three men to adjourn to the lounge for a brandy. The major was apologetic.

"You must forgive Matilda," he said. "We've been in India for so long now that she has grave misgivings about going back to England. It makes her tense and waspish."

"Do *you* have any reservations about going home?" said Dillman.

"Dozens, sir."

"Why?"

"Because the country is going to the dogs."

"I wouldn't entirely agree with that, Major," said Nevin.

"Then you obviously haven't kept track of what's going on. These past few years have been nothing short of disastrous. England now has a Liberal government with a huge majority to create what mischief they will, a confounded Labor Party pouring its poison into the ears of the lower orders, and strident women demanding the vote. Then there's all this dangerous talk of an eight-hour day, old age pensions, health insurance, free school meals, and—God forbid—a measure of independence for Ireland. Yes," concluded Kinnersley, after sipping his brandy, "and there's even a move to stop religion being taught to the children. It's scandalous."

"Oh, I don't know about that," Nevin said easily. "I had far too much Christianity rammed down my throat at Winchester. And we all got chilblains from sitting in that icy cathedral during winter months."

"That's neither here nor there, Mr. Nevin."

"Yes, it is. Those chilblains were painful."

"If you ask me," continued the major, darkly, "the rot set in when some fools elected an Indian to the House of Commons. A foreigner, for heaven's sake! An alien in the seat of government."

"India has aliens in *its* seat of government," argued Dillman.

"That's a false comparison."

"I don't think so. It has a viceroy imposed upon it."

"For its own good, man. Can't you understand that?"

"Frankly, no."

"I told you that he was a political agitator," said Nevin, amused.

"As a matter of fact," returned Dillman, "I admire some aspects of your parliamentary system—now that we're free from its dictates. But I think that it's only right that India should be represented in the

House of Commons. That's where decisions are made about their country. Indians should be able to take part in those decisions."

"Poppycock, sir!" snapped Kinnersley.

"Yes," said Nevin. "Follow that specious line of argument and you'd have members of Parliament from every corner of the Empire. Black faces would outnumber the white. That would be intolerable."

"Indecent!"

"You'll be suggesting that we become a republic next."

"No, Mr. Nevin," said Dillman. "I'd never advocate that. You have a system that's evolved over the years and that suits you perfectly. In America, we prefer to do things differently, that's all."

"Differently and ruinously," asserted the major.

"That's a matter of opinion."

"You've heard mine."

"We're a young country, Major. We're still finding our feet."

"America is also a backward country," said Nevins, rolling his glass between his palms. "Let's face it. Fifty years ago, you still had slavery."

"Granted," said Dillman sadly, "and it was a mark of disgrace upon us. But, unlike you, we had the sense to put an end to it. You still have slavery in India."

"That's a monstrous suggestion!" protested the major.

"What else would you call it?"

"A civilizing process."

"There's nothing very civilized about a turning a vast population into nothing more than servants. You may not keep them in chains," said Dillman, reasonably, "but you keep them in subjection. If that's not a form of slavery, what is it?"

The major rose to his feet. "I'll hear no more of this nonsense."

"Don't go," urged Nevin, enjoying the argument. "Stay and fight your corner, Major. We can't give in to all this American twaddle."

"It's too late," the other man said curtly. "Good night, gentlemen." With a nod of his head, he turned on his heel and walked off.

"I think that you upset him, Mr. Dillman," said Nevin.

"It was quite unintentional."

"Such a pity. I was really starting to enjoy his company now that his wife was no longer with us. What did you make of her?"

"She seemed a rather unhappy woman."

"Unhappy? That's putting it mildly. I thought that Mrs. Kinnersley was sour to the core. No wonder her husband has doubts about going back home. With a wife like that in tow, I'd be terrified."

"I'm sure that the lady has her virtues."

"I dread to think what they might be!" Nevin drained his glass with satisfaction. "Another brandy?"

"Not for me, thank you," said Dillman. "I think I'll turn in." He was about to get up when he remembered something. "Unless, of course, this is the right moment."

"For what?"

"For you to tell me the reason you left England under a cloud."

Nevin laughed. "Oh, that!" he said. "No, not this evening. If you want to hear about that little peccadillo, you'll have to share a lot more than one brandy with me."

First to arrive, they were the last to leave the dining saloon. Constance Simcoe preferred to be helped into the Bath chair with a degree of privacy so that she did not have an audience. Genevieve Masefield waited with her friends until Morelli was summoned to wheel the older woman back to her cabin. It had been a pleasant evening. Both Tabitha and Genevieve had been enthralled by what they had been told by Wilbur Rollins, and they hoped to hear more about women at sea. Constance, on the other hand, still found it too incredible to take seriously.

After an exchange of farewells, Genevieve went off to her own cabin. When she found a letter awaiting her, she hoped that it was from Dillman but it turned out to be a summons from Max Cannadine. She went straight off to the purser's office. He was glad to see her.

"I'm sorry to call you so late," he said, indicating a seat, "but we have a slight problem on our hands."

Genevieve sat down. "That's what we're here for, Mr. Cannadine," she said. "Night and day, George and I are always on duty."

" 'We Never Sleep.' Isn't that the Pinkerton motto?"

"It applies to us as well. Have you sent for George?"

"No, Miss Masefield," he told her. "I thought that you were the person to handle this assignment. How good is your French?"

"It's passable."

"Excellent. I'll need you to interview a lady called Madame Roussel in second class. She had some valuables stolen from her cabin."

"Why didn't she ask you to lock them away in your safe?"

"She didn't think that it was necessary," he explained. "Ordinarily, she would have been right. The *Salsette* has a reputation for its security. As a rule, you could leave the Crown Jewels in your cabin with impunity. But not tonight, it seems."

"What was taken?"

"Some money and several items of jewelry."

"I'll need a full list," said Genevieve.

"Yes, I told Madame Roussel that you'd call on her first thing in the morning. She was too distressed to talk any more about it this evening."

"What sort of woman is she?"

"Rather theatrical, Miss Masefield. She came storming in here and gabbled at me in French. It took me some time to calm her down. With luck, she may be less hysterical tomorrow."

"When did she discover the theft?"

"When she got back from dinner," said Cannadine. "She took off her necklace to put it with the rest of her jewelry and found that it wasn't in its hiding place."

"Hiding place?"

"Tucked away at the bottom of a hatbox."

"That narrows down the time when it must have been stolen," said Genevieve. "We'll have to start looking at any passengers who were not in either of the dining saloons."

"It's not as easy as that, I'm afraid. Madame Roussel was out of her cabin for a couple of hours *before* dinner. I'm not sure of the details, because she was in a highly emotional state, but what it amounts to is this. She has an admirer aboard. Madame Roussel was with him for some time. In fact," he went on, "my guess is that she may have gone back to his cabin after dinner."

"What makes you think that?"

"She's a very desirable lady, and she did drop more than a few hints. Anyway, Miss Masefield," he said, "you can see why I want you to handle this case. It requires tact, diplomacy, and the feminine touch."

"I'll speak to her tomorrow."

"Thank you."

"And I'll talk to this admirer of hers, as well."

"Why?"

"Because he may be implicated," said Genevieve. "If he lured her away for a couple of hours before dinner, he may have been distracting her so that a confederate could search her cabin."

"But she spoke so fondly of the man."

"We have to consider all the options, Mr. Cannadine. He may turn out to be completely innocent—I hope that he is—but he still has to go on my list." She got up from the chair with a sigh. "Oh, dear! And there you were, saying that we'd have a quiet time of it on the *Salsette*."

"I prefer to take a more positive attitude."

"What do you mean?"

"Well, I'm very upset that this has happened, naturally. It reflects badly on us. However," he said with a grin, "it will give me the chance to see you in action, so I regard that as a bonus."

It was quite late when Dillman left the lounge but he had no intention of going to bed yet. That was just an excuse to detach himself from Dudley Nevin's company. What the detective really wanted to do was to explore the ship when almost nobody was about, so that he could familiarize himself with its layout. To that end, he began with the orlop deck and worked his way slowly upward, checking the accommodations, looking into all the public rooms, establishing where the kitchens were, and generally getting his bearings.

Dillman was on the promenade deck when the accident happened. It was a fine night but the place seemed deserted. There were no couples enjoying a romantic moment under the moon, and no members of the crew visible. Standing at the rail, Dillman gazed out across the water, picking out the lights of another vessel in the distance. A rumbling sound then came into his ears, getting closer and louder all the time. Before he could work out what had produced the noise, he was too late. Someone came hurtling around the angle of a bulkhead on roller skates and collided with him.

Thrown backward against the rail, Dillman put out both arms instinctively and found that he was holding a vivacious young woman. Torn between amusement and dismay, Lois Greenwood gave an apology that was punctuated with loud giggles.

"Look," she said, disentangling herself from Dillman, "I'm awfully sorry to run into you like that. I didn't expect anyone to be here at this time of night. I thought the coast was clear."

"It was my fault," said Dillman. "I should have got out of the way."

"I didn't give you much chance."

"No, I suppose that you didn't."

"Are you all right?" she asked. "I hope I didn't hurt you."

"I think I'll survive."

They introduced themselves. Lois was tickled by the fact that the person she had inadvertently hit was a courteous American, and for his part, Dillman was pleased to meet such a friendly and open young woman. After spending dinner sitting opposite the Kinnersleys, he found Lois an absolute delight. She was so exuberant. Sixteen years old, she came from London and was traveling with her parents.

"What were you doing, Miss Greenwood?" he asked.

"Practicing."

"I wouldn't have thought that roller-skating was quite the thing for a young lady to take up. Isn't it rather hazardous?"

"Only when someone gets in the way," she said, bringing a hand up to stifle a giggle. "I don't simply skate, Mr. Dillman. I play for a team."

"What sort of team?"

"You wouldn't believe me if I told you."

"Yes, I would. You have an honest face."

"Are you teasing me?"

"Of course not," he assured her. "I'm genuinely interested. Now tell me what sort of team it is."

"We play football on roller skates."

Dillman was taken aback. "Are you serious, Miss Greenwood?"

"Never more so. We have a league. You'd be surprised how many teams there are. The standard is really quite high."

"Where on earth do you play?"

"On a roller-skating rink," she explained. "Having to kick a football makes it much more difficult. It's a wonderful sport. The only trouble is that we have a few cheats in it."

"Cheats?"

51

"Girls who skate into you on purpose, or trip you up when you go for the ball. If you take a tumble, it can be very painful."

Dillman rubbed his back. "You don't need to tell me that."

"Of course, Mummy and Daddy think that I'm mad even wanting to play. They've done everything they can to stop me but it's what I want to do. It's so much more fun than just skating around."

"Wouldn't it be safer to play football on grass?"

"Yes, but not nearly as exciting," she said scornfully. "I tried ice hockey, but the rink is miles away and I was never really good enough. I'm much better on wheels. I scored two goals in the last match I played."

"I'd like to hear more about this new sport," decided Dillman, "only not now. I think I'll take my bruises off to bed and leave the field clear for you, Miss Greenwood."

"Thank you. I'm so glad it was you that I hit."

"Why?"

"There are so many stuffy people aboard. They wouldn't have been as nice about it as you are, Mr. Dillman." She looked worried. "You won't tell my parents about this, will you?"

"I've no reason to do so."

"That's a relief. It would give Daddy just the excuse he needs to confiscate my skates. He doesn't even realize that I'm out on deck. He and Mummy went to bed early." She grinned up at him. "It was lovely to meet you. I don't know any Americans. I do hope we'll bump into each other again."

"Not if you're wearing those roller skates. It hurts too much."

Lois Greenwood went off into another series of giggles. As he made his way up the steps to the boat deck, Dillman could hear her girlish laughter echoing in the half-dark behind him.

After an early breakfast, Genevieve went into the second-class area of the ship to call on Madame Berthe Roussel. Though she

52

had been warned that the lady was inclined to histrionics, she found her very subdued that morning. Madame Roussel was a buxom woman in her thirties who wore a flamboyant silk dressing gown, and whose lustrous brown hair was brushed back neatly into a chignon. Her face was disfigured by a morose expression but Genevieve could see why the purser had found her desirable. The Frenchwoman had a mature beauty that, allied to her poise, would turn most male heads.

Madame Roussel was surprised that her visitor was a detective.

"But you do not look like the policeman," she said.

"That's the idea, Madame Roussel. My appearance is my disguise. By the way," offered Genevieve, "I can try to talk in French, if you prefer."

"No, no. My English, it is good, I think. Is only when I get excited that I need to speak in my own language. Last night, with the purser, I could not get all the English words out. You understand me now. Yes?"

"Perfectly."

Her accent was thick but her speech intelligible. As they sat opposite each other in the cabin, Genevieve observed how much jewelry the other woman was wearing. Apart from half a dozen rings, she had a gold watch, a gold bracelet on each wrist, a gold necklace, and a large gold brooch in the shape of a cockerel pinned on her dressing gown. An elaborate gold slide glistened in her hair.

"Is all I have left," explained Madame Roussel, touching the brooch and the necklace. "I wear them for the safety."

"And you had them on last night, presumably?"

"Yes, Miss Masefield."

"When did you last see the items that you kept in your hatbox?"

"Maybe, I think, yesterday at five o'clock."

"And you left your cabin soon after?"

"I meet with a friend to share the drink before dinner."

"May I have the friend's name?" asked Genevieve, taking a pencil and pad from her purse. The Frenchwoman hesitated. "Well?"

"Is necessary?"

"I think so, madame."

"But this theft, it is nothing to do with him, no?"

"Perhaps not," said Genevieve, "but he might be able to confirm the time when you actually met."

"I will ask him."

"Why not let me do that?"

"Just find my jewelry for me, mademoiselle."

"I'll do my best," promised Genevieve, wondering why she was so unwilling to give the man's name. "What I simply must have, however, is a list of the items stolen and the amount of money taken."

"I have this here," said Madame Roussel, picking up a sheet of paper from the table and handing it over. "As you see, for some things, I do the little drawing for you."

"That will be very helpful."

"Is the diamond pendant I miss most, you see. My husband, he give it to me for my birthday. Six weeks later, he die."

"I'm sorry to hear that, Madame Roussel."

"This pendant, it is very special to me."

"Sentimental value."

"Is right."

"What time did you return to your cabin?"

"It was late," said the other. "Maybe eleven o'clock."

"And were you alone?"

Madame Roussel flashed her eyes. *"Bien entendu,"* she said with a touch of annoyance. "I would not let anyone else in, mademoiselle. I always travel in the first class, but it was full up when I book the cabin, so they put me in here. Ha!" she snapped with a dismissive gesture of her hand. "Is not good enough for me."

"You'll have to take that up with Mr. Cannadine."

"I tell him last night. I blame the P and O. In first class, my jewelry would have been very safe, no?"

"Not if you kept it in your hatbox, Madame Roussel. It's standard practice for passengers to leave their valuables under lock and key. They should have been in the ship's safe."

"I sail many times with P and O and nothing is ever stolen."

"Then you've been fortunate. As you know, it's company policy to advise passengers about the safety of their personal belongings. They can be insured, of course, but you really should have handed them over to the purser for safekeeping."

"Do not tell me what to do!" said the other, rising to her feet in anger. "What do you say—that this crime is my fault?"

"No, of course not."

"I think you come to help me, not to give the insults."

"I'm sorry," said Genevieve. "I didn't mean to upset you."

"I am the victim, mademoiselle. Remember that."

"I will. Thanks to this list of yours, I now know what we're looking for, and I'm fairly certain that we'll be able to recover the items. One way or another, we usually do."

"We?"

"I have a partner, Madame Roussel."

"Next time, I think, I prefer to talk to this other lady."

"It's a man, actually."

"Then you can send him, please. Maybe he will be on my side."

"We're *all* on your side," said Genevieve, earnestly, "and we'll do out utmost to solve this crime quickly." She got up from her chair. "I'll make sure that you're kept in touch with any developments— and I apologize again for upsetting you."

Madame Roussel folded her arms defiantly to show that she was not appeased. Sunlight slanted through the porthole and made her jewelry gleam even more brightly.

"Good-bye, mademoiselle," she said flatly.

"One last question."

"Do not ask for any names. I not give them."

"I just need to be certain of one thing," said Genevieve softly. "What puzzles me is that the thief was able to get into your cabin so easily. There's no sign of forced entry—so how did he open the door?" She took a deep breath before speaking again. "I take it that you did lock the cabin?"

Madame Roussel glared at her for a moment and seemed to be on the point of exploding. Genevieve braced herself for an attack that never came. Instead, the Frenchwoman swung round abruptly and went off into her bathroom, slamming the door behind her.

Genevieve had her answer.

George Dillman listened to the details of the crime with interest. He had been on the point of leaving his cabin when his partner called on him. Like Genevieve, he wanted to know the name of the friend with whom Madame Roussel had spent time the previous evening.

"I'll speak to the head waiter in the second-class dining saloon," he said. "This lady sounds as if she'd attract attention. One of the catering staff may have noticed the man with whom she dined."

"Thank you, George."

"It's the least I can do. Mind you, if I do track him down, Madame Roussel is going to be angry with you when she hears about it."

"That depends on how you put it to her."

"Me?"

"Yes," Genevieve said sweetly. "She and I got off on the wrong foot, I'm afraid. I'll leave the diplomacy to you from now on."

"As you wish," he said obligingly. "At least, I'll be involved in helping to solve the crime. When you told me that the case had fallen into your lap, I must admit that I was envious. The only drama that I've found on the *Salsette* came in the shape of a pretty girl on roller skates."

He told her about his meeting with Lois Greenwood, expecting her to be astonished by the news that women played football on roller skates. Genevieve showed no surprise at all.

"It's been happening for years," she said. "The last time we were in England, I saw a photograph in the *Illustrated London News* that showed women playing football on a roller-skating rink. When we put our minds to it, there's very little we can't do, you know."

"You've proved that," he said, slipping his arms around her. "Shall I see if Miss Greenwood has room for you on her team?"

"No, thank you. The only team I want to be on is yours."

"In that case," he said, kissing her, "let's get out there and play."

Leaving the cabin, they went off in different directions. Dillman made his way to the second-class dining saloon where the catering staff was cleaning everything away after breakfast. The waiter was a short, squat Welshman in his forties, with a bald pate and a walrus mustache so thick and luxuriant that it looked as if his hair had migrated from his head to take refuge on his upper lip. He was very helpful.

"I remember the lady well," he said with a twinkle in his eye. "There's something about the French that sets them apart—and I don't mean that strange lingo they speak. No, Madame Roussel had style. I always notice that kind of thing."

"Do you happen to remember where she sat?" asked Dillman.

The waiter pointed. "On that table over there," he said. "Directly under the chandelier so that the light fell on her. She knew how be the center of attention."

"What about the man who was sitting next to her?"

"There wasn't one, Mr. Dillman."

"Then he must have been seated opposite."

57

"No," said the Welshman, "that was the funny thing. Madame Roussel was the most handsome woman in the room, yet she was surrounded by other ladies."

Dillman was disappointed. The anonymous friend might be a little more difficult to track down. He wondered why she had not dined with the man. Did she not wish to be seen in public with him? Had the two of them fallen out? Was he, perhaps, traveling in first class? Or had he deliberately missed dinner in order to plunder her cabin? There was another possible explanation. The man was married and wished to keep his liaison with Madame Roussel secret from his wife. Dillman's visit to the dining saloon gave him food for thought.

Still pondering, he came out on to the main deck and felt a welcome breeze coming off the sea. There were several passengers about, walking, reclining in deck chairs, or playing various games, but the two who caught his eye were no more than five yards away. Guljar Singh, the old Sikh, was listening to a small, waiflike Indian girl and nodding in sympathy. At first glance, Dillman took him to be her grandfather, but the only Sikh women he had seen in Bombay had worn a sari, and this child had on *salwar kameez,* baggy trousers, and a loose tunic. The girl's oval face had a kind of sad beauty and her large, brown eyes were filled with gratitude that someone was taking her seriously.

Guljar Singh became aware that Dillman was watching them. He broke off and turned to the American with a welcoming smile. The girl was more cautious, stepping back and lowering her head deferentially.

"Come and meet my new friend," said the old man. "This is Suki, who is going all the way to England. Isn't she a brave girl, Mr. Dillman?"

"Very brave," agreed Dillman. "Hello, Suki."

She gave him a nod but said nothing. Guljar Singh chuckled.

"In Hindi, she can talk all day," he explained, "but she is still shy of speaking in English. That will soon change when she gets to London."

"Are you looking forward to it, Suki?" asked Dillman. She shook her head. "Why not?"

"She would rather stay in her own country," said Singh.

"Then why is she going?"

"Her mother thinks that she will have a better life there."

"Is she being sent against her will?"

"I am not sure, Mr. Dillman. Her story is a little confusing. I have not heard all of it yet. My only worry for her is the English climate. I think it will be too cold for her in winter."

"Where does she come from?"

"Suki was born in the Punjab."

"How old is she?"

"Twelve."

"That's very young to make such a long journey."

"I know, Mr. Dillman."

"Who is she traveling with?"

It was Matilda Kinnersley who provided the answer. Appearing on cue, she looked around, saw the girl, then pointed an accusing finger at her. Dillman saw the look of fear in the child's eyes.

"Sukinder!" cried Mrs. Kinnersley. "What on earth are you doing out here when I need you? Get back to our cabin at once."

"Yes, *memsahib*," the girl mumbled before running off obediently.

Mrs. Kinnersley turned on Dillman. "Don't believe a word she told you," she said, ignoring Singh as if he were not there. "The girl is a congenital liar."

FIVE

Tabitha Simcoe was very disappointed when they spoke outside the first-class lounge. She clearly had been banking on
the fact that Genevieve Masefield would accept the invitation, but
the latter had turned it down with her customary politeness.
Tabitha was distressed.

"I was so hoping that you could join us," she said.

"Under other circumstances, I would."

"Mother specifically asked for you."

"That's nice," said Genevieve, "But I'm rather busy this morning, and to tell you the truth, Tabby, I'm not very good at bridge."

"I don't believe that for a moment. You're the sort of person
who's good at everything."

"Not when it comes to card games."

"The only way to improve at bridge is to play it."

"Another time, maybe. You'll have to find someone else."

"Who?" said Tabitha.

"Well, you've already roped in this Mr. Nevin," Genevieve reminded her. "How did you meet *him*?"

"Over breakfast."

"Perhaps he can bring along a partner."

"I thought it was going to be you," sighed Tabitha. "It's one of the reasons I had breakfast in the saloon. I expected to see you there. Mother had her breakfast in our cabin, while I went off in search of you."

"And you found this Dudley Nevin instead."

"It's not a fair exchange, Genevieve."

"Why—what's wrong with him?"

"Nothing, I suppose. He's pleasant enough in his own way and we had a very civilized breakfast together, but I'm not sure if Mother will like him. She's very selective."

"So I noticed."

"With you at the table, we'd have had no problem."

"I would have," said Genevieve. "I'd have lost every game and let my partner down." She snapped her fingers. "Wait a moment. I know the perfect substitute for me."

"Do you?"

"Yes. Why don't you round up Mr. Rollins?"

"Oh, no, that wouldn't do at all."

"I thought you found him interesting."

"I did, Genevieve. I could have listened to him all night. Mother took a different view, however," she said, pulling a face. "She has a prejudice against Americans, I'm afraid. And she thought him far too earnest."

"That still leaves scores of other people to choose from, Tabby," said Genevieve, pointing to the lounge. "All you have to do is to go in there and ask if anyone would like a game of bridge. I daresay that you'll have dozens of offers."

Tabitha squeezed her arm. "But not the one I want."

Genevieve did not wish to upset her but she had no choice. Now that she had a crime to solve, her time was mortgaged and she could not indulge in the kinds of pursuits that other passengers used to pass the time. Playing bridge could take hours that she could ill afford.

"How is your mother this morning?" she asked.

"Very well, thank you."

"I was so worried when I heard about her fall."

"It happens occasionally," said Tabitha wearily. "It's the reason that I can't leave her on her own for too long. Last time, she bruised her leg badly. She was very lucky yesterday."

"Yes," agreed Genevieve. "Your mother had the good fortune to fall on that lovely thick carpet. P and O deserves credit for that. Well," she went on, glancing at her watch, "I must be off. Enjoy your game."

"Will I see you at lunch?"

"Probably."

"I hope we can sit together again—and at dinner."

"Perhaps."

"I thought that we were friends."

"We are, Tabby, but I don't want to hold you back."

"From what?"

"Meeting people," said Genevieve, deciding it was time to be direct. "To be more exact, making a few male friends. It's unfair that you should play nursemaid to your mother all the time when there are so many other people on board. You should enjoy their company."

Tabitha was hurt. "It's the other way around, isn't it?"

"What do you mean?"

"Be honest, Genevieve. You're not holding *me* back at all. I'm the one who's getting in *your* way." Her eyes moistened. "At least I know where we stand now. You want more freedom onboard the ship."

"That's not what I meant at all, Tabby."

"Wasn't it?"

"I was thinking of you."

"What chance do I have of meeting a man?" said the other, bitterly.

"You befriended Mr. Nevin this morning."

"Only to get someone to play bridge with us."

"He must have been attracted to you."

"But I wasn't remotely attracted to him. And even if I had been, what would have been the point? I have Mother to look after and that's a full-time job. The only person who could have made it bearable on this voyage is you, Genevieve," she said, biting her lip, "and you don't want us to be friends."

"That's not true, Tabby."

"Well, if you wish me to keep out of your way, I will."

"Don't say that. Let me explain."

But the words went unheard. Close to tears, Tabitha hurried away in the direction of the cabins, leaving Genevieve to squirm with guilt.

Dillman's reasoning was sound. All he had heard about Madame Roussel suggested that she was a woman who enjoyed being seen in public, and who would sooner or later appear. He chose the second-class lounge as the most likely place she would head for, and he sat there patiently with his newspaper. Though he had never seen her before, he recognized her instantly when she did arrive. Genevieve's description had been accurate. Wearing a blue-and-gold silk dress with a floral pattern on it, she swept into the room and took a seat from which she could watch the doorway. Her jewelry looked far too lavish for morning wear. Dillman hoped that she was waiting for the man with whom she had spent time on the previous day.

When someone did join her, however, it was a young couple, who spoke to her in French. They were soon sharing a pot of coffee with her. Dillman contented himself with watching Madame Roussel, noting her easy self-confidence, her aplomb, and her studied gestures. Glancing around, he saw that a number of other men in the room were also keeping an eye on her. One of them was Dudley Nevin. The civil servant excused himself from his companions, got up from his chair, and came across to Dillman.

"What are you doing in second class?" he wondered.

"Oh, meeting a friend for tea, Mr. Nevin. And you?"

"Same reason," he said, glancing over his shoulder at the elderly couple he had just left. "Except that they're acquaintances rather than friends. They're not allowed in first class so I had to come to them."

"Noblesse oblige."

"It was well worth the visit," he remarked, nodding toward Madame Roussel. "I wouldn't have missed seeing her. What a remarkable woman she is! Portuguese?"

"French, I think," said Dillman, pretending to look across at her for the first time. "But you're right, Mr. Nevin. A most attractive lady."

"I thought she might be from Goa. It's been a Portuguese colony for almost four hundred years. *We* should have moved in to take it over ourselves," he said arrogantly. "But I shouldn't be telling *you* that, should I?" he added with a chortle. "You don't approve of our imperial ambitions."

"I dislike imperialism of all kinds."

"We'll have to argue about that another time."

"What's the point?" Dillman said with a smile. "You know where I stand, and I know that you belong to the Major Kinnersley persuasion."

"I always enjoy a lively debate."

"You certainly manage to exert more self-control than the major."

"I feel sorry for the chap," said Nevin, eyes still on Madame Roussel. "Being married to a wife like that is enough to make anyone short-tempered. Now, if he had someone like *her* in his bed," he went on, indicating the Frenchwoman, "he'd be a different man."

"What possible appeal would Major Kinnersley have for her?"

"Status. Income. A house in London."

"Yes, Mr. Nevin, but the lady has a fatal defect in his eyes."

"Does she?"

"Of course," said Dillman. "She's not English. She's French. That's the stumbling block. The major has a very low opinion of foreigners."

"Especially if they happen to be Americans," teased Nevin.

"Really? I thought that I was slowly winning him over."

Nevin laughed. "I'll have to go," he said, taking a watch from his waistcoat pocket and consulting it. "Playing bridge."

"With the major and his wife?"

"Heavens, no! I don't wish to stare across a card table at that lady. She'd ruin my concentration. I'm playing with a Miss Tabitha Simcoe and her mother. And I understand that a third lady will be joining us." He glanced across at Madame Roussel once more. "What a pity it isn't her!"

His gaze then shifted to the door and his manner changed at once. Nevin's grin was replaced by an expression of utter dismay. Dillman looked toward the door and saw a thickset, bearded, middle-aged man in a white suit, who was scowling at Nevin. The civil servant was frozen to the spot. After a moment, the man straightened his shoulders, spun on his heel, and marched off. Nevin was still staring at the doorway.

"Someone you know?" asked Dillman.

"No, no," said the other. "Never set eyes on him before."

Anxious to please her employers, Sukinder poured the tea with great care, then stepped back. Major Kinnersley gave her a nod of approval but his wife did not even look at the girl. Reaching for the sugar, Mrs. Kinnerseley put two spoonfuls into her cup and stirred it.

"That is all?" Sukinder asked meekly.

"Yes," said the major. "We'll call you if we need you."

"Thank you, *sahib*."

"Be sure to work on your exercises," ordered Mrs. Kinnersley.

"Yes, *memsahib*."

"And don't you dare go wandering off again."

"No, *memsahib*."

The girl withdrew gratefully and shut the cabin door behind her.

"You're too hard on Sukinder, my dear," said the major.

"Servants need a firm hand."

"She's still very young."

"That makes no difference," argued his wife. "They have to be taught properly from the start or they get into bad habits. Look at her mother. She was so lazy at times. I won't tolerate that kind of thing from Sukinder."

"Her mother was a good servant."

"Only because I tamed her in the end."

"They're human beings, Matilda, not animals."

"They're servants. Nothing more."

"That doesn't mean they don't have feelings."

"Feelings?" she echoed with disdain. "A girl like Sukinder doesn't have real feelings—just childish impulses that have to be contained. If she's to live in our home, she must be brought up to scratch."

"I agree with that," he said, "and I know that she's trying hard."

"She wasn't trying hard earlier on, Romford. Instead of working on her English, she went up on deck as if she was just another passenger. I caught her talking to that odious Mr. Dillman."

"We can't have that."

"Whatever happens, we must not dine with *him* again."

"And we must keep him away from Suki—from Sukinder. We don't want him filling her head with all that balderdash about how everyone is born equal. When she goes on deck again, I'll take her."

"Why should she be allowed out there at all?"

"We can't keep her locked up in her cabin, Matilda."

"It's one sure way to make her read her books."

"That may be," he said, "but it's not healthy. Besides, it's the first time she's ever been on a ship. Sukinder ought to get some pleasure out of it. Leave it to me. I'll take charge of her."

"As long as you don't let her talk to her own kind. There are far too many Indians onboard," she said with disgust. "Some even have the gall to travel first-class."

"They're high caste, my dear. They'd have no interest in Sukinder."

"Mr. Dillman did."

"That's another matter."

"So did this elderly Sikh. The three of them were together."

"I'll make sure that she speaks to nobody," vowed Kinnersley. "Except me, of course. I'll walk her round the deck so that she gets some kind of recreation, and we'll work on her English at the same time." He sipped his tea and adopted a quieter tone. "How do you feel now?"

"About what?"

"Going home after all these years."

"I'm not sure."

"It will be a big change."

"That's what frightens me, Romford."

"It's not like you to be frightened of anything."

"We're giving up so much," she said with a sigh. "It just won't be the same in England. How can it be? We'll be so *ordinary* there. That's what unnerves me. Frankly, there are moments when the prospect terrifies me."

When she had taken morning tea, Madame Roussel went for a stroll on the promenade deck, using her parasol to keep off the sun. Dillman followed at a discreet distance, wondering if she was about to make contact with her mystery admirer. The French-woman had obviously made friends since she had been on the *Salsette*. She stopped to chat to a number of people and waved to a few others as she passed, but Dillman could not identify the man he was after. It was a friend of the detective's who forced him to call off his pursuit.

"I thought so," said Lois Greenwood, bounding up to him. "I wasn't sure at first but . . . it is you, Mr. Dillman, isn't it?"

"I hope so, Miss Greenwood."

"You look so different in daylight."

"So do you—no roller skates."

Lois was wearing a calf-length cotton dress with long sleeves and a straw hat with a floppy brim. Now that he could see her face properly, he noticed how pretty she was. Her smile was infectious.

"Do you know anything about geography?" she asked.

"A little. Why?"

"You can settle an argument I had with Daddy. He thinks we're sailing across the Indian Ocean but I believe it's the Arabian Sea. The thing is, I don't know where the dividing line between the two of them is."

"It's a question of latitude, Miss Greenwood."

"That's a bit technical for me."

"I can't give you precise bearings," said Dillman, "but my guess is that you're right. We are crossing the Arabian Sea."

"Wonderful! I'll be able to crow over Daddy for once."

"Not exactly. The Arabian Sea is only the northwest arm of the Indian Ocean so, in that sense, your father is correct, as well."

"Oh, phooey!"

"Let's call it a dead heat, shall we?"

"I wanted to win."

"Then play football with your father on roller skates." She giggled happily. "What are you doing in this part of the world, anyway?"

"We had a holiday with my uncle and aunt."

"Where do they live?"

"In Bombay. Uncle David is the manager of a company that exports cotton. They have more servants than I could count. They did everything for us. It was a marvelous experience," she said. "The girls at school will be green with envy when I tell them."

"There can't be many of them who get to visit India."

"Only me. What about you, Mr. Dillman—why are you here?"

"I stopped off in Bombay on my way back from Australia."

"You've been *there*," she cried, eyes widening in wonder. "You must be an explorer or something."

"Just a tourist, seeing the sights."

"Do they have any sights in Australia? I thought it was full of ostriches, kangaroos, and those funny little black men."

"Aborigines."

"That's right—oh, and all those convicts we transported there."

Dillman was amused. "It's not a penal colony anymore, Miss Greenwood," he said with a tolerant smile. "Some of those convicts went on to live useful lives and start all kinds of flourishing enterprises. Their descendants are still enjoying the fruits of their efforts."

"Daddy says that Australia is still very primitive."

"They don't play football on roller skates, if that's what you mean."

She giggled again. "I've always liked sports," she confided.

"What else do you play?"

"Tennis, lacrosse, rounders—that's a kind of baseball. I also cycle, swim, and I've started taking fencing lessons at school."

"When do you find time to do any work?"

"I don't, if I can help it," she said. "Oh, the other thing I love doing is tobogganing. When there's an icy spell, the hill behind our house makes the most wonderful slide. It's like being in Switzerland."

"You obviously keep yourself fit, Miss Greenwood."

"What sports do you play?"

"Sailing is my real passion," he told her. "You might say that I was born with a rudder in my hands. My father makes a living building large yachts. I was lucky enough to take many of them on sea trials."

Lois was impressed. "I say! You're an explorer and a navigator!"

"Not quite."

"I wish that Daddy did something as exciting as that."

"Doesn't he?"

"No," she complained. "He has the most boring job in the world. I don't know how he puts up with it. All those meetings, all those people he has to be nice to when he can't possibly like them. Mummy says that he's an important man, but I think his work is tedious."

"Why—what does he do?"

"He's a member of Parliament."

Genevieve spent the whole morning on the case, interviewing the steward who looked after Madame Roussel's cabin, checking to see if any passengers had been absent from the second-class dining saloon on the previous evening, and puzzling over the identity of the Frenchwoman's male admirer. But she never completely forgot her conversation with Tabitha Simcoe. Filled with remorse for having upset her, she hoped that she would have the opportunity to make amends over luncheon.

On her way to the dining saloon, however, she was intercepted by Paulo Morelli. The Italian was patently delighted with his assignment. He handed her an envelope and gave her a dazzling grin.

"I was just about to push this under your door, Miss Masefield."

"Thank you," she said, glancing at the envelope.

"It's from Mr. Cannadine."

"So I see."

"I think, maybe, that he wishes to see you."

"Why—have you read the contents?"

"No, no," said Morelli, holding up his hands. "I would never do that. We are forbidden to open any mail belonging to passengers. We are only allowed to go into the cabins by request."

"Yet you went into Mrs. Simcoe's cabin yesterday," she noted.

"That was only by chance, *signorina*. I knock on the door to introduce myself, and I hear these groans from inside. Somebody needed help," he said, changing the facts to make himself look like a savior. "I had to let myself in."

"It's a good job that you did, Paulo."

"I know. Since then, I go in and out of that door many times."

"Yes, I understand that Mrs. Simcoe had breakfast in her cabin."

"The two ladies, they have lunch there, as well."

"Oh," said Genevieve, realizing that she would have to postpone her attempted reconciliation with Tabitha. "I didn't know that."

"They send for me all morning," explained Morelli, as if it were a mark of favor. "They play the card game with friends. They call for tea, then more tea, then more tea again. This bridge, it is a thirsty game."

"With whom did they play?"

"Mr. Nevin and a nice English lady, Mrs. Ackroyd. I am her steward, as well. Her husband speaks a little Italian, so we talk together." He beamed at her. "I have to go now. Mrs. Simcoe and her daughter will want to see the menu."

"Thank you for this, Paulo," said Genevieve, holding up the letter.

"Is my pleasure."

He clicked his heels, gave her an elaborate bow, then walked away. Genevieve slit open the envelope and read the note inside.

"Oh, no!" she sighed. "Not again."

George Dillman seized his opportunity. Seeing her alone in the second-class lounge that afternoon, he introduced himself to Madame Roussel and was invited to sit beside her. She ran an appraising eye over him and was clearly impressed with what she saw.

"I am glad that you come and not the English lady."

"Miss Masefield is a very competent detective," he assured her.

"Is her manner that I not like, monsieur."

"There was obviously a misunderstanding. She asked me to apologize on her behalf, and to talk to you about the case."

"My jewelry, it is found?"

"Not yet, I fear," he said, "but there's been a development. I've just come from the purser. There's been another theft. A lady from second class was on deck this morning when her purse was taken."

"What interest is that to me? All I care for is my jewelry."

"We think that the same thief may be responsible."

"So?"

"He must be a second-class passenger and will probably strike again a number of times. That means he will accumulate quite a haul by the end of the voyage, Madame Roussel," he pointed out.

"He'll have far too many valuables to hide easily. When we search baggage as people disembark, we are certain to find him."

"I cannot do without my things until then!"

"I thought it might comfort you."

"I want my jewelry now, monsieur."

"I only wish that I could oblige, but these things take time."

"If I do not get my jewelry back, my lawyer will sue P and O."

"There'll be no need for that," said Dillman firmly. "In any case, you have to accept some of the blame yourself. According to my partner, you left the door of your cabin unlocked."

"I was in a hurry when I leave."

"Yes, that's the other thing. You had cocktails with a friend, I hear. Miss Masefield wondered if he'd be able to give us a clear idea of what time you went to his cabin."

"I speak to him. It was not long after five o'clock."

"Then you were out of your own cabin for all of six hours. The thief could have struck at any time during that period." He rubbed his chin in thought before turning back to her. "I don't suppose that it would be possible for me to talk to your friend?"

"No, monsieur."

"Is there any particular reason?"

"I not wish it. That is enough."

"May I ask how long you've known this gentleman?"

"Why?"

"Because it would be instructive to hear if he's an old friend or a recent acquaintance. If it's someone you've only just met," said Dillman, choosing his words with care, "someone whom you don't really know, we have to consider the outside possibility that he may have been involved in the crime."

"Ridiculous, monsieur!"

"Thieves often work in harness. One distracts, the other strikes."

"My friend is not a thief."

"You can vouch for him, then?"

"Yes," she said, vehemently, "I can. You insult me as much as that lady I talk to this morning. She tell me it is all *my* fault."

"That's not what Miss Masefield said."

"Now you ask if I go into the cabin of a man I only just meet." She sat forward angrily in her deck chair. "What sort of woman you think I am, monsieur? One who has a drink with strangers?"

"No, Madame Roussel," he said, trying to mollify her. "That's not what I think at all. Let's forget all about it, shall we?"

"Is only one way to make me do that."

"What is it?"

"Find my jewelry."

"I will," promised Dillman.

"Before the end of the voyage?" she insisted.

He swallowed hard. "You have my word on it."

Dinner that evening was a formal affair. European men wore white tie and tails and the women appeared in a variety of evening gowns, some sober, others arresting, and a few quite daring. Indian wives aboard were not to be outdone. Bedecked in gold bangles and wearing their best saris or *salwar kameez,* they brought a blaze of color and exoticism to the occasion. Genevieve Masefield had selected a gown of cream satin that was trimmed with *chine* ribbon at the hem and the sleeves. She had brushed her hair up and held it in position with two ivory slides. Her only item of jewelry was the beautiful opal necklace that Dillman had bought for her in Australia. It set off her whole outfit.

Music was playing as she entered the dining saloon. Still eager to smooth Tabitha Simcoe's ruffled feathers, she intended to sit at her table but saw that she was too late. Constance Simcoe and her daughter already had dining companions. Though they acknowledged Genevieve as she walked past, there was no warmth in their smiles. She could see that Tabitha was still wounded by her earlier remarks.

At another table, Genevieve received a more cordial welcome.

"Would you care to join us, Miss Masefield?" said Wilbur Rollins.

"Oh, thank you," she replied, taking the chair that he held out for her. "That's very kind of you, Mr. Rollins."

"Allow me to introduce Mr. and Mrs. Ackroyd."

Genevieve was interested to meet Phoebe Ackroyd. The latter was a small, fussy woman in a green dress and coils of pearls. She peered at the newcomer through spectacles. Her husband, Gerald Ackroyd, was a silver-haired man in his sixties with a goatee. Since he had a hearing problem, he missed a great deal of the conversation but his wife talked enough for both of them.

"I understand that you played bridge this morning, Mrs. Ackroyd," said Genevieve. "With Mrs. Simcoe and her daughter."

"How do you know that?" asked the other woman.

"Tabitha asked me to play but I was unable to accept her offer."

"I wish that you had, Miss Masefield. You'd have been a better partner than the one I had."

"Mr. Nevin?"

"That was him. He couldn't seem to keep his mind on the game. It was most frustrating. We never won a single penny."

"You played for *money*?" said Rollins in surprise.

"Of course. It adds piquancy to the game."

"I didn't realize I was dining with a professional gambler."

"I played like an amateur this morning, Mr. Rollins," she said. "Thanks to Mr. Nevin. I was so irritated that I went back again this afternoon with Gerald. He can hear quite well with his ear trumpet."

"What's that, my dear?" asked her husband.

She raised her voice. "Your ear trumpet, dear!"

"Left it in the cabin."

"I'm talking about the game of bridge we played."

"Ah, yes, capital. Charming ladies."

"We have a system, you see," explained Mrs. Ackroyd to the others. "It worked quite well at first. But Mrs. Simcoe and her daughter had the most outrageous run of luck, and, if truth be told, Gerald was not at his most alert as the afternoon wore on."

"But he was an improvement on Mr. Nevin," said Genevieve.

"Oh, yes. A vast improvement."

Inclined to be garrulous, Mrs. Ackroyd could also listen when a subject engaged her, and she was mesmerized by what she heard of the forthcoming book by Wilbur Rollins. She elbowed her husband.

"We must get a copy, Gerald."

"A copy of what?"

"*Women at Sea.*"

"Yes," he said, looking around. "There are lots of them here and what a charming picture they make." He raised his wineglass. "To the ladies—God bless them!"

"I'll drink to that," said Rollins, reaching for his own glass.

It was an excellent meal and the Ackroyds were pleasant company. Gerald Ackroyd was a retired diplomat who had worked in India and he had come on a valedictory visit with his wife. Rollins was as engaging as ever on his favorite subject, but Genevieve was somehow unable to enjoy the evening. Apart from her discomfort over Tabitha Simcoe, she was concerned by the second theft that had been reported, and disturbed to learn that her partner had assured Madame Roussel that her jewelry would soon be returned. Genevieve did not share his confidence.

George Dillman was not dining in the first-class saloon that evening, wanting to be in the part of the ship where the two thefts had occurred and patrolling the second-class corridors in the guise of a steward. His absence was another reason for Genevieve's relative unease. When he was near, she always felt reassured even if she could not actually speak to him. She brought a hand up to caress the opal at her neck. Now that he was her husband, every moment away from Dillman was painful, but she knew that their work took precedence. She was also grateful that he was the one who was keeping Madame Roussel under surveillance and not her. Dining in first class was infinitely preferable.

"Will we be in your book, Mr. Rollins?" pressed Mrs. Ackroyd.

"I'm afraid not," he replied.

"But Miss Masefield and I are women at sea."

"You are ladies at leisure," he corrected with a gracious smile. "My interest is in women who actually become sailors. It happened more often than you can imagine. There were sailors who smuggled their wives aboard, and captains who turned a blind eye to the occasional woman who lacked a wedding ring. No," he went on, "the only modern instance I may include is what we saw outside Bombay harbor. Dozens of women who accompanied the coolies out to a cargo ship. I'll probably mention them in an appendix."

"What's he saying, my dear?" asked Gerald Ackroyd.

"Appendix," said his wife.

"Ah, yes. Nasty operation. You have my sympathies, old chap."

"I'm not having my appendix removed, Mr. Ackroyd," said Rollins.

"Oh, but you should. Otherwise, there are complications."

"Forgive him," said his wife. "I think my husband heard most of it. And that's more than can be said for Mr. Nevin this morning," she went on, clicking her tongue. "I don't believe he listened to a word that I said to him. Bridge is a game that you must play properly or not at all. I meant to say as much to Mr. Nevin this evening."

"Where is he sitting?" asked Genevieve.

"He doesn't appear to be here, Miss Masefield."

"Are you sure?"

"Quite sure. I've watched everyone who came through that door and he was not among them. After what happened this morning, Mr. Nevin is too ashamed to face me. He's keeping out of my way."

Dudley Nevin lay on his back in the darkness of his cabin. A pool of blood had congealed on his white shirt. There was an expression of complete surprise on his face, as if he were still trying to work out why he had been stabbed to death.

SIX

Genevieve Masefield was so relieved to see him when he called at her cabin that night, she flung herself into his arms. Dillman, now in formal wear, was pleased with the warmth of his reception. Pulling her close, he grinned appreciatively.

"I take it that you missed me."

"Very much," she said, nestling into his shoulder.

"What I missed was having dinner in first class."

"Is that all?" she protested. "What about me?"

"Oh, I missed you, as well, darling. That goes without saying."

"I like you to say it anyway."

"I just did," he pointed out. "What was on the menu this evening?"

"Everything you could possibly want. It was a wonderful feast. The best meal we've had on a P and O vessel. The dessert was mouthwatering."

"Don't rub it in," he said, wincing slightly. "I had to make do with a cup of tea and a sandwich. The life of a steward in second class leaves a lot to be desired, I can tell you."

"What did you find?"

"That the irascible Madame Roussel had the sense to lock her door this evening. I checked every cabin in second class while I was at it. All securely locked. No thief waiting to pounce."

"A wasted exercise, then," she said, stepping back.

"Not at all, Genevieve. My simply being there acted as a deterrent. I fancy that we're dealing with an opportunist. If a door is unlocked, he goes through it. If a purse is left unguarded on deck, he steals it. Do you see what I mean?" he said, easing her gently away from him. "A professional would target a victim more carefully, only going for someone who would give them rich pickings."

"Madame Roussel would fit that description."

"I think that the thief was lucky there. When he let himself into her cabin, he couldn't have known what he'd find. Madame Roussel had only been on the ship for a couple of hours."

"That's true."

"How could anyone have learned that she kept valuables in her cabin? No," he decided. "Everything points to an opportunist's crime. The thief didn't realize that he'd strike oil on his first attempt."

"That rules out our theory about her mysterious friend," she said. "He wasn't distracting her so that a confederate could search her cabin."

"I think not, Genevieve. How could he possibly know that she'd be foolish enough to leave her door unlocked? Mind you, I'd still like to find out who he is," he went on, scratching his head. "Why does a woman need to keep the name of her admirer secret? I find that odd."

"I have to do it all the time, George."

"That's different."

"Is it? I wonder."

"We have good reason to conceal our relationship."

"Madame Roussel may have an equally good reason."

"I doubt that. She actually volunteered the information that she'd been drinking with a friend, remember, so we know the man exists. The problem is that she won't divulge his name."

"There's one obvious explanation, George."

"I agree," he said. "And to some extent, she looks the part. Madame Roussel wouldn't be the first courtesan we've met in the course of our work. Yet somehow I don't feel that's the answer. If it had been, she'd never have mentioned this admirer of hers in the first place."

"No, discretion would be part of her trade."

"I daresay we'll unmask the fellow in the end."

"Until then, they keep their secret. Just like us."

"Nobody must know that we're man and wife, Genevieve."

"As long as *you* don't forget."

"How could I?" He kissed her on the lips. "Happy?"

"Very happy, George. When we're together."

"I only wish that I could stay."

"Why don't you?"

"Because it would be too big a risk. If a problem occurs in the middle of the night, Mr. Cannadine would send someone to my cabin. How do I explain that I didn't sleep there?"

"In that case," she suggested, "I'll come to you."

"No, darling," he said with regret. "We agreed on a plan and we must stick to it. Aden is only a few days away. We'll have a whole week there before we pick up another ship. We can be together properly then."

"I can't wait."

"All we have to do is to catch this thief in the meantime."

"And hope that no more crimes are committed aboard."

Dillman was confident. "I have a feeling that the worst is over," he said airily. "If we can reclaim the stolen goods, and get Madame Roussel off our backs, I fancy that we're going to have a restful voyage."

As instructed, the steward arrived early at the cabin with the breakfast. Balancing the tray on one hand, he knocked on the door with the other.

"Breakfast, Mr. Nevin," he called.

He used his key to unlock the door and went in, expecting to find the passenger still in his bunk. Instead, Dudley Nevin was sprawled out on the floor. The steward gaped in horror and almost dropped the tray. He backed out of the cabin as fast as he could.

It was shortly after seven in the morning. George Dillman had just finished dressing when the purser called at his cabin. He could see from Max Cannadine's face that something very serious had happened.

"Trouble?" asked Dillman.

"The worst kind," said the purser. "A murder."

"Oh, dear! Who was the victim?"

"A first-class passenger—Mr. Dudley Nevin."

Dillman was shocked. "Mr. Nevin? But I know him."

"Not anymore, I fear."

"Where did it happen?"

"In his cabin."

"How was he killed?"

"Stabbed through the heart."

"Who discovered the body?"

"The steward," said Cannadine. "He was badly shaken by what

he saw. If I'm honest, so was I. This is a bad business, Mr. Dillman."

"I'd like to take a look for myself. Have you called the doctor?"

"He's examining the body right now."

They hurried along to the cabin and the purser let them in with his master key. Down on one knee, Dr. Rory McNeil was still looking at the wound that had killed Dudley Nevin. When he was introduced to Dillman, he gave him a nod. McNeil was a slight, stringy man in his fifties with close-cropped ginger hair and a freckled face. The detective came over to kneel beside him.

"What was the murder weapon?" he said.

"That," replied the doctor, pointing to a blood-covered knife on the other side of the cabin. "It's a *kukri*—a weapon used by Gurkhas."

"Why is it lying over there and not beside the body?"

"You're the detective, Mr. Dillman. I'm just a ship's doctor,"

"How long has he been dead?"

"Difficult to be exact," said McNeil. "Twelve hours at least."

Dillman took a closer look at the corpse. Dudley Nevin was wearing only a shirt, trousers, and shoes. One of his suspenders had broken and his collar had been torn. Dr. McNeil had opened the shirt to expose the ugly wound in the man's chest. There were also lacerations on the hands of the corpse. Dillman stood up.

"It looks as if he put up something of a struggle," he concluded.

"Then it's possible that the people in the adjoining cabins may have heard something," said Cannadine.

"Not if they'd gone off to dinner. Besides, if a violent disturbance had been overheard, someone would have reported it." Taking out a handkerchief, he crossed to the knife and picked it up by the handle. "Curved blade, thickening towards the end, and as sharp as a razor. This is designed to kill. It's not the kind of thing you'd buy to peel an orange."

"Does that mean we're looking for an Indian?"

"I'm not so sure, Mr. Cannadine."

"Who else would use a *kukri* but a Gurkha?" asked McNeil.

"It's their preferred weapon," conceded Dillman.

"That narrows the field immediately."

"No, Doctor. I don't think it does. A man who owned this knife wouldn't discard it easily. He certainly wouldn't leave it close to a murder victim so that we could find it."

"What are you suggesting?" asked the purser.

"That somebody fled in a hurry. Look where the knife was lying. It's almost as if the killer stabbed his victim, backed away from him, dropped the knife here, then beat a hasty retreat."

"I still think we might be looking for an Indian attacker— someone with a grudge against Mr. Nevin. Do you know what he did for a living?"

"He was a civil servant in Delhi."

"There's a possible motive, then," said Cannadine. "We can run their country for them but we can't stop them feeling resentful about it. Perhaps someone saw Mr. Nevin as a symbol of British imperialism."

"There are plenty of those aboard," noted Dillman. "Why choose him when there are far more senior figures in the British administration? I don't see this as a political assassination."

"I hope you're right or we're sitting on a powder keg."

McNeil rose to his feet. "There's nothing more I can do here," he said. "I'd like to move him to a place where I can clean him up properly. Also, he needs to be kept on ice."

"My advice would be to shift him very soon," said Dillman, "while most passengers are still in their cabins. We need to keep this as quiet as possible. If word gets out that a murder has been committed, the whole ship will be in a state of agitation."

"That's the last thing we want," agreed Cannadine.

"Where's the steward who discovered the body?"

"Still in my office. He's been sworn to secrecy."

"What about his duties?"

"I'll have a word with the chief steward, Mr. Dillman. He'll have to be told, and so will the captain. Including us, that makes six people."

"Seven."

"Who else?"

"The killer, Mr. Cannadine. Add my partner and that gives us a total of eight people. Let's keep it to that, shall we?"

"Yes, please."

Dillman turned to McNeil. "Do you have a stretcher, Doctor?"

"In the medical room," said the other.

"If you could fetch it now, we'll carry him out of here under a blanket. Where shall we take him, Mr. Cannadine?"

"I know just the place. It's an empty storage room."

"Then let's get him there as soon as we can," said Dillman. "And we must make sure that nobody comes into this cabin. If they see that blood on the carpet, they may get curious."

"This cabin will be out of bounds till we reach Aden."

"Then what?" asked McNeil.

"We unload Mr. Nevin with the mailbags," said Cannadine, looking down at the corpse. "He must have nearest and dearest in England. The body will need to be shipped back there." He glanced at Dillman. "Did you say that you knew the chap?"

"Yes, we met in Bombay as we were about to embark."

"What sort of character was he?"

Dillman recalled the last time he had met Dudley Nevin. They were in the second-class lounge together and the Englishman had reacted to the appearance at the door of a thickset man with a beard.

"He was a frightened man," said Dillman, gazing down sadly at the body. "With good cause, it seems."

Quickening her pace, Genevieve Masefield caught up with the other woman outside the first-class dining saloon. Tabitha Simcoe did not look overjoyed to see her.

"Good morning," said Genevieve. "How are you this morning?"

"Fine, thank you."

"Your mother is having breakfast in her cabin, I assume."

"Yes, Genevieve. Mother is not at her best first thing."

"Which of us is? But I'm glad that I've caught you alone at last, Tabby. I wanted to apologize properly."

"There's no need," Tabitha said petulantly.

"I think that there is. I gave you completely the wrong impression."

"Yes, you led me to believe that we were friends."

"We are," insisted Genevieve, "I promise you."

"Then what was all that about not getting in my way?"

"I was only trying to help, Tabby. I know that looking after your mother takes priority, but you are entitled to *some* time on your own. You've got Paulo to help now," she pointed out. "He can't do enough for Mrs. Simcoe. Ever since he found her collapsed on the floor, he somehow feels responsible for her."

"Paulo does take the load off me," admitted Tabitha.

"Then make use of your free time. Spread your wings."

"It's easy for you to say that, Genevieve."

"What do you mean?"

"Well, you're so beautiful and sophisticated. Wherever you go, you win compliments. I don't have your confidence. When people look at me, all they see is this pathetic creature who pushes a Bath chair around."

"No, they don't," said Genevieve, touching her arm. "They see an intelligent and attractive young woman."

"They might—if they had the chance."

"The chance?"

"Yes," said Tabitha seriously. "I don't believe that most people give me a second look. Not when I'm alone, that is. But when I'm with you, it's very different."

"In what way?"

"Well, to start with, I *feel* different. I know that I can never compete with you but that doesn't matter. In your company, I have more self-assurance. That means I start to get some attention."

"It's no more than you deserve, Tabby."

"But it doesn't happen when you're not around."

"I'm sure that it does."

"No, Genevieve. I know my limitations. It's all very well for you to tell me to spread my wings. Don't you understand?" said Tabitha, taking her by both hands. "I can only do that when I'm with you. I enjoy a sort of reflected glory, if you like, and it gives me such pleasure."

Genevieve was puzzled. The other woman seemed to be in a strange mood. When she had been free from her mother before, Tabitha had been spirited and almost gleeful, like a child being let out on school holidays. There was no sign of that animation now. She seemed to be at the mercy of conflicting emotions and was, by turns, anxious, hostile, affectionate, embittered, and envious. There was also more than a hint of desperation in her manner. When Genevieve saw the confusion in her eyes, she felt sorry for her.

"It gave me pleasure as well, Tabby," she said.

"Really?"

"There's no reason why we shouldn't spend time together."

"Yes, there is," Tabitha said gloomily.

"Oh?"

"We're playing bridge with the Ackroyds again this morning. Mother is talking about a game this afternoon with some people we met at dinner last night." Tabitha shrugged hopelessly. "When will I see *you*?"

"We can at least have breakfast together."

"I hoped for so much more than that."

The transfer of the body went off without incident. As they carried the stretcher along the corridors, Dillman and Dr. McNeil had met only two passengers, and neither had been overly inquisitive. The body of Dudley Nevin was now lying in a storeroom on a bed of ice. Dillman was able to return to the man's cabin to search it for clues. The scene of the crime was still and empty now, but its atmosphere was charged. The detective could almost feel that a violent death had occurred there.

Dillman was systematic. Beginning with the wardrobe, he went carefully through everything that he found to see what information it might yield about the murder victim. There was nothing unusual. Dudley Nevin was traveling with exactly the clothing that might be expected. He had also brought a small case containing some paperwork that related to his job, writing materials, a couple of novels—*The Man of Property* by Galsworthy and *The Secret Agent* by Conrad—a pack of playing cards, a passport, and a map of the Aden Protectorate.

The most interesting find in the case was a letter from Michael Carew, the cousin whom Nevin had intended to visit in Aden. Couched in rather formal language, the missive was short but it did contain one sentence that leapt up at Dillman: *"If things in Delhi really are getting on top of you in the way that you describe, then, by all means, visit me here in Aden."* Was Nevin under some pressure at work or were there personal reasons why he wanted to get away from Delhi? Dillman sifted through his memories of the man. Nevin had been keen to escape India. Was he running away from something more than the boredom of his job?

The letter was a useful starting point. It gave Dillman the name and address of a family member who could arrange the transport of the body back to England, and who might be able to shed some light on the problems that Nevin was battling against in Delhi. By the time they met, the detective hoped, the crime would be solved. The one fact on which he could rely was that the killer was still aboard the ship. Once the *Salsette* docked in Aden and the passengers disembarked, the chances of finding the culprit would become extremely slim.

The dead man's billfold provided Dillman with a possible motive for the murder. Lying open on the cabinet, it had clearly been searched and any cash had been taken. Nevin certainly carried money with him. On the first evening at sea, when he had shared a brandy with Dillman and Major Kinnersley, the civil servant had given the waiter a generous tip from a wad of notes in his billfold. That money had now gone and so had his pocket watch. In their place, all that had been left was the *kukri*, the vicious-looking knife that Dillman cleaned off under the faucet. The other items in the billfold—two photographs, a ticket stub from a piano recital, and a membership card for a club in Delhi— had been of no value to the killer.

Each photograph showed a young woman, smiling at the camera. One of them wore a ball gown and was pictured in the doorway of a Regency house, the other, more attractive female, dressed for an outing, was in the passenger seat of an automobile, one hand on her hat to stop it from being blown off in the wind. If Nevin had treasured the photographs enough to carry them all the way to India, the young women must have been important in his life and, reasoned Dillman, they would be equally fond of him. The two of them would be deeply saddened when news of his brutal murder eventually reached them.

Dillman remembered what Nevin had told him about leaving

England under a cloud, and he wondered if either of the young women had anything to do with his departure. Had they been rivals for his affection? Did they, in fact, know of each other's existence? Were the sepia photographs being kept as trophies, marks of conquest to flatter his vanity? Nevin certainly had a keen interest in the opposite sex, as his comments about Madame Roussel had shown. Dillman suspected that the murder investigation would produce a few surprises about the private life of Dudley Nevin.

At least he knew where to begin. Agitated when they had first met, the civil servant had started to relax and enjoy himself once the ship was under way. He had been in good humor until that moment in the second-class lounge when he recognized someone in the doorway. Dillman's first task was to track down the bearded individual who had scowled at Nevin. The enmity between the two men had been palpable. It was the detective's job to find if it had been strong enough to make one of them stab the other to death.

Hurrying along to the purser's office in response to his note, Genevieve Masefield had assumed that another theft has occurred. She soon learned the hideous truth.

"A murder!" she exclaimed.

"I'm afraid so."

"When? Where? Who was the victim?"

"Sit down and I'll tell you," said Max Cannadine.

Genevieve took a seat. "Have you told George yet?"

"He's been working on the case for the past hour or so."

The purser gave her a concise but accurate account of what had happened, and what early deductions had been made about the crime. Listening intently throughout, Genevieve weighed each new detail in her mind, seizing on Dr. McNeil's judgment that the murder must have been committed at some time in the early evening of the previous day.

"That explains why we didn't see Mr. Nevin at dinner," she said.

"You met the gentleman?"

"No, Mr. Cannadine, but the lady with whom I dined knew him. Mrs. Ackroyd had partnered him in a game of bridge, apparently, and had felt terribly let down by him."

"Let down?"

"She said that Mr. Nevin was hopelessly distracted. He simply couldn't concentrate on the game," explained Genevieve, "and since they were playing for money, that really rankled."

"Did this Mrs. Ackroyd say *why* Nevin was distracted?"

"No—just that his mind was obviously elsewhere."

"Perhaps he felt in danger."

"At the end of the last game, he simply rushed off."

"Who else was involved?"

"Mrs. Simcoe and her daughter, Tabitha," she explained. "It was Tabby who recruited Nevin in the first place."

"I wonder what sort of state he was in when she did that."

"Why don't I find out?"

"Yes, of course," he recalled. "You know these ladies, don't you? It might be helpful if you made discreet inquiries, Miss Masefield. They mustn't be told what happened to Mr. Nevin, obviously. Neither must anyone else. The captain agrees—we must keep this from the passengers at all costs, or they'll start looking over their shoulders in fear." He shook his head in dismay. "This kind of thing has never happened on the *Salsette* before. I feel that she's been tainted."

"We can remove any stigma by solving the murder."

"I'm relying on you and Mr. Dillman to do that."

"There are still the other crimes to consider, as well."

"Yes," he sighed. "I haven't forgotten the lady whose purse went astray on deck. And I certainly haven't forgotten the French lady."

"No," said Genevieve with a rueful grin. "Madame Roussel would never allow us to do that."

Madame Berthe Roussel arrived precisely on time. She looked up and down the corridor to ensure that she was not seen, then she tapped on the door of a cabin. It opened almost immediately. Smiling happily, the Frenchwoman stepped quickly into the cabin.

Dillman began his search in the public rooms in second class. Unable to find the bearded man there, he went out onto the main deck and strolled along the starboard side. Two figures were walking towards him. Dillman was surprised to see that one of them was Major Kinnersley. By his side, timid and ill at ease, was Sukinder.

"Good morning, Major Kinnersley," said Dillman.

"Good morning," replied the other without enthusiasm.

"Hello, Suki."

"Her name is Sukinder, Mr. Dillman."

"I beg her pardon." He smiled at the girl. "How are you today?" She was about to reply but Kinnersley jumped in too quickly.

"She's rather shy," he said, "and her English is not what it should be. That's one of the things we're working on, isn't it, Sukinder?" The girl nodded. "She's getting better slowly."

Dillman was struck by the difference in tone between Kinnersley and his wife. While she had treated the child harshly, the major was a little more tolerant. His lofty disdain for his servant was tempered with a distant kindness. It was almost as if he were taking his dog for a walk.

"England will be rather overwhelming for her," said Dillman.

"We're aware of that, sir."

"How will she get on with your other domestics?"

"Sukinder will do what she's told."

"I think that she'll be very homesick."

"What business is it of yours, Mr. Dillman?" said the major.

"I feel sorry for Sukinder, that's all."

"Only because you know nothing of India. How can you feel sorry for someone who's rescued from poverty, and taken to a more civilized country where she'll be free from want? In time," he went on, "Sukinder will be very grateful to us. We're giving her a decent life."

"That's debatable."

"What do you mean?"

"Be honest, Major. Domestic service is nothing short of drudgery."

Kinnersley frowned. "Good-bye, Mr. Dillman."

"And she'll be cut off from her family and friends."

"You'll have to excuse us, sir."

Putting a hand on Sukinder's shoulder, he eased her past Dillman. The detective watched them go, thinking how incongruous they looked together. He then became aware that someone was standing beside him. It was Guljar Singh, his broad grin exposing a few missing teeth and his white beard dancing in the stiff breeze.

"Good morning, Mr. Dillman," he said. "Suki is not happy, is she?"

"No, Mr. Singh. I'm afraid not."

"You know the gentleman with her?"

"Yes," said Dillman. "Major Kinnersley. Retired from the army after a long spell in Simla. He and I are not what you might call close friends."

"I noticed that."

"The major seems to think that Americans are a lower form of life."

"Then what must he think of Sikhs?" asked the old man with a self-deprecating chuckle. "We must be subterranean."

"Not in my eyes, Mr. Singh."

"Thank you, Mr. Dillman. And you may like to know," he added, beaming at him, "that I do not look down on Americans."

"Then I think we have the basis for an *entente cordiale.*"

"What is that?"

"A friendship between two nations. Or, in this case, two people."

Dillman realized that the old man might be able to help him. Guljar Singh was not only held in high esteem for his great age, but for his wisdom and mystical powers. The knife that had killed Dudley Nevin was now in the detective's cabin. He wondered if Singh could give him some idea who might have brought it on board.

"What can you tell me about Gurkhas?" he asked.

"You should have put that question to the major."

"Why?"

"Because they will have served beside him in the British army," said Singh. "Gurkhas originally came from the Gurung, Limbu, Magar, Raj, and Tamang tribes of the Himalayas. They are hardy mountain warriors."

"I thought they came from Nepal."

"They conquered that country a long, long time ago. In the army, they are given rifles to shoot but they have their own weapon as well—the *kukri.* It is a very sharp knife and they can do terrible things with it."

"I'm sure," said Dillman, thinking of the wound in Nevin's chest.

"Why are you interested in Gurkhas?"

"No particular reason."

"That is a pity, my friend."

"Is it?"

"Yes," said Guljar Singh. "The people who can tell you most about Gurkhas are the Gurkhas themselves. We have three or four of them sailing on this ship."

Paulo Morelli enjoyed being in charge of the Bath chair. It was a novelty for him. Constance Simcoe made the most of his services, relishing the idea of being pushed along by the handsome little Italian. They were on their way to the promenade deck when they encountered Genevieve Masefield. The steward flashed a smile at her.

"Good morning, Mrs. Simcoe," said Genevieve. "I thought that you were playing bridge this morning."

"Not until ten-thirty," replied the other. "I need my constitutional before then. Paulo is going to take me around the deck."

"Is my favorite duty," said Morelli.

"I think that he says that to all the ladies."

"No, no, Mrs. Simcoe. This chair on wheels, I like."

"I can't say that I do," complained Constance. "I'd much prefer to get around on my own two feet."

Genevieve was pleased that her manner was so friendly now, and she guessed that Tabitha must have told her mother about their reconciliation over breakfast. It made conversation with the older woman much easier. Genevieve probed for information.

"I gather that you played cards with Mr. Nevin yesterday," she said.

"We tried, Miss Masefield. The rest of us played bridge, but he was in a world of his own. Do you know the man?"

"No, but I had dinner with the Ackroyds last night."

"Ah, yes. Poor Mrs. Ackroyd!"

"She felt horribly let down by her partner."

"She was," agreed Constance. "Mr. Nevin was appalling. I began to wonder if he'd ever played the game before."

"It was your daughter who invited him to play, wasn't it?"

"Yes, it was so peculiar. Over breakfast, apparently, he boasted about how he played bridge regularly in Delhi. According to Tabby, he couldn't wait to join us."

"So he was obviously in a happy mood over breakfast."

"There was no sign of it when he came into our cabin," said the other. "Mr. Nevin was nervous and preoccupied. He kept asking for tea."

"I bring it," said Morelli, proudly. "Mr. Nevin, a silly man."

"Why?" asked Genevieve.

"Is in a room with three beautiful women, and he pay no attention to them. Any other man would love to be where he is."

"Listen to him," Constance said indulgently. "Three beautiful women, indeed. Tabby might qualify, but I certainly don't at my age. And you've seen Phoebe Ackroyd."

Morelli grinned. "To me, all women is beautiful."

"He'll start to serenade us with a mandolin next!"

"Have you any idea *why* Mr. Nevin was distracted?" said Genevieve. "I mean, did he offer any explanation?"

"He mumbled something about problems at work but I didn't catch what he said. The worst of it was that he didn't even apologize to Mrs. Ackroyd. When we'd finished," recalled Constance, "he simply jumped up from the table and scurried off. Good riddance, I say!" She slapped the arm of the Bath chair. "Full speed, Paulo. I need some fresh air."

Genevieve stood aside so that they could get past her.

Dillman was perplexed. The man he was after was nowhere to be seen on any of the decks, yet he had to be on the vessel somewhere. The only explanation was that he was still in his cabin. The detective resigned himself to the fact that he might have to wait until luncheon before he caught up with the bearded man who had given Dudley Nevin such a jolt. Deciding to make one last circuit, Dillman went up the steps to the main deck. Footsteps echoed on the steel steps as someone came hurrying down toward him, and he all but collided with her. When he saw that it was Lois Greenwood, he laughed.

"I'll have to start wearing protective clothing," he said. "I think that you're determined to knock me over."

"I'm sorry, Mr. Dillman. I wasn't looking where I was going."

"At least you weren't on roller skates this time."

"I only put those on at night," said Lois. "But if you think I play a strange sport, you should see that man up on the main deck."

"Why—what's he doing?"

"Playing golf without any golf balls. He's swinging his driver as if he means to send the ball ten miles, but the only thing he's hitting is fresh air. He looks ridiculous."

"That's the mark of a true fanatic, Miss Greenwood. In pursuit of their sport, they never mind looking ridiculous. You can't expect him to hit golf balls. He'd lose them in the sea."

"I suppose not," she admitted. "Listen, have you seen that wonderful old Indian gentleman with the white beard—the one that predicts the future?"

"Yes, his name if Gulgar Singh. He's a mystic."

"I watched him earlier. People were giving him one rupee to hear him tell their fortunes. He went off into this trance for a long time. When he came out of it, he seemed to know exactly what was going to happen to people."

"He has a gift," affirmed Dillman, conscious that the Sikh had predicted a dreadful event aboard. "No doubt about that."

"Oh, I believed every word he told me, Mr. Dillman."

"You've spoken to him?"

"Yes," she said. "When he saw me watching him, he said that he'd tell me my fortune for nothing. All that he did was to stare deep into my eyes—he didn't look at my palm, or examine my tea leaves, or anything like that."

"What did he tell you?"

"That something very pleasant would happen to me."

"And it was true," noted Dillman. "You ran into me again."

"This was at school," she explained. "How did he even know that I was still there? Mr. Singh told me that I would go back to a very nice surprise." She giggled. "That'll make a change. I'm usually in trouble with Miss Carisbroke—she's our house mistress."

"Did Guljar Singh say anything else to you?"

"Only that I'd do something very special on this voyage, something that I could be proud of—and I don't think he meant roller-skating."

"What did he mean? Have you any idea?"

"None at all, Mr. Dillman. I'll just have to wait until I do it."

"It sounds as if you had nothing but good news from Mr. Singh."

"And it didn't cost me a penny. Oh," she said, looking over his shoulder. "I'll have to go, I'm afraid. Daddy is looking for me."

Dillman turned round and scanned the deck behind him.

"Which one is your father, Miss Greenwood?" he said.

"The one with the beard. He's just coming past that life belt."

Dillman was startled. The thickset individual in a white suit, who was picking his way along the crowded deck, was none other than the man whose presence on the ship had upset Dudley Nevin so much.

SEVEN

It was ironic. Dillman had spent well over an hour looking in vain for the man, yet the moment he abandoned his search, the person he most wanted to speak to actually came up to him. The fact that he was Lois Greenwood's father, however, posed a problem. Dillman was very fond of the girl and enjoyed his conversations with her. Unlike some English passengers, she was neither reserved nor condescending. He hated to think that her father might somehow be involved in the murder of Dudley Nevin. If true—and he had no firm evidence as yet—it would be a terrible shock for Lois to absorb.

The approach of a parent put her on her best behavior. Coming to the bottom of the steps, she stood there demurely until her father reached her, then performed the introductions with great composure. Dillman shook hands with Sylvester Greenwood, whose grip was firm and whose sharp eyes searched the American's face.

"How do you do, Mr. Dillman?" he said.

"Pleased to meet you, sir."

"Mr. Dillman is an explorer," declared Lois. "He's been *everywhere*."

"That's not strictly true," said Dillman.

"Yes, it is. You've even been to Australia."

"Your mother is looking for you, Lois," said her father. "You always disappear when she needs you. Now go back to the cabin and see what she wants, will you?"

"I prefer to be out on deck where all the fun happens."

"Do as you're told, please."

"In a minute."

"Now," insisted her father.

Lois gave up. "Yes, Daddy," she said, obediently. "Good-bye, Mr. Dillman. I hope to see you later on."

"I look forward to that," said Dillman. As the girl scampered off, he turned to her father. "You have a charming daughter, Mr. Greenwood."

"We think so," said Greenwood. "How did you meet Lois?"

"Out here on deck."

"I trust that she hasn't been annoying you."

"Not in the least."

"Lois is inclined to be a little forward and impetuous at times."

"We were all like that at her age," observed Dillman.

"I wasn't," Greenwood said sternly. "I wasn't allowed to be."

"Well, I think your daughter is a credit to you. It's a pleasure to meet her. She tells me that you're a politician."

"I have the honor to be a member of Parliament."

"May I ask on which side of the House of Commons you sit?"

"On the government benches, Mr. Dillman. I'm a Liberal."

"Your party seems to have a very radical agenda, Mr. Greenwood."

"Of necessity."

"I don't know enough about British politics to make a comment, but I do admire your determination. You have to be courageous to take on entrenched attitudes."

"Change must come if we're to have a more equitable society."

"England has always been so conservative by nature."

"It's our major national defect, Mr. Dillman."

"How does your daughter like having an M.P. in the family?"

"I think she's rather embarrassed about it," said Greenwood with a smile. "Or at least she pretends to be. I suspect that she has a hard time of it at her boarding school. The parents of the other girls tend to support the Conservative Party. Lois has to endure a lot of teasing."

"She strikes me as a resilient young lady."

"She handles it very well."

If he had met Greenwood under other circumstances, Dillman felt that he would have liked the man. The politician was intense, but he was also pleasant, intelligent, and committed to his work. His affection for his daughter came through whenever he talked about her. Greenwood had a round face and a high domed forehead. The dark beard made him look like an Old Testament prophet. He seemed to exude integrity.

"Actually," said Dillman, "I'm very glad that I've met you like this."

"Why is that?"

"I believe that you know a friend of mine."

"And who might that be, Mr. Dillman?"

"Dudley Nevin."

"I can't really claim to know him," Greenwood said evasively. "I only met the man on one occasion."

"When was that?"

"You'll have to ask Mr. Nevin."

"Did you know that he was onboard this ship?"

"I believe that I did glimpse him briefly. Why do you ask?"

"No particular reason," said Dillman, watching him carefully. "It was just that Mr. Nevin mentioned your name."

"I'm not sure that I'd have recalled *his* name if you hadn't told me what it was. Politics is a hectic business, Mr. Dillman. I meet dozens of people every day. It's impossible to keep track of them all. What I can tell you about Mr. Nevin is this," he continued. "He belongs to my past. I've no reason to seek his company ever again."

When the Ackroyds arrived at the cabin, Constance Simcoe was already seated at the table with the playing cards in front of her. Tabitha let the visitors in and exchanged niceties with them. Gerald Ackroyd had brought his ear trumpet with him. His wife had a competitive glint in her eye. They moved across to take their seats at the table.

"I hope to have a better morning this time," said Mrs. Ackroyd. "I was handicapped by my partner yesterday."

"We'll not be inviting Mr. Nevin back, I assure you," said Constance.

"I'm delighted to hear it."

"Your husband will be our honorary male today."

"What's that?" asked Ackroyd, trumpet to his ear.

"You're an honorary male, dear," said his wife.

"Am I? That's nice."

"As long as you don't mind being outnumbered by us."

"Good lord—no!" he said. "A dream come true, what? Spent a whole lifetime dealing with other men. Quite a treat to be surrounded by the fairer sex."

"Would anyone like refreshments?" asked Tabitha, still on her feet.

Ackroyd was hopeful. "Alcohol, you mean?"

"Too early for that, Gerald," said his wife.

"Pity."

"I'd like some tea, please."

"Then you shall have some, Mrs. Ackroyd," said Constance, "and so will I. Paulo will be here directly. He knows that we're playing bridge."

"You have a very obliging steward, Mrs. Simcoe."

"Yes, Paulo is a gem."

"Mother always knows how to handle stewards," said Tabitha.

"It's something I've worked hard on over the years," said Constance.

"Like your skill at the card table," noted Mrs. Ackroyd.

"That's largely a combination of luck and guesswork."

"I wonder."

"You'll probably beat us easily this morning."

"We intend to," said the other woman, grimly. "Don't we, Gerald?"

Ackroyd blinked. "Didn't quite catch what you said, Phoebe."

"We're here to *win*, dear."

"Oh, yes. We want revenge. No prisoners taken, eh?"

He chortled merrily to himself as Tabitha took her seat opposite her mother. When Constance reached for the cards, Phoebe Ackroyd put a hand on them and smiled sweetly.

"I wonder if we might play with *our* cards today," she said, opening her purse. "Unlike Mr. Nevin, they never let us down." She put her own playing cards on the table. "Do you have any objection?"

"None at all," said Constance.

"Nor me," added Tabitha.

"And I have no objection either," announced Ackroyd, laughing. "I mean to say, it's not as if the cards are marked, is it?"

They met in her cabin to review the case and to discuss the way forward. Dillman gave her a more detailed account of the murder, and showed her the two photographs he had found in Nevin's billfold. He also told her about his suspicion of Sylvester Greenwood. Listening to the evidence, Genevieve was uncertain.

"A member of Parliament, involved in a murder?"

"Why not?"

"It seems so unlikely, George."

"I'm not saying that he actually committed it," said Dillman.

"Then who did?"

"I don't know yet. An associate of his, perhaps?"

"What was the motive?"

"Hatred. I saw it clearly in Greenwood's eyes when he spotted Mr. Nevin in the second-class lounge. Nevin saw it, as well. That's why he was so rattled."

"There's no question about that, George," she said. "I spoke earlier to Constance Simcoe. According to her, Mr. Nevin was far too upset to play bridge properly. Yet, when he had breakfast with her daughter, he'd been in a very friendly mood. What happened in between?"

"The encounter with Sylvester Greenwood."

"There might have been something else."

"I don't rule it out," said Dillman, "but I intend to keep Lois's father under scrutiny. For her sake, I hope that he turns out to be innocent."

"When you searched the cabin, cash had been stolen."

"Yes, Mr. Nevin's billfold was empty."

"Monetary gain is just as strong a motive as hatred," she argued. "I wonder if all the crimes—the two thefts and the murder—can be the work of the same person."

"I think that's highly unlikely."

"Is it? Supposing that the thief was caught in the act of stealing by Mr. Nevin? There may have been a struggle, and in the course of that a fatal wound was inflicted."

"You're forgetting something, Genevieve."

"Am I?"

"Mr. Nevin was already in the cabin," said Dillman. "Look at what he was wearing. He'd never be seen in public like that. And no matter how distracted he was, he wouldn't have left his billfold unguarded for any thief to walk in and take. Mr. Nevin was killed by someone he knew."

"How can you be so sure?"

"Because he wouldn't have let a stranger into his cabin. The door hadn't been forced. The lock was sound. The only way that the killer could have got in was by invitation."

"Unless he was already in there when Mr. Nevin returned."

"In that case, he'd have been more likely to stab his victim in the back. No assassin gives his man a chance to defend himself. And what killer would wait for Nevin to take off his coat and tie before attacking him? No, Genevieve," he said. "It had to be someone *known* to him."

"Sylvester Greenwood?"

"He's our only suspect at the moment."

"But there was bad blood between him and Mr. Nevin."

"Definitely. I could sense the antagonism between them."

"Why would Mr. Nevin let an enemy into his cabin?"

"Good question."

"What's the answer?"

"I don't know," confessed Dillman. "I just have this strong feeling that Mr. Greenwood was lying to me. There's a definite history between the two of them. I'm wondering if he went to Nevin's cabin yesterday to resolve their quarrel, and talked his way in there."

"Was the murder premeditated?"

"Somehow I don't think so."

"Whoever went into that cabin was carrying a weapon."

"That doesn't mean they intended to use it, Genevieve. We've had to deal with homicides before. As you know, killers very rarely oblige us by leaving a murder weapon behind for us to find."

"No," she agreed. "It's such a valuable clue."

"My guess is that an argument developed, the knife was drawn, and Mr. Nevin was killed in the ensuing struggle. Discarding the *kukri,* the murderer then grabbed the money in the billfold and vanished."

"That doesn't sound like the action of an M.P."

"He's a powerful man, Genevieve. Strong enough to get the better of someone like Nevin. I could see that."

"But he has too much to lose."

"Only if he's caught," said Dillman. "Mr. Greenwood doesn't even know that there are detectives aboard—I was very careful not to break cover. If he is somehow implicated in the crime, he thinks he's got away with it. I want to keep him in that frame of mind."

"How will you go about stalking him?"

"I may have to use his daughter. It's not something I want to do because I'd be deceiving her, but friendship goes by the board in a murder investigation."

"What about me?"

"I fear that you'll have to concentrate on the thefts, Genevieve. From now on, I'm going to have my hands full." He gave an apologetic grin. "Madame Roussel is all yours."

"I was afraid you'd say that."

"What about the lady whose purse was taken?"

"That was Mrs. Lundgren," she said. "I'd much rather deal with her. She's the first to admit that it was partly her own fault. She left her purse on a bench on deck while she stood at the rail.

Mrs. Lundgren is not the problem. The one who'll hound me is Madame Roussel."

"It may be time to call on her neighbors," he suggested. "See if anyone in the adjoining cabins saw anything on the evening when the crime was committed. It means that you lose your anonymity, but only in second class. Nobody in first is aware of your real reason for sailing on the *Salsette*."

"It was to be close to my husband."

"And to help him uphold the reputation of P and O."

"That, too, of course."

"So let's get on with it, shall we?"

"What's your next step?"

"To track down that elderly couple I saw talking to Mr. Nevin."

"Were they friends of his?"

"He called them acquaintances," said Dillman, "and I'll settle for that. Right now, I'm ready to talk to anyone who can give me information of any kind about Mr. Dudley Nevin."

Sylvester Greenwood was still strolling around the deck when his daughter rejoined him. Delighted to be back out in the fresh air again, Lois looked around to see if she recognized anyone. She gave a cheery wave to Guljar Singh, who responded with a dignified bow. Greenwood noted the exchange of greetings.

"Who was that?" he asked.

"Guljar Singh," she replied. "He's a mystic."

"How do you know?"

"I've talked to him, Daddy. He's also a fortune-teller. When he saw me watching him earlier, he made some predictions about my future."

"Indeed?"

"He said that I'd do something to be proud of on this ship, and that I'd have a pleasant surprise when I got back to school."

"How much did he charge you for this fortune-telling?"

"Nothing, Daddy. It wasn't like that."

Her father was cynical. "He's just a confidence trickster."

"No, he isn't!"

"Nobody can predict the future with any accuracy."

"Guljar Singh can. You can *feel* this strange power that he has."

"I think you were taken in," said Greenwood. "The old man is probably a fraud. Forget him, anyway. Did you do what your mother asked you?"

The girl sighed. "Yes, I did."

"Your uncle deserves a letter of thanks."

"But Mummy was writing one already," complained Lois. "Why did I have to write to Uncle David, as well?"

"Simple courtesy. He went out of his way to make your visit a memorable one. When we get to Aden, the two letters can go straight back to Bombay on the *Salsette*."

"I wish that I could."

"So do I, Lois. The trip was a revelation." He glanced across at Guljar Singh, who was now talking to a group of Indian passengers. "Perhaps the old man was right. You *have* done something to be proud of on this vessel. After two days of putting it off, you finally wrote to thank your uncle."

"I want to do something much more special than that, Daddy!"

"I was only teasing."

"I want to save someone's life," she said with passion.

"Calm down, Lois."

"Guljar Singh is a genuine seer. What he told me will come true. Look at the respect those men are showing him," she went on, pointing to the little entourage. "You ask Mr. Dillman. He believes in Mr. Singh."

"I'm glad that you mentioned Mr. Dillman."

"Did you talk to him?"

"Yes, I did."

"He's such an interesting man, isn't it?"

"Very personable," conceded Greenwood. "What does the fellow do exactly?"

"He works for the family firm, I think," explained Lois. "They make large yachts. Mr. Dillman crossed the Atlantic on one when he was only ten. He's a real sailor. That's why he seems so at ease on a ship."

"What was that about Australia?"

"That's where he went before he came to Bombay. He must be very rich if he can afford to travel round the world like that."

"How did you meet him?" said her father.

"Out here on deck."

"Did he approach you?"

"Oh, no," replied Lois, thinking of the nocturnal collision with Dillman. "I sort of got into conversation with him. He's such a charming man, isn't he?"

"That's beside the point," her father said seriously. "I've warned you before about speaking to strangers. You must be more careful, Lois. You're far too unguarded."

"Mr. Dillman was a perfect gentleman."

"It was still wrong of you to befriend him like that."

"Why?"

"And to get involved with that old man over there."

"Guljar Singh told me my fortune. It was exciting."

"That's what I'm complaining about," Greenwood said patiently. "Your constant need for excitement. It worries your mother to death."

"Mummy worries about *everything*."

"Lois!"

"Well, she does," insisted the girl. "When she read my letter to Uncle David, she worried that I'd been too effusive. It was the best

109

holiday I've ever had, and I wanted Uncle David to know that."

"Coming back to the point at issue," he said, "I want you to restrain yourself in public. We're on show as a family, Lois. If you shake hands with every Tom, Dick, and Harry that you meet on the ship, it lets us down badly. Don't you understand that?"

"No. Where's the harm in making new friends?"

"It's the *way* that you make them that disturbs me. If it goes on like this, you'll have to spend more time with us."

"That's unfair!" she protested. "I love strolling around on my own."

"Then be more discreet."

"You mean, that I can only talk to innocuous old ladies?"

"That's not what I mean at all," said Greenwood, raising an admonitory finger. "There are people of your own age onboard. If you need company, get to know some of them."

"But they all look so dull," she said scornfully, "especially the boys. I prefer to be with people who've *done* something in life. People like Guljar Singh, who has a kind of holiness about him. Or like that nice Mr. Dillman. I've never met an American before."

"I think that you should keep away from both of them, Lois."

"But they're my *friends*."

"No, Lois," he corrected. "They're casual acquaintances, and that's a very different thing. They're complete strangers to whom you had no business talking in the first place. I won't tell you again," he went on, raising his finger once more. "You're a young lady, remember. It's high time you started behaving like one."

Genevieve had little success. When she called at the cabins adjoining the one occupied by Madame Roussel, she found only one person there. He was a pale-faced Dutchman, who suffered from seasickness and who had hardly ventured outside his cabin since they had set sail. He was unable to help Genevieve. She was about to knock on another door when Madame Roussel came around the corner. The complacent smile on the Frenchwoman's face disappeared at once.

"What are you doing, mademoiselle?" she demanded.

"Pursuing my investigation."

"You have news for me?"

"Not yet," replied Genevieve. "But we are making progress."

"That other detective, your partner, he say he get my jewelry back."

"We will, Madame Roussel."

"When?"

"In the fullness of time. Please try to be patient."

"I will not wait much longer."

"We won't let you down."

"I am told this thief, he strike again."

"That's right," said Genevieve. "A Norwegian lady named Mrs. Lundgren had her purse stolen on deck. She left it on a bench for a couple of minutes while she stood at the rail with her husband. When she came back, the purse had gone."

"How many more things will this thief steal?"

"None, I hope."

"Then catch him and lock him up."

"It's not as straightforward as that, Madame Roussel. We have to watch and wait. We have to build up intelligence about the two thefts."

"What more do you need?" asked the Frenchwoman with a dramatic gesture. "I leave my cabin, the thief goes in and steals my jewelry. Find this criminal and punish him."

"We're on his trail, I assure you."

Madame Roussel was unconvinced. "You have done this before?" she said, clearly doubting Genevieve's competence.

"Done what?"

"Worked on the ship as a detective?"

"Yes, Madame," replied Genevieve. "I was employed by Cunard for over eighteen months and made dozens of Atlantic crossings in that time. Mr. Dillman and I have worked for P and O since last autumn."

"And you have actually *caught* thieves?"

"Without fail—thieves, pickpockets, cardsharps, blackmailers, and we've even solved a number of murders."

"Murders!" gasped Madame Roussel, a hand to her neck. "Such things happen onboard a cruise ship?"

"Only very rarely."

"I thought I am safe when I step on the *Salsette*."

"You are," Genevieve reassured her. "Completely safe."

"*Mon Dieu!* I just have the terrible idea."

"About what?"

"That thief, the one in my cabin. What if I come back and find him with my hatbox? Is possible he might have attacked me."

"Luckily, that didn't happen."

"No," said the other with a shudder, "but it make me think. When we sail to Bombay from Aden, we have no trouble. No thieves, nothing. I feel very safe. But now, is different."

"Does that mean you sailed on the *Salsette* before?"

"Yes, mademoiselle. In first class."

"Why were you going to Bombay?"

"Is not for you to know," retorted the other, tartly. "Just do your job, please, and leave my private life alone."

"Of course, Madame Roussel."

"And get my things back soon or I make the complaint."

"Mr. Cannadine is all too aware of the difficulties we face."

"I not bother with the purser," Madame Roussel said grandly. "I speak to the person in charge and tell him what I think of his detectives. I report you and your partner to the captain!"

Dillman found him in the second-class lounge. The man was so absorbed in what he was reading that he did not see the detective approach. It was only when a shadow fell across the book that he looked up.

"Can I help you?" he asked.

"I believe so," replied Dillman. "I wonder if I might have a few minutes of your time, please. My name is George Dillman."

"Then you'd better sit down, Mr. Dillman."

"Thank you." He took a seat. "May I know your name, sir?"

"Archibald Sinclair."

"Well, Mr. Sinclair, I couldn't help noticing that you were talking in here yesterday to someone with whom I've become acquainted."

"Oh, and who was that?"

"Dudley Nevin."

"Yes," sighed the other. "Poor Dudley. Not one of my successes."

"Successes?"

"He was a Wykehamist, you know."

"I didn't know," admitted Dillman. "To be honest, I only met him recently. What exactly is a Wykehamist?"

"A former pupil of Winchester College—it was founded by William of Wykeham in the fourteenth century, you see. He was Chancellor of England for a time, and Bishop of Winchester for over thirty-five years." He lifted up his book. "I taught classics there. That's why I'm the only person on this ship with his head in a copy of Cicero's *De Inventione*."

Dillman was not surprised to hear that the man had an academic background. Sinclair had a long, thin, earnest face with intelligent eyes, peering through wire-framed eyeglasses and surmounted by wispy silver eyebrows. Silver hair was scattered indiscriminately across his pate. There was a scholarly roundness to his shoulders and a cultured tone to his voice. Dillman could understand why Nevin had not described his old classics master as his friend. Even in retirement, Sinclair maintained the authority gap between master and pupil.

"I take it that Mr. Nevin was not the most gifted student you ever taught," said Dillman.

"Oh, he was gifted," explained the other, "but far too wayward. Dudley could never apply himself. He was interested largely in the pleasures of life and, as Cicero has warned us, *voluptas est illecebra turpidinis.*"

"You'll have to translate for me, Mr. Sinclair."

"Pleasure is an incitement to vileness. I became so frustrated with him that I made Dudley write it out three hundred times. It did not, alas, do the trick. He continued to go astray."

"It's something of a coincidence, you running into him like this."

"Not really, Mr. Dillman," said the other. "I've always tried to keep track of my former pupils—even the more slothful ones. Paradoxically, it's often the latter who shine in later life, while the true scholars waste their talents in unworthy professions like popular journalism."

"Would you say that Mr. Nevin shone?"

"Fitfully. But he was a Wykehamist, so I followed his career. My wife and I had always promised ourselves that, on my retirement, we'd visit India. Since I knew that we'd be in Delhi for a short time, I wrote to Dudley to forewarn him."

"Did he reply?"

"Yes," said Sinclair. "Eventually. He offered to buy us dinner one evening. And—*mirabile dictu*—he proved that he had learned something during my lessons, after all. On the back of the envelope, he wrote the Latin tag from Cicero that I made him copy out three hundred times."

"He obviously didn't hold a grudge against you."

"I found that heartening."

"When did you discover that you'd be sailing together from Bombay on the *Salsette*?"

Sinclair removed his glasses and studied Dillman for a moment. "Why are you asking me all these questions?" he wondered.

"Purely out of interest."

"There's more to it than that, Mr. Dillman. There's nothing I've told you that Dudley couldn't have volunteered for himself."

"All he ever talked about was his job in Delhi. He hated it."

"You're evading my question, sir."

Sinclair was too clever a man to be fooled by glib answers. As a former teacher, he had spent a lifetime listening to excuses dreamed up by erring pupils and his instincts had been sharpened in the process. Dillman decided that he would have to tell him a measure of truth if he wanted any further cooperation.

"I work for P and O," confessed Dillman. "I'm a detective."

"Dear me! Is Dudley in some kind of trouble?"

"That's what I'm trying to find out, Mr. Sinclair. Needless to say, I'm speaking to you in the strictest confidence. I can do my job much more effectively if the passengers are unaware of my role on the ship."

"Yes, yes," said Sinclair, putting on his glasses again, "I appreciate that. Have no worries on that score, Mr. Dillman. I'm as close as the grave. Our conversation will go no further than this lounge."

"Thank you."

"What precisely has Dudley done?"

"He seems to have fallen in with bad company," said Dillman. "That's why your remarks about his time at school were so valuable. You've been a sort of character witness."

"His character did have severe defects, I fear."

"What did he do when he left Winchester?"

"He went up to Cambridge to read jurisprudence, and spent

three years indulging in the very pleasures that Cicero and I had warned him against. He got a poor degree. We don't expect that of Wykehamists."

"And afterwards?"

"He drifted from one job to another."

"In the law?"

"For the most part, Mr. Dillman. Then he dabbled in politics."

"Supporting the Conservative Party, I assume."

"Of course," replied the other. "For all his faults, he hadn't allowed himself to be corrupted by Liberal values. His father and grandfather were military men who'd both served in India. It was a family with real backbone. When he stirred himself into action, Dudley displayed authentic Nevin spirit. I think it's the one thing he did that his father could approve of wholeheartedly."

"His dabbling in politics?"

"To do him justice, it was rather more than that."

"Oh?"

"He stood for Parliament in a by-election."

"Really?" said Dillman in surprise. "I would have thought his attitude a little too flippant for something as serious as that."

"Dudley gave a good account of himself, I'm told. He fought hard to retain the seat for the Conservatives but he was beaten by a small majority. Now, if you really want a coincidence, Mr. Dillman," he went on with a high-pitched laugh, "I can offer you one that will astound you."

"Can you, Mr. Sinclair?"

"The Liberal candidate who actually won that by-election is also on the ship—a fellow by the name of Sylvester Greenwood. What do you make of that, eh? Old adversaries, locking horns once again."

Sitting in the purser's office, the woman was in tears. When she was introduced to Genevieve Masefield, she dabbed at her eyes with a scented handkerchief and made an effort to control herself.

"Will you get it back for me?" she pleaded. "Everything of any real value to me was in that purse, Miss Masefield. It's not the money I worry about but the photographs. Some of them are irreplaceable."

"We'll do all we can to retrieve them, Mrs. Verney," said Genevieve.

"Just give us the details," suggested Max Cannadine.

"Where and when did this theft occur?"

May Verney blew her nose into the handkerchief before launching into her tale. She was a stout Englishwoman in her forties with a pudgy face that was furrowed by anxiety, and a habit of adjusting her hair with her right hand as she spoke. Her story bore some similarity to that of Mrs. Lundgren. Like the Norwegian passenger, she had had her purse stolen on deck.

"It was right beside me," she explained. "I was reading in a deck chair, and I must have drifted off to sleep. When I woke up, the book was still in my lap but my purse had gone."

"And you reported the theft instantly?" said Genevieve.

"Yes, Miss Masefield."

"I can confirm that," said the purser. "Mrs. Verney came in here a few minutes ago and I sent for you at once. The theft must have occurred sometime in the last half hour."

"I couldn't have been asleep for more than twenty minutes or so," insisted Mrs. Verney. "I never doze off for any longer than that."

"Were there many people on deck?" asked Genevieve.

"Dozens."

"Was anyone sitting or standing close to you?"

"Lots of people."

"Can you remember any of them, Mrs. Verney."

"Only that ancient Indian gentleman."

"Who was that?" said Cannadine.

"And old man with a white beard. My husband said that he must be a Sikh because of his turban. The man is a fortune-teller, it seems. I heard him saying that he could predict the future."

"How close was he standing to you?"

"Very close, Mr. Cannadine," she said, brushing a curl back from her forehead. "When I fell asleep, he was no more than a couple of yards away. When I opened my eyes, both he and my purse had vanished."

EIGHT

Though her face remained impassive, Matilda Kinnersley was actually impressed with the girl for once. As she checked her appearance in the mirror in her cabin, she tossed a compliment over her shoulder.

"Well done, Sukinder," she said. "You've obviously worked hard."

"Thank you, *memsahib.*"

"You can read the language so much better now."

"I try," said Sukinder, clutching the book to her chest.

"It's your conversational English that needs attention."

"We'll work on it every day, my dear," said Major Kinnersley. "By the time we get home, Sukinder will be almost word perfect. In time, she'll blend in with the rest of the household."

"I sincerely hope so, Romford."

"She's looking forward to it—aren't you, Sukinder?"

"Yes, *sahib,*" said the girl without conviction.

"Off you go, then," Mrs. Kinnersley told her, turning round.

"Look at the next chapter this afternoon. You can read that aloud to us later on."

"Yes, *memsahib.*" Sukinder gave a servile nod and let herself out of the cabin.

"I told you that she'd improve," said the major.

"Only because I exerted a little pressure on her."

"I did the opposite, my dear. I encouraged her very gently. Push her too hard and Sukinder withdraws into herself. You mustn't frighten her so much."

"It's the only way to get results."

"I don't accept that."

"Well, it was with her mother," said Mrs. Kinnersley. "If I hadn't shouted at her so much, we'd have got no work out of her. It was the same with the other servants. You have to be tough and un-compromising with them. They interpret any kindness as a sign of weakness."

"I disagree, Matilda."

"I'm the one who'll spend the most time with the girl."

"True."

"I expect her to take her place with the rest of the domestic staff."

"Sukinder understands that. I explained it to her once again during our walk around the deck."

"You were gone a very long time, I must say."

"We bumped into various people."

"Such as?"

"The Ackroyds were the first."

"Oh, yes," she said with approval. "Gerald and Phoebe are very agreeable types. He must be in line for a knighthood sooner or later. Do you remember that time he introduced us to Lord Curzon?"

"Do I?" he echoed. "Never forget it, my dear. Lord Curzon was my idea of what a viceroy ought to be. He understood the country and its importance to us. Do you know what he told Prime Minister Balfour?"

"What?"

"The plain truth. That as long as Britain ruled India, we were the greatest power in the world."

"Nobody disputes our supremacy, surely?"

"The Boers did, my dear. So did the Zulus. That's why we had to teach them a lesson in South Africa. I know that they both had freakish victories against us, but they were vanquished in the end. Anyway," he went on, "to come back to the Ackroyds. They were having a stroll on deck before playing bridge with the Simcoes."

His wife sniffed. "Those dreadful people from Cheltenham?"

"I think you were a little unkind to them, Matilda. The mother is crippled. You should have been more gracious."

"I didn't *feel* gracious."

"That doesn't mean you had to be rude to them."

"They're not our sort of people, Romford."

"I'd go along with that," he agreed. "When I left the Ackroyds, I came across someone else whom I'd never wish to meet socially again."

"And who might that be?"

"Mr. Dillman. The American gentleman."

"That's a contradiction in terms."

"Had the nerve to engage me in conversation, but I wasn't standing for that. I gave him short shrift. We must ensure that we never get stuck at a table with him again."

"We should make an effort to sit with the Ackroyds," she decided. "I know that Gerald's deafness is a nuisance at times, but at least they're our equals. They talk the same language as us. You can't say that for anyone else aboard this ship."

While continuing her investigations, Genevieve Masefield still had to maintain an appearance of normality. She could not simply disappear from sight in order to do her work. Luncheon found her filing into the first-class dining saloon with the rest of the passengers. She had intended to eat with the Simcoes, but when they did not show up, she sat at a table that included Wilbur Rollins and the Ackroyds. To make sure that he missed nothing, Gerald Ackroyd kept his ear trumpet in position. The American author was soon broaching his favorite subject.

"Grace Darling is the most famous heroine of the waves," he said, "but my book will also dwell on the bravery of Ida Lewis, who rescued two soldiers from drowning in Newport Harbor when they were returning from Fort Adams."

"Those women are surely the exception to the rule," said Ackroyd.

"No, sir. Their example spurred on others."

Phoebe Ackroyd was critical. "I'm not sure that it's right for a young woman like Grace Darling to be working in a lighthouse."

"She was born to it, Mrs. Ackroyd."

"I'm glad that I wasn't. What about you, Miss Masefield?"

"Oh, I don't think that I'd ever qualify for inclusion in Mr. Rollins's book," Genevieve said modestly, "but I shall nevertheless look forward to reading it."

"Wonderful!" said Rollins. "I've sold one copy already."

Having given her order to the waiter, Genevieve scanned the room.

"If you're looking for the Simcoes," said Mrs. Ackroyd, "you're out of luck. They're still in their cabin, licking their wounds."

"You played bridge with them again, didn't you?" said Genevieve.

"We did," said Ackroyd. "Splendid session."

His wife smiled. "Gerald and I had our revenge against them."

"Not true, Phoebe. It was a case of honors even."

"No," she corrected. "We ended up with a profit of five pounds. It might not have made up for what we lost yesterday afternoon, but it taught Mrs. Simcoe and her daughter that we're formidable opponents."

"You sound as if it were a military engagement," said Rollins.

"To some extent, it is."

"In the nicest possible way," added Ackroyd. "It's not so much cut and thrust as clever tactical maneuvering. Rather like chess, only with more speed and less deliberation. Do you play bridge?"

"No," replied Rollins. "I don't play any card games."

"You would if you'd been based in India," Mrs. Ackroyd said soulfully. "What else is there to do during those long evenings? Card games were our salvation. One develops an addiction for them."

"I prefer to study women at sea."

Ackroyd chortled. "Fruitful subject of study wherever they are!"

"Don't be coarse, Gerald," chided his wife.

"Harmless remark, Phoebe. Meant no offence."

"None taken, Mr. Ackroyd," said Genevieve. "So Mrs. Simcoe and her daughter were not pleased to be beaten, you say?"

"No," returned Mrs. Ackroyd, "though they were more surprised than upset. They thought their system was invincible."

"Not when we're around," said Ackroyd.

"Yesterday, we were trounced. Today, we fought back. The Simcoes made us promise to have a deciding battle tomorrow."

"What's the choice of weapons?" asked Rollins. "Swords or pistols?"

"We simply pit intellects against each other."

"They must be keen," commented Genevieve. "I gather that Mrs. Simcoe and her daughter will be playing another couple this afternoon. That will make four sessions of bridge in two days—with another to come tomorrow. I wouldn't have the stamina for that."

"We would," boasted Mrs. Ackroyd. "Wouldn't we, Gerald?"

"Yes," he said. "We could play bridge all day and every day."

"Don't you ever get bored?" asked Genevieve.

"Never, Miss Masefield."

"There's two ways to stave off boredom," said his wife with an air of authority. "First, you make sure that you play for money."

Ackroyd nodded. "Adds real spice to a game. Gives you incentive."

"And what's the second way?" said Genevieve.

"That's easy," explained Mrs. Ackroyd. "You keep on winning."

Constance Simcoe lay back in her Bath chair as she was wheeled around the main deck. After lunching with her daughter in their cabin, she had instructed their steward to take her out into the fresh sea air before an afternoon devoted to bridge. Paulo Morelli parked her in the stern of the ship, so that she could watch the water being churned up by the two propellers, spreading out into an ever widening triangle behind them. Clouds were scudding across the sky but there was no prospect of rain. A cool breeze was sweeping the decks.

"Is it always like this, Paulo?" she asked with exasperation.

"Like what?"

"Can't you feel the way the ship rocks to and fro?"

"Is much worse during a storm."

"Then I hope we don't get caught in one. This is bad enough. I just wish that the *Salsette* was a little more stable."

"She is like a woman," said Morelli, grinning. "Very pretty, but she will shake you up a little." He bent solicitously over the Bath chair. "You not happy out here?"

"We'll stay for a while. It's the first time today that I've left the cabin, and I need a change of scene. My daughter and I have been too busy playing cards."

"It helps to pass the time."

"And to exercise the mind, Paulo."

"I cannot say about that. I no learn to play."

"They must have card games in Italy."

"When I was a boy," he explained, "the only game that I like is to run after the girls. Is how I meet my wife, Sophia. We go to the same school. We know each other many years."

"Childhood sweethearts?"

"Is right."

"How often do you see her?"

"Not enough. To be a steward, I have to travel."

"What does your wife think of that?"

"Sophia accept this."

"But you write to her, presumably."

"All the time. I write, I send money, I tell her I love her."

"I can think of one or two wives in England who'd prefer to have a husband on that basis," observed Constance with a smile. "There's a lot to be said for time apart in a marriage."

"Does your daughter think that, as well?"

"I don't know."

"She is a beautiful young lady."

"I think so, as well."

"Every man who sees her, he like her."

"Perhaps," she said, not wishing to pursue the subject.

"In Italy, she would have been married years ago."

"That's immaterial, Paulo."

"It show the difference between my country and yours," he argued, unaware that he was annoying her. "In Italy, your daughter, she would have had *bambinos* by now."

Constance was icy. "Fortunately, we are not Italians."

"You no like Italy?"

"Only to visit."

"What about children? You no want to be a grandmother?"

"That's not something I'm prepared to discuss with you, Paulo."

"But the best age for a woman to have a *bambino* is when—"

"Enough!" she interrupted. "I did not come out here to talk about my private life. All you have to do is to push me."

Morelli was hurt. "I thought you like us to speak together."

"On certain topics, perhaps. This is not one of them."

"I very sorry."

"Take me back to the cabin."

"Already? We only just arrive."

"The roll of the ship is making me feel seasick."

"Then I move you somewhere else on the deck, yes?"

"No, Paulo. You move me back to my cabin—now."

"Why you so angry with me?" he asked, standing beside her. "Is it because you lose at cards today?"

"No!" she snapped.

"What I say to upset you?"

"Just do as you're told, man."

"But I think we are friends."

"I am a passenger," she emphasized, "and you are steward. That means you do what I ask you to do without arguing about it. Now, wheel me back to my cabin—or I'll ask for a steward who can obey orders."

"I do whatever you tell me," he promised.

"Then do it!"

Morelli was bewildered. Hitherto pleasant toward him, Constance Simcoe had suddenly turned on him and he could not understand why. What he wanted to avoid, however, was being reported to the chief steward again. Responding to her command, therefore, he took hold of the Bath chair, swung it gently round, then pushed it back in the direction of her cabin, fearful that it might be the last time she asked him bring her up on deck. When he reached the cabin, he took out the key from his pocket.

"Just knock on the door," Constance said pointedly, "then you can leave me. My daughter will take over from here."

"Thank you for bringing me up to date, Mr. Dillman," said the purser.

"I wish that I had more to report."

"You're obviously making some headway."

"I still have no hard evidence," said Dillman. "That worries me."

"You've established a firm connection between the murder victim and a member of Parliament, who happens to be onboard. I think it was disingenuous of Mr. Greenwood to tell you that he only met Mr. Nevin on one occasion." Max Cannadine scratched his head reflectively. "Though, technically, I suppose, he may be correct."

"In what sense?"

"Parliamentary candidates don't necessarily meet each other during the contest. They and their supporters canvass independently. The only time they do come face-to-face is when the count is made and the returning officer declares the results."

"Mr. Greenwood deliberately tried to mislead me," asserted Dillman, "and I want to know why. He knew perfectly well who Dudley Nevin was yet he pretended even to have forgotten his name."

"I wouldn't forget the name of someone *I* beat in a by-election."

"Neither would I, Mr. Cannadine."

"The rivalry between them sounds as if it was more than political."

"It was deeply personal," said Dillman. "It was only after I left him that I realized Mr. Greenwood had given himself away."

"Oh?"

"He told me that he'd only met Mr. Nevin once. I asked him when."

"And?"

"He suggested that I ask Mr. Nevin himself. Don't you see?" he went on. "If I'd done that—and if Nevin had been alive—I might have learned the truth. Sylvester Greenwood must have known that I couldn't speak to him because Nevin was dead."

"That's clever reasoning, Mr. Dillman."

Besieged as he was by other duties, Cannadine had made time for a chat in his office with the detective. He was pleased with what he saw as the first sign of progress. Like Genevieve, however, he found it difficult to believe that Sylvester Greenwood had actually committed the murder, even though there were possible indications of his involvement in the crime.

"What he couldn't know was that this Mr. Sinclair was aboard."

"That was a stroke of fortune," said Dillman. "Were he still here, I'm not convinced that Mr. Nevin *would* have told me about his relationship with Mr. Greenwood. He denied even knowing him."

"His old classics master put paid to that lie."

"And he taught me some Latin into the bargain."

"What sort of M.P. would Dudley Nevin have made, do you think?"

"Not a very good one, I suspect," decided Dillman. "Having met them both, I have to say I'd have more faith in Sylvester Greenwood. He has more presence and is a much better speaker. Now that I know he's a liar, of course—and may even be a party to murder—I don't think he'd get my vote, even if I had one."

"Politicians are all one to me," declared Cannadine.

"Untrustworthy?"

"That's a kind word for it."

"Their reputation in America is not much better."

"I can imagine. Returning to Greenwood, what's the next stage?"

"I dig a little deeper, Mr. Cannadine. His daughter, Lois, is a friend of mine, so I'm going to talk to her about her father."

"Won't Greenwood mind?"

"With luck, he won't know about it," said Dillman. "I'll talk to Lois in a place where she's not supposed to be."

"And where's that?"

"Skating around the deck last thing at night."

The purser laughed. "She sounds like an adventurous young lady."

"Oh, she is. Lois plays football on roller skates, apparently."

"What is the weaker sex coming to!"

"Getting stronger all the time," said Dillman with a grin. "More power to their elbow. Well," he added, rising from his chair, "I'll get back to it. Now that Genevieve has her hands full with the thefts, I'm on my own. I gather that there's been a third incident."

"You've spoken to Miss Masefield?"

"No, but I saw her across the dining saloon earlier on."

"How do you communicate—by semaphore?"

"We have our own system of signals, Mr. Cannadine. That's why we always sit where we can see each other. I don't know the details, of course, but Genevieve made one thing very clear to me. She's dealing with another crime."

When luncheon was over, Genevieve accompanied May Verney to the place on the main deck where the latter's purse had been stolen. Cursing herself for having fallen asleep, Mrs. Verney pointed to her deck chair.

"That's where I was sitting," she said. "In the shade."

"Reading a novel?"

"Yes. It was *Moths* by Ouida. I love her books."

"And where was the Sikh gentleman standing?"

129

"Just here," said Mrs. Verney, taking up a position. "He couldn't help but notice when I dozed off."

"That gives me something to work on."

"Mr. Cannadine told me there was another theft on deck."

"Yes," said Genevieve. "That was an opportunist's crime, as well. So was the first theft, as a matter of fact. It was from a cabin whose door had been left unlocked."

"Was the same person responsible for all three crimes?"

"I think so. In each case, a woman was the target."

"What does that tell you?"

"That the thief is careful not to steal from men. If they catch him in the act, they're likely to take him on. Most women wouldn't do that. Also, of course, we do tend to have more valuables with us than men—jewelry, keepsakes, and so on. A thief stands to gain more from preying on female passengers."

"Especially if we're stupid enough to leave our purse unguarded, as I did," Mrs. Verney said bitterly. "No man would leave his billfold on a deck chair while he took a nap. Oh, I had such a nasty shock when I woke up, Miss Masefield."

Genevieve was sympathetic. "It must have been dreadful for you."

"It was. I don't mind about the money—there wasn't a great deal in my purse. It's the photographs and the other items. Be honest with me. What are the chances of getting them back?"

"They're rather slim, I'm afraid."

"Why?"

"Most thieves would simply take the money and throw the purse overboard. That way they destroy evidence that could lead to their arrest."

"So I might as well give up hope?" the other said gloomily.

"Never do that, Mrs. Verney. We could be lucky."

"My husband was so angry with me."

"He had no right to be," said Genevieve. "The vast majority of passengers are very honest. They wouldn't dream of stealing anything. Nine times out of ten, you could sleep for an hour and find your purse untouched beside you."

"I won't put that to the test, if you don't mind."

"Once bitten?"

"Quite, Miss Masefield."

"The next thing I need to see is this man who was standing so close to you," said Genevieve. "Point him out if you will, please."

"I don't see him on this side of the ship," said Mrs. Verney, gazing up and down the deck. "Shall we go round to the port side?"

"Yes, but let's do it as if we're having an afternoon stroll. We don't want to look as if we're searching for someone. If you do spot him, just nudge my arm."

"Very well."

They walked the length of the starboard side until they reached the stern, then made their way at a leisurely pace up the other side of the deck. Almost immediately, Mrs. Verney saw the man they were after and she gave Genevieve a nudge. Sitting cross-legged on the deck, staring ahead of him, was Guljar Singh. Two Indians stood patiently beside him. When he emerged from his trance, he held out his hand and one of the men slipped a coin into his palm. Guljar Singh spoke to him at length, using both hands expressively. Pleased with what he heard, the man pressed a second coin into his palm and went off happily with his friend.

Having seen it all, Genevieve and her companion walked on past. May Verney waited until they were out of earshot before she spoke.

"That was him," she said. "I'm certain he was the thief."

Even in second class, dinner was a formal occasion and Lois Greenwood enjoyed dressing up for it. When she was ready that evening, she studied herself in the full-length mirror, made a final adjustment to her shoulder strap, then swept out of the cabin in her pink satin gown. As soon as she knocked on the door of the adjoining cabin, her father let her in. He and his wife were both delighted with her appearance. Daphne Greenwood, a thin, handsome, dark-haired woman, was wearing a tomato-colored frock of Liberty velveteen and Indian muslin, with an elaborate lace fichu.

"Mummy!" said Lois. "You look wonderful!"

"That's what I've been trying to tell her," said Greenwood.

His wife was dubious. "I'm wondering if it's more suitable for a younger woman," she said, turning to the mirror again. "I'm not sure that it's altogether right."

"Of course, it is, Daphne."

"Yes," Lois cried enthusiastically. "It makes you look almost regal."

"I don't want people staring at me," her mother said nervously.

"They'll look at you, whatever you wear," said Greenwood with a touch of gallantry. "You'll be the most attractive woman in the room."

"What about me?" protested Lois.

"You'll have to take second place to your mother this evening."

"As long as I can have that frock when Mummy's finished with it."

"Of course, darling," said Mrs. Greenwood.

Lois put a hand to her stomach. "I'm starving. Shall we go?"

"In a moment," replied her father. "I just want to remind you about what I said earlier. We'll be on show in the dining saloon. Good behavior is paramount. I don't want anyone to think that my daughter hasn't been brought up properly. Remember my position, Lois."

"Oh, Daddy," she said wearily, "you're always chastising me

about that. Ever since you became an M.P., you've been obsessed with keeping up appearances."

"Only because it's important. I'm a public figure now."

"In England, maybe—not in the middle of the Arabian Sea. By the way," she went on excitedly, "I asked Mr. Dillman about that. He's a sailor. According to him, we *are* crossing the Arabian Sea, so I was right about that. Except that it's part of the Indian Ocean, of course."

"Never mind that, Lois. Do as I told you. I don't want you speaking so freely to the Mr. Dillmans of this world."

"But he's such good company."

"Listen to your father, dear," advised Mrs. Greenwood.

"He's far and away the nicest person I've met on this ship."

"That's irrelevant," said her father, straightening his white bow tie and brushing some dust from his lapel. "The fact is that you went up to a total stranger and engaged him in conversation. That's not the way things are done, Lois."

"I'd never have got to meet him otherwise."

"What must he have thought of you?" asked her mother anxiously. "A young woman, approaching him in that brazen way. When I was your age, I wouldn't have dared to do such a thing."

"You might if you'd met someone as good-looking as Mr. Dillman."

"Lois!"

"Wait until you see him, Mummy."

"I've no wish to see him."

"Neither have I," decreed Greenwood. "He does not belong to our circle and he never will. I suggest that you forget about Mr. Dillman."

"It's because he's American, isn't it?" challenged Lois.

"What do you mean?"

"If he was English, and lived in your constituency, it would be a very different matter. Mr. Dillman would be able to vote for you then. You'd be as nice as pie to him, Daddy. You'd go out of your way to get to know him."

"That's not true at all."

"And very naughty of you even to suggest it," said Mrs. Greenwood with uncharacteristic sharpness. "I won't have you being so disrespectful to your father, Lois. Apologize at once."

"You're both being so unfair to Mr. Dillman."

"Apologize."

"Do I have to?"

"Unless you'd prefer to eat your dinner in your cabin."

"Mummy, that would be cruel!" cried Lois. She turned a penitent face to her father. "I'm sorry, Daddy. It was very rude of me. I didn't mean that about chasing his vote."

"Then let's hear no more of it," he said peremptorily. "We'll draw a line under the whole business and go into the dining saloon as a family. Do you understand, Lois? What you do reflects on your parents." He crossed to open the door. "Don't you ever forget that."

Since his only suspect was traveling in second class, George Dillman went to the other dining saloon that evening, arriving early so that he could choose a seat from which he could command a view of the whole room. Sitting opposite him, Guljar Singh was pleased to see his friend again.

"Are you enjoying this stage of your journey?" he asked.

"Very much," replied Dillman.

"Where do you go next?"

"Back to England, Mr. Singh."

"Then home to America, I think."

"Everywhere is home to a sailor," said Dillman. "What about you?"

"I am going to Aden to see my son. He works there. When I have spent some time with his family, I must go back to Bombay. There is too much work for me to do."

"At your age? I thought that you'd retired."

"Mystics never retire, my friend. We are at the mercy of our gifts."

"Those gifts have certainly found an audience on the *Salsette*," noted Dillman. "Whenever I've seen you on deck, you have a small audience around you."

"Everyone likes to have their fortune told."

"I prefer not to know what lies ahead."

"Then how can you prepare for bad things?" asked Singh. "What is that saying the English have?"

"Forewarned is forearmed."

"I use my powers to forewarn people."

"But you pass on good news to them, as well, don't you?" said Dillman, remembering Lois Greenwood. "Your prophecies are not always laden with doom."

The old man shook his head. "No, no," he said. "Sometimes I bring happy tidings. This afternoon, I was able to tell a man that his wife would soon bear them a lovely daughter. He was so pleased that he gave me another rupee."

"It's been a profitable voyage for you, then?"

"Very profitable, Mr. Dillman. I do not do it only for the money, of course, but bills have to be paid. The *Salsette* has been kind to me. Well, you saw the way that I won that bet with the officer."

"It served him right for taking you on."

"I had some more unexpected money, as well."

"Wait a moment," said Dillman. "How could it be unexpected when you always know exactly what to expect?" Guljar Singh let out a cackle. "Come on. How do you explain that?"

"Easily, Mr. Dillman. My gift only works for others. I could foretell *your* future, but I cannot foresee my own. It is my blind spot."

"Do you remember a pretty English girl called Lois Greenwood?"

"Was that her name? She did not tell me."

"She was thrilled with what you told *her*."

"Yes," recalled the other. "She has a pleasant surprise waiting for her at school. Before that, on this ship, she will do something very good. Something that will be special."

"Do you have any idea what it is?"

"I only see outlines, Mr. Dillman. Not clear shapes."

"You saw enough to put a smile on her face. Lois was ecstatic."

"She may still suffer along with the rest of us."

"Suffer?"

"Yes, Mr. Dillman," explained the mystic. "Bear in mind what I said about this ship. I believe there will be a terrible event aboard."

"You could be right," agreed Dillman, thinking of the murder of Dudley Nevin. "Is there no way that we can avert this disaster?"

"No, my friend. It may already have happened, you see. We just do not know about it yet."

"I hope that you're wrong about that."

"I am never wrong about such things."

"I'll have to take your word for that," said Dillman, concealing the fact that Guljar Singh's prediction had been remarkably accurate.

"There is evil on the *Salsette*," warned the other. "And it will affect all of us, including that young lady we spoke of just now."

At that moment, Lois Greenwood came into the saloon with her parents. In white tie and tails, her father cut quite a dash and her mother gained many admiring glances, as well. Lois herself was basking in the attention that she was getting. What puzzled Dillman was that she never even acknowledged his smile of welcome. Though she definitely saw him there, Lois deliberately ignored him.

Dining in first class that evening, Genevieve Masefield had selected a dress of ivory-colored taffeta that displayed her figure at its best, and she carried an ivory fan. Tortoiseshell slides kept her hair in place. As she stepped out of her cabin, she was startled to see Paulo Morelli waiting for her. For once, his face was not split into an ingratiating grin. The Italian heaved a sigh of relief.

"I pray that you come out first, Miss Masefield," he said.

"Why?"

"I need to ask you the favor."

"What kind of favor, Paulo?"

"Is Mrs. Simcoe. She no like me anymore."

"I'm sure that you're imagining things," said Genevieve. "Only yesterday, she told me what an accommodating steward you've been."

"That was yesterday. Today, is different."

"In what way?"

"I take her on deck in the chair with wheels, and all is well at first. Then I say something nice about her daughter and—poof!" he said, smacking his palms together. "Mrs. Simcoe, she turn on me."

"Why? What did you say?"

"I tell the truth, that is all. Miss Simcoe, she is a lovely young lady. In Italy, she would be married by now with *bambinos*. Is true. All women of that age have a husband."

"And Mrs. Simcoe took exception to your comments?"

"She did. She warn me she will get another steward."

"In that case, she must have taken umbrage."

Morelli blinked. "Umbrage? I no hear that word before."

"It means that she took offense. She was resentful."

"Oh, yes," he said. "Is a lot of resentment. While they play the cards this afternoon, she send for me twice to bring refreshment but she speak very unkindly to me. Her daughter, she is the same. She not say anything, but she look at me as if I am not wanted anymore." Morelli was obviously distressed. "Please, Miss Masefield. I like my job. I love to serve you and your friends. I need your help."

"What can I do, Paulo?" asked Genevieve.

"Talk to them. Find out what I did wrong. Do not tell them that I ask you to do this," he added quickly. "I just want everything to be like it was before. I am a good steward."

Genevieve felt sorry for him. She could see his anguish. Morelli had a tendency to be overfamiliar with the passengers he looked after, but she did not condemn him for that. Without knowing why, he had somehow alienated Constance and Tabitha Simcoe.

"I'll see what I can do," she promised.

"Thank you, Miss Masefield. Thank you very much."

Before he could say anything else, a door opened farther down the corridor and Tabitha Simcoe put her head out. When she saw Morelli, she snapped her fingers.

"Mother is ready now," she said curtly.

"You see what I mean," he murmured to Genevieve.

Morelli hurried along to the cabin, went inside, and reappeared almost at once, pushing the Bath chair. Resplendent in a dress of burgundy-colored silk, Constance Simcoe waved to Genevieve as she was wheeled past. She then ordered Morelli to push her faster. Afraid of saying the wrong thing, the steward remained silent. Tabitha fell in beside her friend as they followed the Bath chair.

"We're a little late this evening," she said. "The bridge game went on much longer than we anticipated."

"Who were you playing, Tabby?"

"The Kingtons. Have you met Mr. and Mrs. Kington yet?"

"I don't believe that I have," said Genevieve.

"Arthur Kington is a retired businessman of some sort," explained Tabitha. "He promised his wife that he'd take her to see the Taj Mahal one day, and he was finally in a position to keep that promise."

"How nice!"

"Yes, they're a pleasant couple. Mother met them yesterday when she was being wheeled around the deck. Before they knew it, she'd persuaded them to join us for a game of bridge."

"How did you get on?"

"Oh," Tabitha said briskly, "we won, of course."

"Were you playing for money?"

"Mr. Kington insisted. He said that it gave him incentive."

"I gather that you had a slightly harder time against the Ackroyds."

Tabitha bridled slightly. "Why do you ask?" she said. "Has Phoebe Ackroyd been boasting about it?"

"She was a trifle expansive over luncheon," admitted Genevieve.

"They had a good run," conceded the other. "That sort of thing happens in cards. It may be a different story when we play them again tomorrow. Especially as Gerald Ackroyd wants to raise the stakes."

"Really?"

"Yes, that mild-mannered man is something of a gambler. Mother can always pick them out. She has this sixth sense."

"Talking of your mother," said Genevieve, looking at the Bath chair as it turned a corner ahead of them, "I couldn't help noticing that her manner towards Paulo has altered. The same goes for you, Tabby. Both of you seemed rather annoyed with him."

"We are, Genevieve. Very annoyed."

"Why—what has the man done?"

"He overstepped the mark."

"Did he?"

"Yes," said Tabitha. "When he wheeled Mother around the deck this afternoon, he made some very improper remarks to her."

"That doesn't sound like Paulo."

"I can only tell you what Mother said to me. She's still simmering with rage. I think you've seen the last of Paulo Morelli."

"Have I?"

"Yes, Genevieve. Mother has sent a note of complaint to the chief steward. It was very explicit. After today, she doesn't want Paulo anywhere near her."

NINE

His visit to the second-class dining saloon was a productive one. While he was still mystified by Lois Greenwood's apparent rebuff, Dillman was glad that he had decided to forsake an evening meal in first class once more. At least he did not have to pose as a steward and tramp the corridors on this occasion. Instead he was extremely well fed in congenial company. Dining in second class not only gave him a chance to get to know Guljar Singh better, it enabled him to watch Sylvester Greenwood. Nothing about the man's behavior suggested that he was capable of committing a serious crime. To all outward appearances, Greenwood was essentially a family man, affectionate toward his wife, attentive to the needs of his daughter, and clearly taking pride in both. Dillman also noted the ease with which Greenwood was able to hold a conversation with the people around him.

Looking at him now, it seemed incredible that the Englishman had stabbed a man to death, and Dillman had to remind himself that Greenwood had lied to him earlier. He was also the same man whose eyes had burned with hatred when they fell on Dudley Nevin, inducing visible fear in the civil servant. Dillman was determined to find out the true nature of the relationship between them.

Guljar Singh broke off from his meal to lean across to his friend.

"The other day," he said, "you ask me about Gurkhas."

"That's right," agreed Dillman. "Why?"

"You are dining with some of them, Mr. Dillman."

"Am I?"

"Yes. Look at the far end of the other table."

Guljar Singh used a bony finger to point at three men, who, like him, were eating food that met with the rules of their religion. All three of them were young men in their twenties, bearded, wearing turbans and tribal dress, and having the weathered look of mountain warriors. There were other Indians in the room, and several Arabs, but the trio stood out because of the intensity with which they were discussing something, and the way in which they were excluding everyone close to them from the debate. Their faces were serious, their gestures emphatic. The detective was bound to wonder if one of the men was missing his *kukri*.

"Never pick a fight with a Gurkha," advised Guljar Singh.

"I've no intention of doing so."

"They are fearsome soldiers. They fight to the death."

"I know of their reputation in the British Army."

"They are a loyal people."

"Loyal to whom, Mr. Singh?"

"Whoever they pledge themselves to," said the old man.

Dillman's eyes flicked back to Greenwood. Unlike his daughter, he had not even glanced in Dillman's direction and appeared to be unaware of his presence. What he did do, however, was to keep Lois under close scrutiny, showing a fatherly concern that the detective took for a means of control. Greenwood had the look of a man who would react badly if he knew that his daughter had been roller-skating at night under the stars. Dillman realized how brave Lois must be to defy her father.

When the meal was over, most people drifted off to the lounge or to the smoking room. Others went out on deck; a few returned to their cabins. Greenwood and his family were among the first to leave, making their way to the lounge for a last drink before they took to their bunks. Dillman saw no value in pursuing them. In the smaller confines of the lounge, Greenwood might become aware that he was under surveillance. The detective did not wish to put him on his guard.

Instead, therefore, Dillman decided to shift his interest briefly to the other crimes that had been committed. Since the major theft had occurred in second class, he assumed that the thief would also be traveling in that part of the ship, looking for further opportunities to steal. Accordingly, he chose to patrol the corridors for a while, ambling slowly along and checking once again to see if all the doors were locked. He was about to turn the doorknob on one cabin when a voice cried out behind him.

"*Arretez-vous!*"

Dillman swung round to see Madame Roussel, brandishing a fan and bustling toward him in a beautiful cream-colored gown of lace, velvet, and chiffon. When she recognized him, her hostile manner changed at once. The anger drained out of her face.

"Oh," she said. "Is you, monsieur."

"Good evening, Madame Roussel. I was just keeping an eye on these cabins to make sure that they have no unwelcome visitors." Dillman indicated her door. "I'm pleased to see that it is now locked."

"Is too late now."

"What do you mean."

"I might as well leave the door wide open," she said, waving an arm. "Is nothing left to take."

Madame Roussel was clearly wearing all her surviving jewelry. He had glimpsed her from a distance in the dining saloon. Close to, Dillman saw how imposing she was. The long, flowing, elaborate frock was an ideal choice for such a full-bodied woman, and she had used cosmetics very subtly to enhance an already striking face. She, in turn, was clearly impressed by his appearance. It was the first time that she had seen him in formal wear and his elegance brought a smile to her lips.

"I see you are no Englishman, monsieur."

"Do you?"

"They are never really smart," she said contemptuously. "They do not look after their bodies and do not know how to dress. But you are different. You might almost pass for the Frenchman."

"I take that as a compliment."

"I mean it."

"Needless to say," he replied, sensing that she expected a compliment in return, "you put most of the other ladies in the dining saloon to shame. I could see the envy in their eyes."

She laughed lightly. *"Merci."*

"French fashion always seems to be in advance of everyone else."

"It is not the clothes, monsieur," she said, striking a pose. "It is the way that a lady wears them."

"I couldn't agree more. However," he went on, "I'm glad that our paths have crossed again. I feel that I owe you an apology."

"Why?"

"When we last met, I made an unfortunate remark."

"Pah! No more of that," she said with a flick of her wrist. "All I wish is to get my jewelry back."

"Miss Masefield and I are working on the case."

"I speak to her earlier," said the other. "She tell me that you always solve crimes on other ships. Is true?"

"Yes, Madame Roussel. We do have a good record."

"Is correct that you deal with murders, as well?"

"Not too often, luckily."

"But such things happen on P and O ships?"

"Regrettably, they do."

She shuddered. "I hope it will not happen on the *Salsette*."

"You can rest easy on that score," he said, forcing a smile. "Still, I won't delay you, madam. I can see that you wish to retire for the night."

"As long as you do not forget your promise."

"Promise?"

"To find my jewelry before we reach Aden," she reminded him. Her voice softened. "And when you have it, I want *you* to return it, monsieur, not your partner. You must promise that as well."

"Very well."

Their eyes locked for a moment and Dillman saw more than a flicker of interest. He thought that Madame Roussel was about to say something else, but she changed her mind. After bidding him farewell, she let herself into her cabin and locked it behind her. It was a strange encounter. Relieved to find her in such a mellow mood, he wondered what had brought it on, but unless they recovered her possessions, he knew that it would not last.

When he came to a companionway, he went down the steps and walked along another corridor. The lighting was dim and his mind was still very much on his exchange with Madame Roussel. As he walked past an alcove, therefore, he did not even glance into it. It was only when he was yards past it that he had the feeling that someone had been lurking in the shadows. The sound of hasty footsteps confirmed his instinct. He turned round but he was too late. Whoever had been hiding in the alcove had disappeared around a corner.

Dillman gave chase, covering the ground in long strides, hoping that he might at least catch sight of the person he had put to flight. But he was too late. When he reached the corner, he saw that the corridor ahead of him was completely deserted. Dillman blamed himself for his lapse in concentration. He felt certain of one thing.

The thief was on the prowl again.

Paulo Morelli was on the verge of tears. Standing in the purser's office, he was pleading for help but Max Cannadine was unable to give it.

"This is a matter between you and the chief steward," he said.

"But you are the senior man, sir."

"My duties are circumscribed, Paulo. They do not include sorting out the mess that you seem to have got yourself into."

"That is what I come to tell you, Mr. Cannadine. Is not my fault."

"It never is," the purser observed dryly.

"I swear it," said Morelli. "This time, I am innocent."

"So you admit that you were guilty on the other occasions, do you? That's a step forward, anyway. You've always denied it in the past. Look," he went on, adopting a more sympathetic tone. "Why don't you sit down and tell me what exactly happened?" He looked at his watch. "Only make it quick, Paulo. It's late."

"Yes, sir," said Morelli, lowering himself onto the chair in front of the desk. "Is Mrs. Simcoe and her daughter."

"I thought you were getting on well with them."

"So did I, Mr. Cannadine. Both of them, they like what I do. Then today, when I take Mrs. Simcoe out in the chair with wheels, she turn on me like the wildcat. All I do was to say that her daughter, she would be married at her age if she was an Italian girl."

"Are you sure that was all you said, Paulo?"

"I get no chance to say anything else. I am told to take her back to her cabin. From then on," said the steward, "Mrs. Simcoe and her daughter, they treat me badly. While they play the cards, they make me fetch things but they never thank me. Then this evening, Mrs. Simcoe do something very cruel."

"What was that?"

"She let me push her to dinner, then she tell me that she has reported me to the chief steward for insolence." He spread his arms. "I not insolent, Mr. Cannadine. I like ladies. I am always the gentleman."

"Too much so at times."

"Is not fair. I lose my job."

"Then you shouldn't have spoken out of turn."

"But I not do it, sir," insisted Morelli. "I make the comment about her daughter and that was that. Now I am not even allowed to work in first class. The chief steward, he put me in second class from now on."

Tears began to course down his cheeks. Cannadine could see how upset he was. Working in first class was a matter of pride to someone like Morelli. Demotion was a bitter blow. It would mean a reduction in an already low wage. There had been complaints from ladies about the steward before, but never for insolence. Much as he liked the man, the purser did not see what he could do for him.

"Will you speak up for me, please?" begged Morelli.

"I can't get involved in a dispute like this."

"But you know that I always treat ladies with respect."

"I'm sorry, Paulo," said Cannadine. "If it's a case of the passenger's word against yours, the chief steward has to side with the passenger."

"Even when she tell the lie?"

"Mrs. Simcoe must have had some cause for complaint."

"Yes," grumbled the other. "She and her daughter, they lose at the card game this morning. That make her spiky. She in bad mood so I very careful what I say to her."

"Not careful enough, it seems."

"Is not right that I should work in second class."

"Perhaps not. But it may be the answer in the short term."

"The answer?"

"It keeps you and Mrs. Simcoe apart," explained Cannadine. "She and her daughter will disembark at Aden. When that happens, you may be restored to first class."

"No, sir. The chief steward, he say he never put me back there. That's why I need you on my side. In my country, even the worst criminal, he allowed someone to defend him."

"I can't interfere with the chief steward's decisions, Paulo."

"Ask to see the note," implored Morelli. "Find out what Mrs. Simcoe say about me. Please, sir. This means a lot to me."

Cannadine sat back in his chair and scratched his head. With three thefts and a murder to worry about, he did not have time to concern himself with something as trivial as a dispute between a passenger and a steward. To Morelli, of course, it was far from trivial and his dejection was painful to watch. The purser took pity on him.

"I'll speak to the chief steward in the morning," he consented.

"*Grazie, grazie!*"

"But I make no promises," warned Cannadine. "If he's been given good cause to demote you, then I'll support his decision to the hilt."

Genevieve Masefield waited so long for him to come that she began to believe he might not turn up that night. Eventually, however, she heard the familiar tap on her door and she let Dillman in. When she had kissed and hugged him, she sounded a note of reproach.

"Why did you keep me waiting?"

"I'm sorry. I was delayed in second class."

"Eating and drinking to your heart's content, I suppose."

"No, Genevieve," he said. "Chasing the thief, among other things."

Her interest was sparked. "You *saw* him?"

"Not exactly. But I was aware of his presence."

When he told her about his futile chase, Genevieve pondered. "What makes you so certain that it was our thief?" she asked.

"Who else would hide in the shadows like that?"

"Someone who didn't want to be seen. A man going off to a rendezvous in a lady's cabin, perhaps. Yes, that might have been it," she decided. "Perhaps he was sneaking off to see Madame Roussel."

"I can absolve her of that charge," he said. "I spoke to her only moments before and she didn't look like a woman who was expecting a lover to call. If she had been, she wouldn't have talked to me for so long."

"Did she threaten you, as well, George?"

"No, she was quite pleasant."

"Pleasant?" repeated Genevieve in surprise. "Madame Roussel?"

"Yes."

"I refuse to believe it."

"At one point, she was almost coquettish."

"You're spoken for, Mr. Dillman," she warned.

"And glad to be so," he said, kissing her gently. "When she caught me trying the door of her cabin, I thought she'd rant and rave, but Madame Roussel was in a more forgiving mood. She even complimented me on my appearance."

"I could have done that."

"The only awkward moment was when she said that she hoped we wouldn't have a murder on the *Salsette*. Apparently you told her about some of the crimes we'd solved in the past."

"Only because she challenged me, George. It was time to put her in her place. Madame Roussel was treating me as if I were a complete amateur, and I wasn't standing for that."

"Good for you!"

"It didn't stop her from threatening to report us to the captain, mind you," said Genevieve. "We must stop her doing that." A memory nudged her. "But she did come up with one interesting fact. Did you know that she sailed to Bombay on the *Salsette*?"

"No," he replied. "Why did she go to India in the first place?"

"When I asked her that, I was told to mind my own business."

"She's a lady who likes to speak her mind."

"Yet Madame Roussel spared you the lash of her tongue this evening," Genevieve said enviously. "What's your secret, George?"

"Flattery. I told her how wonderful she looked."

"And did she?"

"Yes—compared to the other women in second class. No disrespect to your nation, Genevieve, but most of the English ladies there were either too conventional or simply dowdy. In fairness, Mrs. Greenwood was an exception to that," he recalled, "and so was her daughter. Lois looked quite grown-up."

"Did you learn anything from watching Sylvester Greenwood?"

Dillman told her what had transpired during dinner and how pleased he was to have sat with Guljar Singh. When he described the old Sikh, Genevieve identified him at once.

"That's the man who stole Mrs. Verney's purse," she said.

"Impossible. He's no thief."

"Mrs. Verney thinks he is. Her purse was taken on deck while she slept in her deck chair. This friend of yours—Guljar Singh— was standing nearby at the time."

"That's hardly convincing evidence," argued Dillman.

"It was convincing enough for Mrs. Verney. She pointed him out to me. He was sitting on deck, earning money by fortune-telling."

"What's wrong with that?"

"He was preying on gullible people, George."

"Only if he was tricking them, and I don't believe that he was. Guljar Singh has genuine powers of foresight, Genevieve. He gave me a solemn warning that something terrible would happen on board and—lo and behold—Mr. Nevin was murdered."

"That could have been a lucky guess."

"It wasn't very lucky for Dudley Nevin."

"None of this rules him out as a suspect for the theft."

"It's a ludicrous idea," he said with feeling. "The chances are that all three crimes are the work of the same person, and it certainly wasn't Guljar Singh. He's a frail old man. He'd never have outrun me in the corridor like that. Besides," he added, "he has no interest in money as such. He makes enough for his own immediate needs and that's all that concerns him. As it happens, I watched him win a bet of ten rupees from an officer who was foolish enough to mock him. Yes, and he told me that he had another unexpected sum of money today."

"Did he say where it came from?"

"No, Genevieve."

"Then it might have been from Mrs. Verney's purse."

Dillman was forced at least to consider the possibility. He still believed that his friend was innocent but he now wondered about the origin of Guljar Singh's unheralded windfall.

"Give me the details of this latest theft," he asked.

Genevieve did so, describing Mrs. Verney and explaining how she had visited the scene of the crime with her. Dillman seized on the fact that Mrs. Verney was, like Madame Roussel and Mrs. Lundgrun, the other victims before her, a second-class passenger.

"All three thefts have occurred there, so at least we know in which part of the ship we can look for our thief. He's hidden away somewhere in the passenger list that the purser gave us."

"Unless he's a member of the crew."

"Have you seen where the stewards sleep?" said Dillman. "They don't have individual cabins like us, Genevieve. There are at least four bunks in all of their quarters. There's no chance of hiding jewelry in there."

"Then it has to be a passenger."

"Someone fit enough to sprint along a corridor."

"That must eliminate a lot of people, George."

"It does," he said. "But it still leaves us with a fair number of suspects. There are lots of younger people aboard the ship. You can't watch them all simultaneously. My fear is that I may have frightened the thief off this evening. If he knows someone is after him, he may decide to go to ground."

"If that happens, we'll never find him."

"Yes, we will," he asserted. "Somehow."

"Time is fast running out."

"Then we'll have to redouble our efforts." Seeing her disconsolate expression, he gave her a reassuring hug. "Cheer up, Genevieve. We've been in more difficult situations than this and managed to pull through."

"I suppose so."

"Tell me about *your* evening," he suggested.

"It wasn't as interesting as yours. I dined with the Simcoes."

"Have you made your peace with the daughter?"

"I thought so," she said, "but I'm not quite sure. Tabby is such a creature of moods—and so is her mother. They spent most of the meal talking about their triumph at the card table or complaining about their steward. Some of Tabby's behavior surprised me."

"In what way?"

"Well, she seemed so meek and mild when I first met her."

"And now?"

"She really blossomed over dinner. She was full of confidence. In the past, she's always been rather shy where the opposite sex is concerned, but not last night. Tabby was chatting away to the young man beside her as if he were an old friend."

"Perhaps that's what he was."

"No, George," she said. "He was a complete stranger—a German by the name of Siegfried Voigt. I wouldn't have believed it of Tabby if I hadn't actually seen it happen. She came very close to flirting with him."

Lois Greenwood was circumspect. When she parted from her parents that night, she waited a long time before creeping out of her cabin with her roller skates. After her father's warning, she knew that she had to be especially careful, but she was not going to be denied her exercise. Before she put on her skates, she walked around the deck to make sure that nobody was about. It seemed to be deserted. Perched on a bench, she was reaching for the first skate when someone came out of the gloom to sit down beside her.

"Hello, Miss Greenwood," said Dillman.

"Oh!" she exclaimed, hand on heart. "You gave me such a fright."

"You are speaking to me, then?"

"Of course, Mr. Dillman."

"I thought you'd forgotten who I was," he complained. "In the dining room earlier on, you cut me dead."

"Yes, I'm sorry about that. It was Daddy's fault. He gave me a roasting for being so impetuous. Daddy said I wasn't to befriend people like you and Guljar Singh in the way that I did. So—just to please him—I pretended to ignore you."

"Does he know that you once skated into me?"

"No! He'd crucify me if he found that out."

"It sounds to me as if he's rather strict with you."

"Too strict," she said. "It's been far worse since he became an M.P. Daddy never used to be quite so pompous before. He says that he has a position to maintain and that I mustn't let him down."

"You're a credit to him, and I told him so."

"Thank you, Mr. Dillman."

"How long has he been in Parliament?"

"Only for two years or so," she replied, strapping the first skate to her foot. "He won a by-election in Reading. The one good thing about that was that we had a party to celebrate. Daddy was in great form that night. From then on, Mummy hardly ever saw him."

"Did he spend all his time at the House of Commons?"

"There or abroad. He's always traveled a lot."

"Oh? What did he do before he became a politician?"

"He worked for a newspaper as a foreign correspondent. I used to get letters from all over the place. He even went to South Africa."

"Why?"

"Something he was investigating. I don't know the details."

"Does he like being in Parliament?"

"He loves it."

"What about your mother?"

"She's very proud of him but she'd like to see more of him. Mummy is anxious at the best of times. When Daddy goes abroad," she said, putting on the other skate, "she worries herself sick."

"Why does he have to travel so much?"

"I don't know."

"Does your father have any enemies, Miss Greenwood?"

She giggled. "He's a politician. Everyone hates them."

"Is he the sort of man who has vendettas against people?"

"That's a funny question. Why do you ask?"

"I know that passions can run high in politics," said Dillman. "They certainly do in my country, anyway. What about this by-election? Do you have any idea who stood against your father?"

"Not really. There were two other candidates, that's all I know."

"Can you recall either of their names?"

"No," she said. "I was away at boarding school when it happened. The only time I went home was for the party. If you want all the details, you'll have to ask Daddy. He still has his election poster framed on the wall of his office."

Dillman did not wish to press her any further in case he aroused her suspicion. He had learned some interesting new facts about Sylvester Greenwood and settled for those. Since women were excluded from the political process, Lois clearly had no real curiosity about her father's work. There was little more that he could learn from her.

"Will you tell your father that we had this conversation?" he said.

"Of course not."

"Because you're not supposed to speak to me?"

"That's not the only reason, Mr. Dillman," she said, standing up on her skates. "If I told him we met on deck like this, Daddy would never forgive me. He has a real temper when he's roused."

"He ought to be proud of a daughter with spirit like yours."

"Well, he's not, I'm afraid."

"A pity. Still, you get on with your practice. The deck is yours."

"Good-bye!"

Pushing herself off from the bench, Lois skated along the port side of the vessel with gathering speed. Dillman waited until she had done a complete circuit of the ship and clapped his hands in appreciation. She did not, however, get very far on her second circuit. A burly figure soon emerged from a doorway to block her way and she gave a little cry of alarm. Thinking that she was in danger, Dillman ran swiftly to her aid but his help wasn't needed. When he reached her, he saw that she was gazing up in horror at her father.

Still in his white tie and tails, Sylvester Greenwood was brusque.

"Good night, Mr. Dillman," he said.

Max Cannadine was not enamoured of the idea at all. When it was first put to him in his office that morning, he shook his head doubtfully.

"Will that really be necessary, Miss Masefield?" he asked.

"Only as a last resort."

"You want permission to search the cabins?"

"A selected number of them," said Genevieve. "It may be the only way we can actually track down the jewelry that was stolen."

"Even so, it's a big step."

"It's always proved to be crucial in the past."

"That may well be," said the purser, "but that doesn't make it any more palatable for me. Passengers trust us. They have faith in us to transport them safely from one port to another in the quickest way. When they buy a P and O ticket, they don't expect to have their belongings searched by detectives."

"They won't know anything about it, Mr. Cannadine."

"There'd be an unholy stink, if they did."

"Rely on our discretion."

"How many cabins are we talking about, Miss Masefield?"

"George estimates that it will be somewhere around thirty."

"As many as that?" gasped the purser.

"We don't want to leave any stone unturned."

"I'll need to think about this. It's not something that we can undertake lightly. As you know, we have so many foreigners aboard. If one of them discovers you or Mr. Dillman in his cabin, we could have an international incident."

"You'll certainly have one if Madame Roussel isn't pacified by the return of her jewelry. She's talking of suing P and O."

"That's all we need!" moaned Cannadine with a hollow laugh.

"By the way," remembered Genevieve, "did you know that she sailed to Bombay on the *Salsette*?"

"No, but then I don't keep track of everyone who steps aboard. There are too many of them. When was this, Miss Masefield?"

"I was going to ask you that. Do you keep old passenger lists?"

"Naturally."

"When you have a moment, I'd be grateful if you could look through them to find out when Madame Roussel was on the ship before."

"Right," Cannadine agreed. "I will." He grimaced. "I do wish I hadn't said that I relished the chance of seeing you and your partner at work. I had no idea you'd have your hands this full."

"Neither did we." Genevieve got up from her chair. "But what do you say to my request? Do we have your permission in principle?"

"In principle, Miss Masefield. But try everything else first."

"We will, I assure you."

"Before you go," he said as she moved to the door, "I wanted a word on another matter. It appears there's been a serious rift between Mrs. Simcoe and her steward."

"Yes," said Genevieve. "Paulo told me all about it. He begged me to find out what he'd done wrong."

"Did you know that he's been downgraded to second class?"

"No, I didn't. That will really hurt his pride."

"I had him in here last thing at night. Paulo was weeping. It's taken him so long to get the promotion to first class, and it suddenly vanished before his eyes. I agreed to speak to the chief steward on his behalf."

"What did he say?"

"That there was nothing he could do. Mrs. Simcoe alleges that her steward made improper remarks to her on deck, and she has to be believed. Paulo's behavior has been criticized before, I fear," he confided, "but only by younger women. I can't imagine that he tried to woo Mrs. Simcoe with that charm of his."

"Whatever he said to her, she was deeply offended. I know that. I dined with her last night. Both she and her daughter were still angry with Paulo, though they didn't fully explain why."

"He wondered if it might be to do with a card game."

"Oh?"

"Apparently the Simcoes lost at bridge that morning."

"I heard all about it from Mr. and Mrs. Ackroyd. They beat them."

"Paulo's story is that it put Mrs. Simcoe in a foul mood," said the purser. "He made the mistake of mentioning the loss at cards to her while they were on deck. Mrs. Simcoe rounded on him."

"She and Tabitha do take the game seriously."

"Seriously enough to play for money, I gather."

"Yes," said Genevieve, "but they met their match in the Ackroyds."

"How do you know?"

"Because Mrs. Ackroyd was boasting about it over luncheon. The Simcoes won the first session and the Ackroyds, the second. They're meeting to play the deciding game this morning."

"Really?" said Cannadine with a grin. "I'd love to be a fly on the wall of the cabin when *that* happens."

———

"They can't possibly have a run of luck like that again," said Constance Simcoe, seated at the table as she played patience. "I wouldn't have minded so much if Phoebe Ackroyd hadn't bragged about it to other people."

"What time did you tell them to come?" asked Tabitha.

"Ten o'clock. I thought we'd start earlier today."

"And this afternoon?"

"We're playing the Kingtons again."

"That will be a lot easier. They're relatively new to the game." She heard a tap on the door. "That can't be the Ackroyds already."

"Find out, please."

Tabitha opened the door to admit Phoebe Ackroyd, who waddled into the cabin with an apologetic smile. She went over to Constance.

"We may have to disappoint you, I'm afraid," she said.

"Why?"

"My husband has mislaid his ear trumpet."

"That won't stop him playing bridge, will it?" said Constance.

"Gerald feels at a disadvantage without it."

"I feel at a disadvantage without my legs, Mrs. Ackroyd, but I've learned to live with my problem. Your husband is only partially deaf, after all. That's not a major handicap."

"When did he lose the ear trumpet?" said Tabitha.

"He thinks it must have been in the lounge last night," explained Mrs. Ackroyd, "though he's not certain. Gerald is a little forgetful in his old age. He had the ear trumpet with him at dinner, I know that. Then I went to bed early and left him to have a brandy in the lounge."

"I'm sorry about this," said Constance, "but I really don't think it's fair of you to let us down at the last moment."

"Yes," added Tabitha. "It's too late to rustle up someone else now."

"There are the Kinnersleys. They play bridge."

"Unfortunately," Constance said coldly, "we don't get on all that well with the major and his wife, so that wouldn't be an option. It's you and your husband or nobody."

Phoebe Ackroyd was in two minds. Eager to play, she was worried that her husband would not be at his best without his ear trumpet. When she looked down at the cards, however, she felt very tempted.

"We don't *want* to disappoint you," she said. "And we did promise to give you the chance to recoup your losses."

"Or to increase them," observed Constance with a smile as she collected the cards. "You and your husband are worthy opponents."

"That makes such a difference," said Tabitha.

"If you wish, we could always forget money altogether and simply enjoy the game for its own sake."

"No, no," protested Mrs. Ackroyd. "There must be a financial inducement. That's what makes bridge so thrilling."

"We'll play on any terms that you prefer," offered Constance. "With or without your husband's ear trumpet."

Phoebe Ackroyd needed only a few moments to reach her decision.

"We'll play," she announced. "Gerald and I can't possibly miss an opportunity like this."

The sky was overcast that morning and the wind was gusting. Most of the passengers were discouraged from spending much time on deck. It meant that the second-class lounge was quite full. When Dillman arrived there, however, he saw that Archibald Sinclair had found himself a quiet corner in which to study Cicero.

"May I join you for a short while?" Dillman asked politely.

Sinclair looked up. "Oh, yes. Please do, Mr. Dillman."

The detective sat down. "If you don't mind, I'd like to ask you a few more things about Mr. Nevin."

"Fire away."

"Do you happen to know if he was ever married?"

"Not married, I'm certain of that. But he was engaged at one time."

"Do you happen to know to whom?"

"I don't keep that close a watch on my former pupils, Mr. Dillman."

"Of course not." Dillman took out the two photographs that he had found in the dead man's billfold. "Do you by any chance recognize either of these ladies?"

Sinclair studied the photograph of the young woman sitting in the car and shook his head. When he looked at the second photograph, however, his eyebrows shot up.

"I may have seen this young lady before," he said.

"Where?"

"In Dudley's apartment. My wife and I called there before he took us out to dinner. I'm fairly certain that there was a large photograph of this pretty young creature on a shelf."

"Did he tell you her name?"

"We didn't ask. We were only in the room for a few minutes."

Dillman put the photographs away. "You mentioned that he stood for Parliament and that the candidate who beat him in the by-election was aboard this ship."

"That's right—a Sylvester Greenwood."

"How do you know him?"

"Because his picture was in all the newspapers at the time. Mr. Greenwood is quite memorable. He's a stocky fellow with a black beard and a sense of purpose about him. He and Dudley were pictured together in the *Times*." He sucked in his breath. "An unsavory business."

"What was?"

"The allegations that were flying about, Mr. Dillman."

"Allegations?"

"Of electoral impropriety," explained Sinclair. "Dudley always was one for sailing close to the wind. It seems that he was so desperate to win the seat that he may have bent a few rules."

"Was there a court case?"

"No, thankfully. The charges were dropped in the end. But not before we'd had to endure the sight of a Wykehamist being blackened in public. Dudley denied the allegations, naturally," he went on, "but the speed with which he fled to India suggested that they might have some foundation to them."

"In other words, Mr. Greenwood had good reason to dislike him."

"To detest him, probably. Nobody likes to lose a parliamentary election because of illegal practices. In the event, Sylvester Greenwood did actually win but I suspect that the affair still rankles."

"So do I," said Dillman to himself.

"Dudley made no mention of any of this to me, I have to say."

"I can understand why, Mr. Sinclair."

"Politics is such a dangerous game," said the old man. "Look at my good friend, Marcus Tullius Cicero," he went on, tapping his book. "After he helped to suppress the Cataline conspiracy, he was made consul. Then he supported the senatorial party against Julius Caesar and, after the emperor had been assassinated, he attacked Mark Antony in a series of speeches. Cicero was executed for sincerely held beliefs. The odd thing is this. After his death, his influence became stronger and stronger. Well, I'm still under his spell over two thousand years later." He took off his eyeglasses as he laughed shrilly. "Who knows? Maybe that will happen to Dudley. When he dies, we may come to respect his finer qualities."

Dillman had severe doubts about that but he said nothing. The second interview with Archibald Sinclair had brought important new facts to light, and the detective was grateful that he had taken the trouble to visit the second-class lounge. He was soon given an even stronger reason for gratitude. When he glanced up, he saw Sylvester Greenwood standing in the doorway, deep in conversation with one of the Gurkhas onboard.

TEN

Any fears that Genevieve Masefield might have had about the thief going to ground were soon dispelled. The purser summoned her to his office to meet Ethan Gilbert, a big, barrel-chested man in his fifties with his curly brown hair graying noticeably at the edges. A Texan by birth, Gilbert had a deep voice and a slow drawl. When he had been introduced to the detective, he explained why he was there.

"Martha was too upset to come herself," he said. "That's how much this has shaken my wife. I mean, we travel all round the world without losing so much as a red cent, then *this* happens."

"What does, Mr. Gilbert?" asked Genevieve.

"Martha had her purse taken."

"From where?"

"The main deck."

"When was this?"

"About half an hour ago," he said. "I'd have come sooner but it took me a long time to calm her down. My wife is a very sensitive woman. She *feels* things."

"Nobody enjoys being the victim of theft," remarked Cannadine.

"Were you with Mrs. Gilbert at the time, sir?" said Genevieve.

"No, I wasn't," replied Gilbert, "and I regret that bitterly. If I'd found some guy trying to take her purse, I'd have beaten him to a pulp."

Ethan Gilbert had the physique to fulfill such a threat, and enough anger to want to wreak revenge on his wife's behalf. He was demanding prompt action to recover his wife's purse.

"It's quite windy on deck this morning," noted the purser. "I'm surprised that your wife wanted to sit out there."

"Martha is from Chicago," said Gilbert. "Winds don't bother her."

"Where was the purse when it was taken?" asked Genevieve.

"On the deck chair next to her."

"Was Mrs. Gilbert distracted in some way?"

"She was talking to the lady on the other side of her."

"Were there any people about at the time of the theft?"

"Only a few, apparently," he said. "They were walking briskly along the deck. There weren't many people hardy enough to sit out there."

"I don't suppose that your wife remembers any of the by-standers."

"Only one of them, Miss Masefield."

"Oh? And who was that?"

"This old Indian guy with a white beard," he recalled. "He was talking to someone nearby at one point. By the time that Martha realized that her purse had been taken, this fellow with the turban had gone."

Genevieve was certain that he was referring to Guljar Singh, the elderly Sikh who had been nearby when an earlier theft had taken place.

"I'll need to see the exact spot where the crime occurred," she said.

"Then you'll have to wait until she's recovered."

"Was there much in the purse, Mr. Gilbert?"

"Does it matter?" he said testily. "The fact is that it was stolen from right under Martha's nose. Even if it had been empty, it would have been a shock to lose it."

"I appreciate that," said Genevieve, "but it would be helpful to know if there were any valuable items, things that the thief might keep. The likelihood is that he'll dispose of the purse but retain any cash or items that he can sell. Was there anything distinctive in that purse that he might hang on to?"

"You'll have to ask Martha that. What's making her holler is that she's lost photographs of our children."

"The thief is unlikely to keep those," warned Cannadine.

"He'd better—or he'll answer to me!"

"Let us handle this, Mr. Gilbert."

"Your wife is not the only victim, you see," said Genevieve. "In fact, she's the third person to have a purse taken from the main deck, and we're investigating a theft from a cabin as well."

"What kind of a ship is this?" asked Gilbert, slapping the desk with a palm. "Don't you have any protection against this sort of thing?"

"We have experienced detectives aboard, sir," said the purser, "and they'll stop at nothing to recover any lost property."

"Well, I hope they find it. If they don't," vowed Gilbert, "I'm going to stand at the gangway when we reach Aden and search everyone's luggage till I get back what someone took from my wife."

"We can't allow you to do that, sir."

"Just try and stop me."

"It may not be necessary," said Genevieve in an effort to soothe him. "We know that the man has certain items in his possession, and your wife may be able to tell us of some additional ones. Find those and we find our thief. That means we can return property to four separate passengers."

"Martha's the only one I care about," he stressed, opening the door. "We came on this trip to celebrate our silver wedding anniversary. I'm not taking my wife home with any bad memories of this vacation. She wants her purse back and I mean to get it."

After glaring at the two of them, he went out and closed the door. Max Cannadine looked at Genevieve and raised an eyebrow. She responded with a long sigh.

"If only his wife had come here instead," said Genevieve.

"He was a rather aggressive customer, wasn't he?"

"I think that he could be more trouble than Madame Roussel."

"Not if the crimes are solved."

"They will be if you sanction the search of the cabins."

The purser hesitated. "Has it really come to that, Miss Masefield?"

"I'm afraid so. This thief is light-fingered. We're unlikely to catch him committing a crime, so we have to track down the stolen goods."

"So be it."

"I'll tell George—and I'll mention this latest theft to him."

"There's something else you might care to pass on, as well."

"Is there?"

"You asked me to look at passenger records for you."

"That's right, Mr. Cannadine," she said. "I wanted to know when Madame Roussel sailed to Bombay from Aden."

"The first time or the second time?"

"I don't follow."

"It turns out that this is her fourth voyage on the *Salsette*. She went to Bombay and back to Aden ten days ago—in first class both ways. Now she's doing the same again, except that the return leg is second class this time."

Genevieve was agog. "Four trips in so short a period?"

"Perhaps she likes us," said the purser.

Wrapped up against the wind, Major Romford Kinnersley strode along the main deck with Sukinder by his side. Unlike him, she did not seem to feel the cold, though the roll of the ship made her slightly queasy and she put a hand to her stomach from time to time. Kinnersley was in a censorious mood.

"You must learn to be more punctual, Suki," he told her.

"I sorry, *sahib*."

"Mrs. Kinnersley was very cross when you turned up late this morning. She expected you to be there on time."

"Yes, I know."

"What kept you?"

"I sleep too long."

"Then it's a habit you're going to have to break," he pointed out. "I know it would have been easier if your cabin had been closer to ours, but that couldn't be arranged. There are clocks in all the public rooms. You can tell the time from those." Sukinder nodded. "And you must try not to upset Mrs. Kinnersley," he continued. "When you get to England, you'll take all your orders from my wife."

"Yes, *sahib*," she said mournfully.

"It will be a big opportunity for you. I hope you realize that."

"I do."

"Most girls of your age would love to be taken to England to work. The standard of living is much higher there, even for those in domestic service. Your mother understood that, Suki. That's why she was keen to send you there in our care."

"I am missing Mother."

"That's only natural."

"I am missing her now when I no feel well."

"What's wrong with you?" She rubbed her stomach. "A touch of seasickness, eh? That will soon pass. Lie down in your cabin for a while."

"Yes, *sahib*."

"But don't forget that we'll expect you to read to us this afternoon."

"I remember."

"Your mother read English very well."

"She like to speak it."

"So should you. There'll be no opportunity to use your native language when you get to England—unless you write to your mother, that is."

"I am writing all the time."

"Learn to do it in English. It's what your mother would expect." He saw how crestfallen she was. "Yes, I know," he said considerately. "It's rather overpowering for you, isn't it? Taken away from your home, your family, your friends. Going to a strange country so far away. But you'll come to thank us in the end, Sukinder. And one day, perhaps, if you do what you're told, it may be possible to bring your mother over to visit you in England. Would you like that?"

"Yes," said Sukinder, tears in her eyes.

"That will give you something to look forward to, eh?"

"I think so."

"Right. You run along and get some rest. I can see that you're not at your best while the ship is rocking like this. But we'll want you in our cabin this afternoon, remember. Be on time."

"Yes, *sahib*."

Glad to be released, she hurried off up the deck with a hand still on her stomach. Kinnersley was about to retrace his steps when he saw a familiar figure bearing down on him. Gerald Ackroyd was wearing a scarf and a hat to ward off the buffeting wind.

"Good day to you, Romford!" said the other.

"Nice to see you, Gerald."

"Was that your servant toddling off? Pretty little thing."

"Sukinder is not at her best this morning."

"What's that?" asked the other, cupping his hand to his ear. "You'll have to speak up in this wind, old chap."

Kinnersley raised his voice. "I said that Suki is not feeling well."

"Seasickness or homesickness?"

"A mixture of both, I suspect."

"They do make excellent servants, though," said Ackroyd. "It's the thing I really missed when I left India. Along with my friends, of course."

"What are you doing out here on such a blustery day?"

"Working up an appetite for luncheon. And—this is between the two of us, mark you—trying to keep out of Phoebe's way."

"Upset the lady wife, have you?" said Kinnersley with a grin.

"It wasn't my fault, Romford."

"What did you do?"

"Lost my ear trumpet somewhere," replied Ackroyd. "Can't for the life of me think where it is. Anyway, we've just had a couple of dreadful hours, playing bridge with the Simcoes. Have you met them?"

"Yes," said Kinnersley. "Can't say we took to either of the ladies."

"They're pleasant enough in their own way, I suppose. And they do play cards as if they intend to win. I admire that trait in anybody."

"I take it that you and your wife lost?"

"Heavily," said Ackroyd. "Phoebe was so convinced that we'd put the pair of them to the sword again that she raised the stakes—even though she must have realized that I wouldn't be quite so adept without my ear trumpet."

"How much did you lose?"

"Too much, Romford. And, of course, I got the blame."

"Well, you were the one who let the ear trumpet go astray, Gerald."

"Thank heaven I did," said Ackroyd, chortling merrily. "I don't think I'd like to have heard some of the things that my wife called me."

Spurred on by what he saw in the second-class lounge, George Dillman went off in search of Dr. McNeil. Now that he had witnessed a connection between Sylvester Greenwood and one of the Gurkhas aboard, he wanted to know more about the wound that had killed Dudley Nevin. He found Rory McNeil in the medical room, checking supplies against a list. The Scotsman looked up at him.

"I was wondering when you'd come to see me," he said.

"I'm sorry if you feel neglected, Dr. McNeil."

"If only I were. The passengers have kept me busy, treating minor complaints and begging me to cure their seasickness. I also had to put some stitches in a rather nasty gash on someone's leg, so I feel that my presence on the ship is justified."

"You were invaluable when it came to dealing with Mr. Nevin."

"That was a first, Mr. Dillman," he said. "I've had fatalities before, especially on long voyages, but I've never had to handle a murder victim. It was a novel experience and I think I learned from it."

"Did the purser tell you about the letter that I found?"

"Yes—from the man's cousin. At least we'll have someone to take charge of the remains when we dock in Aden."

"Mr. Cannadine has sent a telegraph to the P and O agent there, telling him what to expect. We must just make sure that all the passengers disembark before we unload the corpse."

"Don't forget the ones joining the ship at Aden," said McNeil. "We don't want to frighten them either. I don't think I'd feel too happy about setting off on a voyage if I saw a coffin being carried past me."

"We'll arrange it discreetly," promised Dillman.

"I forgot. You've done this before, haven't you?"

"Once too often, Dr. McNeil."

"How is your investigation going?"

"I've been gathering evidence steadily," said Dillman. "In fact, that's why I'm here. I just wanted to check some details with you."

"About what?"

"The wound, principally. I assume that you cleaned it off to examine it properly." McNeil nodded. "What did you find?"

"Exactly what I expected to find—that a *kukri* is a deadly weapon."

"Do you think that Mr. Nevin put up much of a fight?"

"He did his best, Mr. Dillman, as any of us would in that situation, but he wasn't a strong man. His muscles were slack and he was carrying too much weight. Dudley Nevin was out of condition. Also," said McNeil, "there was another factor that would have slowed him down."

"Was there?"

"He'd been drinking heavily. I could smell the whiskey on him."

"There was a lot of blood," said the other. "Could some of it have got onto his attacker?"

"I'm certain that it did—it probably stained his clothing."

"In that case, he'll have got rid of it somehow."

"It was the wound itself that intrigued me."

"Why?"

"Well, I'm no expert on such things," admitted the doctor, "but I would have expected more proficiency from a Gurkha. You know, one well-aimed thrust and it would all be over. Not in this case, however. The wound was very jagged."

"Perhaps Mr. Nevin put up more of a struggle than we think."

"That's one explanation, I suppose."

"Can you suggest any others?"

"Yes, I think there are two possibilities."

"Go on."

"Well, the killer was either someone who didn't know how to use the knife and just lunged out at him."

"Or?"

"He wanted to *hurt* his victim," said McNeil. "The knife was twisted to inflict maximum pain, Mr. Dillman. When you catch up with this devil, you'll have to be very careful. He's dangerous."

It was late morning before Martha Gilbert felt able to return to the spot where her purse had been taken. She was a short, slight woman with the kind of elfin features that took a decade off her age. Supported by her husband, she pointed out where she had been sitting and where the old man had been standing. Genevieve did not keep her there for long. Thanking the two of them for their help, she went off to confront Guljar Singh. Notwithstanding her partner's comments about him, she felt that he had to be questioned. On two separate occasions, the Sikh had been standing near someone whose property had been stolen. That was too much of a coincidence for Genevieve.

When she eventually found him, Guljar Singh was sitting cross-legged on the deck in the stern of the vessel, impervious to the rolling motion of the ship and to the wind that was making his beard dance so wildly. His eyes were closed and he seemed to be miles away. Not wishing to disturb his contemplation, Genevieve waited patiently for several minutes until he became aware of her presence. When he saw her standing over him, the Sikh gave her a welcoming smile and hauled himself to his feet without any visible effort.

"Mr. Singh?" she said.

"That is my name, lady," he replied. "Guljar Singh of Bombay."

"My name is Genevieve Masefield and I work for P and O."

"Indeed?"

"I'm employed as a detective on the *Salsette*."

"A *lady* detective?" he said with a mixture of wonder and wry amusement. "What will they think of next? In my country, it would never happen. No, I do not believe it. You are too beautiful to be a detective."

"Nevertheless, Mr. Singh," she insisted, "that's what I am."

He gave a polite bow. "Then I stand corrected."

"I need to speak to you with regard to some crimes that were committed on this deck."

"Crimes?" He hunched his shoulders. "It is not a crime to tell fortunes, is it? I do not force anyone to pay me."

"I'm talking about some thefts that occurred, Mr. Singh. Do you have any objection to answering a few questions?"

"None at all."

"The most recent case happened this morning," she told him, "shortly after breakfast. Were you on the main deck at that time?"

"Certainly. I prefer to be in the fresh air whenever I can."

"There's an American passenger called Mrs. Gilbert who was sitting in a deck chair on the starboard side of the ship. You must have noticed her because there were so few people ready to brave this wind."

"I remember two ladies, sitting side by side."

"Talking to each other."

"Yes, I was standing only a short distance away."

"That's what Mrs. Gilbert told me. She's still very perturbed by the loss of her purse but she was able to give a description of you."

"I was only there for a few minutes."

"Did you notice her purse?"

"It was beside her on the empty deck chair."

"Did you see anyone approach it?"

"No," said Singh. "I was talking to a friend at the time. When he left me, I walked off in this direction." A note of indignation came into his voice. "Is this lady saying that *I* am the thief?"

"Not exactly."

"Then why do you look at me with such suspicion?"

"I'm only doing my job, Mr. Singh."

"What do you mean?"

"Yesterday—when you were on this deck again—a lady called Mrs. Verney had her purse taken while she was asleep. According to her, you were very close to her when she dozed off to sleep."

"That may have been so. I did not notice."

"Her purse was on the chair beside her."

"And you think I took *that,* as well?" he said, deeply wounded by the charge. "What sort of person do you take me for?"

"I have to look into what the victims tell me, Mr. Singh."

"Let them come here. Let them accuse me to my face."

"The evidence is only circumstantial," she confessed, "but I must take it seriously. Two thefts occur and the one person whom both ladies remember being in the vicinity is you."

"So?"

"It is significant."

"Only if I steal their purses," he argued. He spread his arms wide. "Search me, if you wish. Search my cabin. Search my belongings. You will find nothing that I take from anyone else."

There was such injured innocence in his voice that Genevieve wondered if she had made a gross error in approaching him.

Guljar Singh neither looked nor behaved like a thief, but that did not exonerate him. Genevieve had arrested older criminals than him before now, and ones with even more blameless appearances. Her suspicion remained.

"I may have to speak to you again in due course," she said.

"You will not arrest me?" he taunted, holding out his wrists. "You will not put the handcuffs on me?"

"No, Mr. Singh."

"But you should. If it is a crime to stand on deck near a lady in a deck chair, then I must ask for dozens of other offences to be taken into account. If this is your justice," he said with disgust, "then I spurn it. I do nothing wrong yet you humiliate me."

"I merely asked you some questions," said Genevieve.

"Yes, but there were questions *behind* those questions. You are thinking that I am guilty before you even talk to me. This is it," he decided, grasping his hands together and looking upward. "I *knew* that a terrible event would occur on this ship—and this is it. Guljar Singh is to be arrested for crimes that he never committed. You do the worst thing possible to me," he said, trembling all over. "You try to take away my good name."

Luncheon in the second-class dining saloon was served with customary speed and courtesy. The meal itself was delicious. Whatever else passengers might complain about, they could not fault the catering staff. Like everyone else in the room, George Dillman enjoyed the food and had no regrets about deserting first class once more. Sitting with Archibald Sinclair and his wife, he listened to them reminiscing about their visit to India, while keeping one eye on Sylvester Greenwood. The latter was seated at the other end of the saloon, saying very little and, judging by the expression on his face, throbbing with suppressed anger.

There was no sign of Lois Greenwood. Her parents were lunching alone. Dillman surmised that their daughter had been confined to her cabin as a punishment for her nighttime outing on the roller skates, and he felt sorry for her. He also regretted the absence of Guljar Singh. Hoping to sit with his friend again, he could not understand why the mystic had missed the meal, as well. The Sinclairs could only talk to him about India. Guljar Singh, on the other hand, symbolized it.

Sylvester Greenwood gave no indication that he even knew that Dillman was there. It enabled the detective to watch him carefully and to switch his attention occasionally to the Gurkha whom he had seen talking earlier to the Englishman. Seated with his friends as before, the Gurkha was involved in another earnest discussion. At one point, he bunched a fist and smashed it into the palm of his other hand for emphasis. Dillman noted the impressive breadth of his shoulders and the determination in his craggy face. Even when sober, Dudley Nevin would have stood little chance against such an attacker, if that, in fact, was what the Gurkha had been. Dillman reserved his judgment.

When the meal was over, the Greenwoods were among the first to leave. After chatting with his companions for a few minutes, Dillman excused himself from the table and headed for the door, expecting to resume his surveillance of Sylvester Greenwood in the lounge. Instead, the man was waiting for him outside. Scowling at Dillman, he pointed a finger at him.

"I'd like a word with you, sir," he demanded.

"Of course, Mr. Greenwood."

"Somewhere a little more private."

"Then I suggest that we go on deck," Dillman said easily. "It's too windy out there for most people this afternoon." He indicated the way. "We should have all the privacy we want."

They went down the corridor to the door that gave access to the deck. When they reached a bulkhead that gave them some protection from the gusts of wind, Greenwood swung round to face him. There was quiet fury in his voice.

"Stay away from my daughter, Mr. Dillman," he ordered.

"But I enjoy her company."

"Lois will not be speaking to you again."

"Is that your decision or hers?" asked Dillman. "I would have thought she was old enough to choose her own friends by now. Where is she, by the way? Locked in her cabin?"

"That's a personal matter."

"Not if I'm indirectly responsible. I'd hate to think that she was being disciplined simply because she spoke to me."

"Lois needs to be curbed," said the other, sharply, "and so do you."

Dillman smiled. "Am I to be locked in my cabin, as well?"

"Who *are* you, Mr. Dillman?"

"An interested bystander."

"No," said Greenwood, eyelids narrowing, "you're much more than that. According to Lois, you questioned her about me."

"Yes, I did," admitted Dillman. "I was trying to find out why you lied to me earlier. When I mentioned the name of Dudley Nevin, you told me that you could hardly remember who he was—yet he actually stood against you in a by-election."

"It's something I prefer to forget."

"Then why do you keep your election poster framed on your wall?"

Greenwood was startled. "How do you know about that?"

"Is it true?"

"My daughter told you, didn't she?"

"Yes," said Dillman, "and it does rather contradict your claim that you'd rather forget the event that brought you and Mr. Nevin together."

"That poster happens to be a souvenir of an important moment in my life," explained Greenwood with dignity. "I'm very proud of being a member of Parliament—and proud of defeating a candidate who tried to cheat his way to victory. Perhaps Mr. Nevin didn't mention that to you. He flouted several electoral rules and was exposed for it."

"I'm aware of that, Mr. Greenwood."

"It's one of the reasons that he packed his bags and left England."

"Yes," said Dillman. "He admitted that he'd left under a cloud."

"That was certainly true!"

"You obviously dislike the man."

"I loathe him, sir."

"Then why did you deny knowing him?"

"What business is it of yours, Mr. Dillman?"

"I'm curious, that's all."

"Far too curious," decided Greenwood, squaring up to him. "First, you befriend my daughter. Then you quiz me about my relationship with someone from my past. Then you go out of your way to interrogate Lois about me—and now you accuse me of lying."

"But that's exactly what you did."

"Nevin has put you up to this, hasn't he?" he challenged.

"My interest in you *was* first aroused by Mr. Nevin," conceded Dillman, thinking of the blood-covered body of the civil servant. "But he's not aware that I'm talking to you now."

"Keep him out of my way!"

"Is that a threat, Mr. Greenwood?"

"And stay away from me yourself."

"Your daughter warned me that you had a temper."

Greenwood was fuming. "You've seen nothing yet, believe me!"

"Just answer one last question."

"Don't push me, Mr. Dillman."

"Were you entirely surprised to see Mr. Nevin onboard this ship?"

There was a long pause. Sylvester Greenwood was torn between rage and embarrassment. Dillman saw him blink involuntarily several times. He believed that he had found a weak spot. He jabbed at it.

"Meeting him again was not a complete coincidence, was it?"

"I've nothing more to say to you, Mr. Dillman."

"Not now, perhaps," the detective said casually, "but I can assure you that we'll be talking again fairly soon."

Greenwood was pugnacious. "No, we won't!" he asserted.

"We'll see."

Dillman met his steely glare. Greenwood's muscles had tensed and his fists tightened. For a moment, Dillman thought that the man was about to throw a punch and he got ready to parry it. Instead, Greenwood looked over the American's shoulder at someone who had glided silently up behind him. Dillman turned around to find himself gazing into the stern face of the Gurkha he had been watching in the dining saloon. The man's dark eyes flashed.

"Are you needing help, Mr. Greenwood?" he asked.

When she shared a table with them in the first-class dining saloon, Genevieve Masefield did not need to ask how they had fared at the card table. Constance and Tabitha were positively glowing with their success, careful to not to gloat but deeply satisfied that they had turned the tables on the Ackroyds. During luncheon, Genevieve did not wish to raise the question of why Paulo Morelli had been dismissed, but she saw her chance at the end of the meal. The Simcoes lingered so that Constance could be helped back into her Bath chair without too many spectators.

"You've lost Paulo, I see," said Genevieve.

"That's right," replied Constance. "We have a new steward, but I prefer Tabby to take me around the deck instead. I haven't had any fresh air all day."

"Then why don't I wheel you?" volunteered Genevieve.

"That's very kind of you. Are you sure you don't mind?"

"Not at all."

"Thank you," said Tabitha, happy to be relieved of the task. "Mother only wants fifteen or twenty minutes out there. We're playing bridge with the Kingtons at three." She tucked a blanket around her mother's legs. "Keep yourself warm. It's quite chilly on deck. This is so sweet of you, Genevieve," she went on, squeezing the latter's arm. "You're a real friend."

"It's a pleasure to help, Tabby."

Genevieve took the handles and shoved the Bath chair off. The first thing she noticed was how heavy it was. Built of wicker, it had a very solid construction and seemed to be weighted underneath to provide stability. The two large wheels turned smoothly. Constance guided the contraption with the handle that was attached to the small wheel at the front. As she rolled along, she pulled up the hood of the chair to shield herself.

The wind seemed to have eased slightly but it was still keeping most passengers indoors. Constance did not have to pick her way through the crowd that sometimes filled the decks. She inhaled deeply.

"It's an article of faith with me that I get out here at some time each day," she said. "Even if it rained, I'd insist on my trip around the deck. I don't know how some passengers can stay entombed in their cabins on a voyage."

"You have a very healthy attitude, Mrs. Simcoe."

"It's vital. The doctor warned me that I mustn't let these wretched legs get the better of me, or I'd just shrivel up and waste away."

"I can't imagine that happening to you."

"I've too many things to live for, Miss Masefield."

"Like beating the Ackroyds at the card table?" said Genevieve.

Constance laughed. "That did give me pleasure, I must admit."

"They certainly enjoyed their win against you yesterday."

"Phoebe Ackroyd is one of those women who likes to crow."

Genevieve pushed her along the port side of the vessel and watched the waves breaking against the hull. Since her passenger was in such a benign mood, she decided to touch on the subject that really interested her.

"Paulo must have been very upset to part company with you."

"It was his own fault," Constance said sharply.

"He always seemed to be very attentive."

"He was at first. Nothing was too much trouble for him. The problem was that he became overfamiliar, Miss Masefield. I suppose that I'm partially to blame for encouraging him. Well," she said, adjusting her blanket, "every woman enjoys the flattery of a handsome man."

"Tabby said that he overstepped the mark."

"He forgot his place."

"What did he do exactly?"

"He made some uncalled for comments about Tabby."

"I'm sure that he didn't mean to give offense."

"Well, he succeeded nevertheless," said Constance. "I'm a very tolerant woman but I have my limits. I reached them with Paulo and made my feelings known to the chief steward."

"No regrets?"

"None at all, Miss Masefield. I wanted the fellow out of my sight. He got to the stage of taking conversational liberties, and I'll not allow that kind of thing. Paulo had no right to pass remarks about our private life."

"Of course not."

"In the final analysis, he's only an underling."

"Well, yes. I suppose so."

"He tried to cross the line," said Constance with asperity. "I'm told that he's only been demoted to second class. If it were left to me, I'd have had him kicked off the ship altogether. I'd have been quite ruthless."

George Dillman was shocked. When he found Guljar Singh on the main deck, looking so despondent, he thought at first that he was ill. The old man's account of what had happened took him by surprise.

"You were accused of stealing the two purses?" he asked.

"Yes, Mr. Dillman," replied Singh. "I was nearby so I must be guilty. That is how the mind of this detective works. Also, of course, I have a brown face so I must be a criminal."

"I'm sure that Miss Masefield wouldn't make that assumption."

"How do you know? You have not met her."

"Would you like me to speak to her on your behalf?"

"What good would that do?" wailed Singh. "She thinks I am the thief. I could see it in her eyes. The only consolation was that nobody else was about when she made these charges. My countrymen *respect* me, Mr. Dillman."

"I know. I've seen how they treat you."

"My reputation will be damaged if I am arrested for these crimes."

"I think I can guarantee that that won't happen," Dillman said firmly. "I don't believe for a second that you could have stolen those purses, Mr. Singh."

"What use would they be to me?"

"Exactly."

"I have all the money that I require."

"Yes, you told me you had an unexpected windfall."

"Oh, it was not very much," said the old man, smiling for the first time, "but it shows that some of us from India do know how to behave. You remember that trick I played on that officer on the first day?"

"Using that sheet of newspaper, you mean? Yes, I do."

"I outwitted him with the power of the mind. One of the people who watched me was a young Parsi from Bombay. He asked me if he could borrow my trick to use on someone else. Of course, I said that he could. And what do you think happened?"

"He probably won a bet as a result."

"Twenty whole rupees! That's twice as much as I had off the officer. Only this friend of mine was very honorable," said Singh. "Since he had learned the trick from me, he insisted on giving me half of his winnings."

Dillman was delighted to hear it. The explanation removed the faint suspicion of the old man that he had himself entertained. He had never been annoyed with Genevieve before, but he felt his irritation rising when he saw how badly she had hurt Guljar Singh's feelings. In accusing him, she was looking in the wrong direction altogether.

"I'll talk to this detective," he resolved. "I'm sure that she made an honest mistake, Mr. Singh, and will be only too ready to apologize."

The old man shook his head. "The English *never* apologize," he declared. "If you can make this lady say that she is sorry, I will believe that it is *you* who have strange powers and not me."

Before he spoke, Sylvester Greenwood waited until the steward removed the tray from his daughter's cabin. Lois was pale and withdrawn.

"You didn't eat very much," he chided.

"I was not hungry."

"You do realize why I had to punish you in this way, don't you?"

"I like roller-skating, Daddy," she protested.

"There's a time and place for recreation, Lois. The time is not close to midnight, and the place is most certainly not the deck of the *Salsette*. What on earth were you thinking about? You might have been *seen*."

"Nobody was there—except Mr. Dillman."

"Yes," he said, "that's what I want to talk to you about. Did you tell him that I have a framed copy of my election poster on the wall?"

"I may have done."

"That was confidential information."

"It's not exactly a state secret, Daddy."

"Don't be impudent!"

"Mr. Dillman was interested in your political career."

"Why?"

"You'll have to ask him that?"

"I did, Lois," he replied, "and I found him very evasive. There's something about that man that I don't trust. My guess is that he wasn't on deck last night by accident."

"He's a friend. He came to have a chat."

"Yes—about *me*."

"What harm is there in that? Honestly, I just don't understand why you're reacting like this. Anybody would think that Mr. Dillman was a spy or something." She saw his grim expression. "Is that what you think?"

"Tell me what he said."

"I've already done that," she said.

"Only in outline," he argued. "I want the fine detail now. Tell me exactly what Mr. Dillman asked you, Lois—word for word."

When he caught up with her, they adjourned to his cabin at once. Genevieve had never been put on the defensive in that way before and she was not enjoying the experience at all.

"I felt I had enough evidence to act," she said, trying to justify her confrontation with Guljar Singh. "Mrs. Verney had no doubt that he was the thief."

"Why—did she actually *see* him steal her purse?"

"Of course not. She was asleep."

"I see. So she dreamed that Guljar Singh was guilty."

"There's no need to be sarcastic, George."

"I've just left the old man. He's in a state of complete dejection."

"He was *there*," insisted Genevieve. "In the case of Mrs. Verney and that of Mrs. Gilbert. Don't you find that odd?"

"Not at all. Guljar Singh virtually lives on the main deck."

"Both times, he was only yards from where the purse was stolen."

"And what about Mrs. Lundgren?" he asked. "She had her purse stolen on deck. Did she mention a phantom Sikh, waiting to pounce?"

"George!"

"No, she didn't. Neither did Madame Roussell. There are four crimes to investigate, Genevieve, and I'd bet anything that they're the work of the same thief. Whatever his name is," he urged, "it's not Guljar Singh."

Genevieve bit back a reply. When he had reproached her before, he had always done it as gently as he could. This time, however, Dillman was letting a touch of anger show. It worried her. For his part, he felt that he had spoken too sharply. He gave an apologetic smile and took her into his arms. The loving embrace reassured her.

"I'm sorry," he said, holding her tight.

"It was my fault, George. I was too hasty."

"That makes two of us."

"You always told me to be absolutely certain before approaching a suspect like that. I suppose the truth is that I was too anxious to solve the crimes. The victims have been bearing down on me for an arrest."

"I know. They expect instant detection. But that was no excuse for me to chide you," he said. "I'm sure that you didn't intend to upset Guljar Singh. The trouble is that he's very sensitive to criticism."

"So am I."

Dillman kissed her on the lips and hugged her to him. "Forgive me?" he asked. "I don't ever want us to fall out, Genevieve."

"There's nothing to forgive."

"I think there is. It won't happen again, I promise."

"I should have consulted you first," she admitted. "I see that now. But you were too busy pursuing your own investigation, and I was under such pressure to do something."

"That was the problem."

"I was too eager."

"You had to look into the matter, Genevieve."

"Yes, but I didn't have to hurt the old man's feelings like that. I tried to be polite but he flew off the handle."

"I can imagine."

"Then you come along and take his side."

"Not exactly," he said. "I'm fond of Guljar Singh, that's all. I hated to see him so disturbed. But the simple fact is that you're my partner, in every way, and I should always support you."

"Supposing that he *had* been the thief?"

"Not a chance."

"But if he had—for the sake of argument."

"Then I'd have arrested him myself."

"Even though you liked him?"

"There's no such thing as a likable thief."

Dillman let her go and brought her up to date with his own movements, telling her about his visit to the medical room, and about his confrontation with Sylvester Greenwood. When she heard mention of the Gurkha who had arrived on the scene, Genevieve was alarmed.

"Don't put yourself in jeopardy."

"I'll happily do so if it will flush out the killer."

"You ought to carry a weapon," she urged. "Ask Mr. Cannadine to authorize the master-at-arms to issue you with a revolver."

"It hasn't come to that stage yet, Genevieve."

"What stage *has* it come to?"

"Well," he sighed, "let's take the thefts first. I've got a feeling that the only way we'll recover the stolen property is to institute a search of selected cabins."

"That's what I told the purser. He was very unhappy about it, but he accepted that we might have to go to that extreme. Mr. Cannadine is as anxious to catch this thief as we are."

"He doesn't want to face an irate Madame Roussel, that's why."

"Oh, I was forgetting. He discovered the most extraordinary thing about her, George."

"That she runs a bordello in Paris?"

"That, too, is possible," she said. "No, I asked him to check his records to see when Madame Roussel had sailed on the *Salsette* before. This turns out to be her fourth voyage in just over a fortnight."

He was amazed. "You mean that she's been going to and fro across the Arabian Sea?"

"Apparently."

"Why?" he asked, rubbing a hand across his chin. "What's the point of going to India if you come straight back again?"

"It doesn't make sense."

"Madame Roussel must have a very good reason to do that."

"I can't think of one."

"I can, Genevieve," he said, trying to work it out in his mind. "Suppose that she pulled the wool over our eyes. Suppose that she's been working this ship because there are such easy pickings."

"Madame Roussel is the *thief*?"

"It's one explanation."

"But she was the first victim, George."

"That's how she presented herself to us. What better way to throw us off the scent? She must have an accomplice—the man she's been careful not to name. He took the jewelry from her cabin and she left the door unlocked to make it easy for him. The other thefts were opportune crimes on deck."

"Hers is the one cabin we'd never think of searching."

"Until now."

"Do you really think she'd devious enough to do this?"

"Yes, I do," he decided. "I think she's a good actress. She can turn that outrage on and off like a tap. It's such a cunning trick."

"What is?"

"Arranging to have her own jewelry stolen then blaming the P and O. She'll get the insurance money and—if she yells loud enough—some added compensation from the company. And all for valuables that are still hers."

"I just can't think of Madame Roussel as a criminal somehow."

"That's because of the way she's deceived us."

"I wonder." She looked at him. "What are we going to do?"

"Watch her very carefully, Genevieve."

"Why?"

"Because if my theory is right," he said, "she won't stop there."

"I'm not sure that your theory *is* right. The other evening, you spoke to her outside her cabin. Shortly afterwards, you were certain that you'd almost brushed shoulders with the thief. How could Madame Roussel be in two places at once?"

"She wasn't—her accomplice was. No wonder she won't tell us his name. All right," he went on, "I know you have reservations and so do I. But I guarantee that we'll soon have another theft on this ship."

Madame Roussel walked quickly along the corridor, checked the number of a cabin, and inserted the key into the lock. Ensuring that nobody could see her, she darted inside.

ELEVEN

After her argument with Dillman, Genevieve had to accept that Guljar Singh was almost certainly not the culprit, and that she therefore had to look elsewhere. The suggestion that Madame Roussel might be a thief—or at the very least that she was working in partnership with one—forced Genevieve Masefield to think very hard about her strategy for solving the crimes. It was true that the Frenchwoman had been the first to report a theft on ship, but Genevieve had encountered such a ruse before. As well as deflecting suspicion from Madame Roussel, it would also enable her to find out who the ship's detectives might be, a crucial piece of information for any criminal.

The problem was that Genevieve could not devote all her time to watching Madame Roussel in the hope that she might give herself away. Unlike Dillman, during his days as a Pinkerton agent, she had not been trained to shadow someone without being seen, and there was the simple fact that the Frenchwoman did not like or trust her. If she became aware of Genevieve's surveillance—and if she proved to be innocent of the crimes—Madame Roussel would report the female detective to the captain, and that would have unpleasant repercussions for her.

Genevieve had to achieve her objective by other means. Left alone in her cabin, she wrestled with her dilemma for some time until she realized that she knew exactly the right person to help her. Hurrying to the second-class area of the ship, she sought out Paulo Morelli. After commiserating at length with him over his dismissal, she asked him if he would like the opportunity to redeem himself.

"I would do *anything,*" he declared, hands together as if in prayer. "I belong in first class. Please tell me how I can get back there."

"I can offer you no firm promises," she said, "but it will advance your case a great deal if you assist me."

"What must I do?"

"First of all, Paulo, you have to keep a secret."

"Oh, I am very good at that, *signorina.* I know how to seal the lips."

"I hope so," she warned. "Because if you divulge what I'm about to tell you, there'll be no chance at all of you returning to first class. Do you understand that?"

"Yes, yes."

He nodded vigorously. They were standing outside the quarters used by second-class stewards. Morelli was now sharing a cabin with five other men, all of whom he considered to be inferior in ability and status. He was desperate to escape from the ignominy of being demoted. For that reason, Genevieve decided that she could put her faith in him.

"I'm not simply a passenger traveling on the *Salsette,*" she said. "I work for P and O as a detective." He was stunned by the news.

"Yes, it may be difficult to believe, Paulo, but it's true. Some thefts have taken place aboard and it's my job to find the thief."

"*You* are a policeman?" he said, incredulously.

"I'm a private detective, working onboard with a partner. There's no need for you to know his identity just yet. Like me, he's been operating quietly behind the scenes."

"This is wonderful, *signorina*. You are not only the most beautiful lady on the ship, you catch the thieves, as well."

"I *try* to catch them, Paulo."

"Why do you tell this to me?"

"Because I need your assistance."

"Me?" The notion delighted him. "I am to help a detective?"

"I hope so, Paulo."

"What must I do?"

"Keep an eye on a second-class passenger for me."

"It will not be easy for me," he explained. "I have many duties."

"I'll speak to the chief steward," she said, "and get him to relieve you of some of them. This investigation is more important than whether or not someone gets the towels changed in their cabin."

"*Grazie, grazie.*"

"The main thing is that you are discreet."

"Oh, I always am."

"Are you sure?"

"Yes!"

"Not according to Mr. Cannadine."

"Do not believe all you hear," he said defensively. "The complaints against me are all from ladies who wish me to pay more attention to them than I am allowed to do. So they report me."

"If you obey my instructions, I'll report you, as well—only my report will show you in the most favorable light."

"I like that very much. Who must I keep the eye on?"

"A French lady named Madame Roussel."

"But I already know her," he said with a laugh. "I meet her before. She is on the *Salsette* again?"

"Yes, Paulo. Apparently, it's her fourth trip."

"She always travel in first class. Madame Roussel is very lovely. Why is she sailing in second class this time?"

"That's something I need to look into," said Genevieve. "Since you already know who she is, it will make your job a little easier. Now, this is what I want you to do, Paulo." And she lowered her voice to a conspiratorial whisper.

George Dillman was leaving the purser's office when he saw her walking toward him down the corridor. Lois Greenwood gave a cry of surprise.

"I was just coming in search of you, Mr. Dillman," she said.

"Were you?"

"Yes, I was going to ask the purser if he could tell me which cabin you were in." She held up an envelope. "I intended to slip this note under your door."

"Why?"

"Because I wanted to say sorry."

"You've no need to do that, Miss Greenwood," he said.

"But I feel that I do. Daddy tells me that he spoke to you."

"That's true."

"And I can guess what he said. He's not a man to mince his words when he's angry. For some reason, he's been caught on the raw. He made me repeat almost every word we've exchanged."

"Did he tell you why?"

"No, Mr. Dillman. It was like being in the Spanish Inquisition."

"Then I should be apologizing to you. If you hadn't talked to me on deck last night, you wouldn't be in such hot water."

"Oh, yes, I would," she told him. "Daddy didn't even know that

I'd brought my roller skates on this trip. He thought that it was disgraceful of me to skate around the deck at night—disgraceful and dangerous. I might have had an accident and broken my leg."

"Or collided with someone," he reminded her gently.

"Exactly—that's why I wanted you to read this." She gave him the envelope. "Though now that I'm here, I might as well tell you what's in it."

Pleased to see her, Dillman was also worried about Lois. Red marks around her eyes showed that she had been crying, and he knew that she had been confined to her cabin as a result of her last meeting with him. Evidently, she was acting in open defiance of her father, and that showed courage on her behalf. However, Dillman did not want to get her into any more trouble.

"Look," he said, "perhaps we shouldn't be seen here like this."

"It's all right. Daddy is in the lounge with some friends."

"Does he know that you've left your cabin?"

"Yes and no."

"In other words, he gave you permission to leave on condition that you wouldn't speak to me again."

"Something like that," she admitted. "But I'm not really breaking my promise, because I didn't expect to find you. I just wanted to put that note under your door. Now that we have met, I don't feel at all guilty. Daddy had no right to criticize you like that," she continued. "I'm to blame. If I hadn't skated into you on that first night, none of this would have happened."

Dillman was in a quandary. Presented with a chance to glean more information from her about Sylvester Greenwood, he was not sure whether it was right to do so. It meant talking to her under false pretences, and perhaps getting her to incriminate her father. On the other hand, he told himself, he would be foolish not to exploit such an unexpected opportunity. The chances of meeting Lois Greenwood again before the end of the voyage were extremely slim.

Dillman had to strike now. When he reminded himself what was at stake—the arrest of a brutal killer—he put aside his affection for the girl. Any detail she could tell him about her father might be valuable.

"Listen," he said, glancing up and down the corridor, "this is not the best place for a chat. Somebody else will be here any moment to bang on Mr. Cannadine's door. Let's find a quieter spot, shall we?"

"Lead the way."

Dillman guided her swiftly through a maze of corridors until they reached some storerooms used by the second-class stewards. Lois was duly impressed.

"You certainly know your way around the ship, Mr. Dillman."

"Professional interest. I like to know exactly what I'm sailing on."

"What's your verdict on the *Salsette*?"

"Sleek and fast, but in need of more stability."

"That sounds like me when I first started skating," she said with a giggle. "Not that I'll be doing any more of that for a while," she went on sadly. "Daddy has locked my skates away."

"Is he always so strict with you?"

"He didn't used to be—well, he was away on assignments for a lot of the time—but he is now. As a rule, Mummy is on my side, but she can't override his authority."

"Was it her brother you visited in Bombay?"

"Yes, Uncle David. Honestly, he's made *so* much money out of exporting cotton. His house is three times the size of ours. He's a true businessman. He knows everyone of any importance in the city."

"How does your mother get on with him?"

"Very well," she replied, "though it was Daddy's idea to go to India."

"Was it?"

"Yes, it was funny, really. I mean, Mummy was dying to see her brother, yet while we were there Uncle David spent far more time with Daddy."

"Why was that, do you think?"

"Something to do with politics, I expect. Uncle David has a lot of contacts in Delhi," she said. "There was one occasion when he showed Daddy a message he got from Delhi by telegraph. That's how we came to change the date we sailed."

"You changed it?"

"Yes, Daddy postponed it by over a week."

"He must have had a good reason to do that," said Dillman.

"I didn't complain. It gave me a longer holiday in the sun. Back in England right now, they're probably shivering from the cold."

"Did your father explain why he changed the departure date?"

"No," she said blithely. "But then, I didn't ask. According to Mummy, someone was going to be sailing on the *Salsette* this week—a man that Daddy was keen to meet."

"What was his name?" asked Dillman, fascinated by the revelation.

"I have no idea."

"Is he a friend of your father's?"

"I suppose that he is. My guess is that he's another politician."

"So you never actually met this man?"

"I didn't," she said, "but I know that Daddy did."

"How?"

"Because I overheard him talking to Mummy about it."

"What did he say?"

"That he'd spotted the man aboard, and that he was going to have it out with him."

"Have it out with him?" repeated Dillman.

"That was the phrase he used."

"What did it mean?"

"I haven't a clue."

"Do you happen to know if he did go to see the man?"

"Oh, yes. There's no doubt about that, Mr. Dillman. I heard him clearly over dinner that night. Daddy said that he'd been to the man's cabin and told him a few home truths." Her face clouded. "Why are you so interested in all this?" She gave a sudden giggle. "I say, you're not *really* a spy, are you?"

"It was humiliating, Matilda," she said. "I'll never forgive Gerald for this."

"It was only a game of bridge," Mrs. Kinnersley pointed out.

"It was much more than that. It was a battle of wills."

"I can see that you'd hate to lose to people like the Simcoes."

"The money was incidental. It was a matter of pride to beat them. And we could have done so," insisted Phoebe Ackroyd, "if only my husband had managed to find his ear trumpet."

"Gerald didn't lose it on purpose."

"Perhaps not, but I blame him for being so careless."

Time had not mellowed Phoebe Ackroyd. Well into the afternoon, she was still smarting over their defeat at the hands of Constance and Tabitha Simcoe. Taking tea with her in the first-class lounge, Matilda Kinnersley was not overly sympathetic.

"You shouldn't have bothered with undesirables like the Simcoes."

"One can't always choose one's partners for bridge."

"Romford and I always do."

"That's why you play so infrequently," said Mrs. Ackroyd. "Gerald and I play all the time—at least three or four times a week back in England. We're not accustomed to losing."

"Did that obnoxious Mrs. Simcoe gloat over their win?"

"No, Matilda. In fairness to her, she was very restrained, and so was her daughter. Of course, my immediate response was to take them on again—when Gerald had found his ear trumpet, that is—but they already have other opponents lined up."

"You wouldn't catch *us* at the same card table as them."

"You're too selective."

"It's a question of class, Phoebe. One must have standards."

"We only played bridge with them," countered Mrs. Ackroyd. "It's not as if we socialized with them. That, I agree, would be unwise."

"What about Gerald's ear trumpet?"

"That's still missing. I sent him off in search of it."

"If he mislaid it somewhere, I'm surprised that nobody has handed it in. An ear trumpet is hardly an object that anyone would want to hang on to. It's bound to turn up soon."

"I hope so, Matilda," said the other, sipping her tea. "Gerald is such a dear. I hate it when I have to remonstrate with him. But where's Romford?" she went on. "I thought he was going to join us in here."

"He'll be along any moment. He's been helping Sukinder with her written English. Romford has far more patience with her than I do."

"How do you think she'll fit in when you get back home?"

"To be candid, I have my doubts."

"I know one or two other families who've taken Indian servants back to England with them," said Mrs. Ackroyd, "and it's worked out quite well. I'm sure that will be the case with Sukinder."

"The girl is so slow—at least, that's one explanation."

"What do you mean?"

"Well, her mother was quite intelligent—lazy, mark you, but she was quick to learn when she put her mind to it. That's why Romford was so eager to take the daughter back with us. If we got the best out of her, he said, we'd have a first-rate servant."

"You don't share that view, obviously."

"Not entirely," said Mrs. Kinnersley. "I'm beginning to wonder if Sukinder is playing games with us. She's only *pretending* to be slow to learn the language. Her mother speaks it very well, so the girl has heard English being used at home for years now. Why is the child so far behind in her lessons?" she asked. "Is it because she's struggling—or is Sukinder trying to deceive us?"

Sukinder was grateful when she found him. Relatively few people were on deck that windy afternoon, but the blustery weather had not deterred Guljar Singh. He was talking to another Sikh on the starboard side of the vessel. Sukinder waited until the other man had left before coming forward. Guljar Singh gave her a welcoming smile.

"Hello, Suki," he said. "How are you today?"

"Cold," she replied, rubbing her hands together.

"It will be much worse than this in England."

"If I get there."

"What do you mean?"

"I do not wish to leave India," she confided. Head to one side, she looked at him quizzically. "Is it true that you can look into the future?"

"Sometimes. Why?"

"I would like you to tell me my fortune, please. Do I have to pay?"

"No, no," he said, holding up a wrinkled hand. "I wouldn't dream of taking money from a child like you. But you must be warned, Suki. I do not see everything clearly. I just sense that certain things will happen."

"How do you do that?"

"I have this gift."

Before he could put it at her disposal, he saw someone walking along the deck toward him and his manner altered. Genevieve Masefield was moving with a purposeful stride. If she had come to arrest him, Guljar Singh hoped that it would not be in front of the girl. That would be a mortifying experience for him.

"Hello, Mr. Singh," said Genevieve when she reached them. "I just wanted a brief word with you, if I may."

"Here?" he asked uneasily.

"I came to apologize."

"For what?"

"Jumping to conclusions earlier on."

Guljar Singh heaved a deep sigh of relief and introduced her to Sukinder. Delighted to be offered an apology, he was glad that it was in front of a witness, albeit only a young girl.

"I'm certain that you were not involved," said Genevieve.

"That is what I told you, Miss Masefield."

"I had to find out for myself."

"So you will be asking me no more questions?"

"None at all."

"Thank you. It was good of you to come out here like this."

"It's the least I came do, Mr. Singh," said Genevieve. "I caused you unnecessary embarrassment. I hope that you'll find it in your heart to forgive me."

"Of course, of course. I bear no ill will."

"I'm so pleased to hear that."

When she offered her hand, Guljar Singh shook it warmly. It had taken an effort for her to make the apology and he appreciated it all the more as a result. He watched her walk away. Sukinder was curious.

"What did the lady do to upset you?" she asked.

"Nothing, Suki. It is all forgotten now."

"Who is she?"

"Someone who made an honest mistake. Now then," he went on, turning to her, "you wanted me to foretell your future, didn't you?"

"And to ask you a big favor, please."

"A favor?"

"You are the only friend I have on this ship."

"I'm sure that's not true, Suki."

"There is nobody else that I can trust to do it."

"To do what?"

She became wary. "Promise me that you will tell nobody."

"You have my word," he said, putting a reassuring hand on her shoulder. "So—what is this favor?"

Wanting to reflect on what Lois Greenwood had told him, Dillman went back to the place where the murder had been committed. Letting himself into Dudley Nevin's cabin with the key, he tried to envisage where the man must have been standing when he was stabbed. The position of the discarded *kukri* again puzzled him. It was nowhere near where the body had fallen. Had it been thrown away on impulse after it had done its work, or had it been deliberately left behind as some kind of symbol? Dr. McNeil believed that the fatal wound had either been inflicted by someone lashing out crazily at Nevin, or by a skilled assassin who was determined to make his victim suffer great pain. Dillman thought of the Gurkha, who was a friend of Sylvester Greenwood.

Lois had unwittingly given him what might turn out to be the breakthrough that was needed. She had overheard her father saying that he had been to a cabin to confront someone. Though she did not provide a name, it had to be Dudley Nevin. By virtue of his contacts in Delhi, Greenwood's brother-in-law had discovered that Nevin was traveling to Bombay by train to embark on the *Salsette*. If Greenwood had altered his own plans in order to be on the same vessel, then he must have had a compulsion to see Nevin, and Dillman knew that it would not have been simply to discuss the result of a by-election in Reading. Something else must have connected the two men.

Thanks to the man's daughter, Dillman could place Greenwood in the cabin, but he had no evidence to put a weapon into his hand, or for that matter, into the more practiced hand of his Gurkha friend. He was still building on supposition. If either of the two men *had* been the killer, Nevin's blood would have stained their clothing. That opened up the possibility that somebody might have seen one of them, returning to his cabin in a disheveled state. Whenever he had seen Greenwood, the man had been dressed with meticulous care. Had he suddenly changed his suit on the day of the murder?

After rehearsing all the possibilities, Dillman decided that he had to confront the member of Parliament with certain facts. He left the cabin and locked it behind him. He was about to walk away when Tabitha Simcoe came gliding along the corridor toward him.

"Excuse me," she said, "but isn't that Mr. Nevin's cabin?"

"Yes, it is."

"We haven't seen him for ages. Not since he played bridge with us, in fact. Is he all right?"

"No," replied Dillman, inventing an excuse to explain his absence, "I'm afraid that he isn't. Mr. Nevin is unwell. Dr. McNeil has told him to rest until we reach Aden."

"What a shame!"

"My name is George Dillman, by the way," he said, extending a hand. "I'm a friend of Dudley's."

She shook his hand. "Tabitha Simcoe."

"I think that he must have been ill when he played bridge with you, Miss Simcoe. He told me that he gave a poor account of himself."

"That was certainly true. He let his partner down badly."

"But you and your mother are formidable opponents, I hear."

"We try, Mr. Dillman," she said with a bland smile. "Do you, by any chance, play bridge?"

"It's not one of my accomplishments, I fear."

"That's a pity. We might have found a partner for you."

"I'd have been a liability, Miss Simcoe."

"I'm sure that you could never be that."

This was not the shy and restrained woman that Genevieve had described to him. Tabitha was brimming with confidence and able to pay him a frank compliment. She was looking at him with the same undisguised approval he had seen in the eyes of Madame Roussel. When she was not burdened with her mother, it seemed, Tabitha Simcoe blossomed into full womanhood.

"Haven't I seen you, pushing a Bath chair around?" he said.

"Mother is crippled."

"I'm sorry to hear that. Actually, the last few times I've noticed her, she was being wheeled along by one of the stewards."

"Mother had to dispense with his services."

"Oh? Was he pushing her too fast?"

"No, Mr. Dillman," she said, "he was getting above himself and Mother would never countenance that. She had the fellow demoted. Paulo Morelli is where he belongs—toiling in second class."

Morelli was thrilled with his new assignment. Overwhelmed with remorse at losing his position in first class, he had now been given the opportunity to make amends and he resolved that he would do so. Apart from Genevieve Masefield herself, there was nobody on board whom he would rather watch than Madame Berthe Roussel. On three previous voyages, she had been a conspicuous figure and he regretted that it had never fallen to him to be her steward. She had the look of a woman who reveled in flattery, and who would give generous tips. It would have been a pleasure to work for her.

Instead, he had been given the task of trailing her as unobtrusively as he could. Morelli did as he was told. Without speculating on why she was under suspicion, he watched her in the second-class lounge, then on a brisk walk around the main deck, and finally going back to her cabin. With a tray under his arm, he lurked nearby in case she came out again. It was twenty minutes before she emerged, wearing a different dress and glancing at her watch. Since she was coming in his direction, Morelli walked toward her as if on some errand, and strode past. She was not even aware of his presence.

Once round the corner, he stopped and went slowly back again. He saw Madame Roussel about to ascend a companionway and trotted along the corridor to catch her up. When she vanished from the top of the steps, he went up them, looking in both directions. He was just in time to see her furtively checking the number of a cabin before letting herself in with a key. Morelli was intrigued. Strolling past the cabin, he made a note of the number, then went around the corner at the far end of the corridor and waited. It was exciting work.

"I am the detective!" he said to himself. "I am good at it."

Mrs. Verney could not understand it. She was quivering with indignation.

"Why haven't you arrested him, Miss Masefield?" she demanded.

"Because I'm not convinced that he's the thief," replied Genevieve.

"He must be—he was there at the time."

"How do you know, if you fell asleep?"

"There was something so shifty about the man."

"I thought he was rather dignified."

"Miss Masefield interviewed this fellow," explained Max Cannadine, "and she came to the conclusion that he was innocent of the charge."

Mrs. Verney was upset. "You let him go?" she said to Genevieve.

"There was no evidence on which to apprehend him."

"You could have searched the man."

"He was hardly likely to have your purse on him, Mrs. Verney."

"No," said Cannadine, "and we have to be careful not to make false accusations against anyone."

The three of them were in the purser's cabin. Mrs. Verney had come to see if her property had been recovered yet, and Genevieve had been brought in to tell her how the investigation was going. Disappointed that there was no sign of her missing purse, the victim was close to tears.

"So, in fact," she said morosely, "you've made no progress at all."

"Yes, we have," Genevieve told her. "We have another suspect who is being kept under close scrutiny."

"Who is it—another Indian?"

"We're not able to tell you that, Mrs. Verney," said the purser, getting up from behind his desk to open the door. "But you can rely on one thing. As soon as we make an arrest, you'll be told."

Giving a resigned nod, May Verney rose to her feet, thanked them for their help, and left the cabin with an air of discontent. Cannadine closed the door behind her and pulled a face.

"One consolation, anyway," he noted. "It wasn't Ethan Gilbert."

"He'd want the pleasure of arresting the thief himself."

"Arresting him—or strangling him with his bare hands?"

"In his mind," said Genevieve, "it amounts to the same thing."

"Are you absolutely certain that this Guljar Singh is innocent?"

"George thinks that *you'd* be a more likely thief."

Cannadine laughed. "That's the nicest thing anyone has said about me all day." He became serious. "We *are* going to solve these crimes, aren't we?" he asked.

"We hope so."

"I was banking on rather more than hope, Miss Masefield."

"This evening will be the critical time."

"When will you conduct the search?"

"During dinner," she told him. "George and I will actually go into the cabin, but we'll have a lookout to help us."

"Oh, and who's that?"

"Paulo Morelli."

"Morelli?" he said anxiously. "Are you sure you can rely on him?"

"I think so. He snatched at the chance to redeem himself."

"As long as he doesn't get overzealous. What do you expect to find in the course of your search?"

"Some or all of the property that was taken," she said. "George thinks we might stumble on some clues about the murder, as well. If someone has bloodstained clothing in his wardrobe, we'll know where the blood came from. I have high hopes of this search, Mr. Cannadine."

"You must, if you're making the supreme sacrifice."

"Sacrifice?"

"Missing a delicious meal in the first-class dining saloon."

"Oh, that doesn't bother me at all," confessed Genevieve. "The truth is that I'm not hungry. When I spoke to Guljar Singh earlier, I had to eat rather a large helping of humble pie."

It was early evening when Dillman was able to seize his opportunity. Seated in the second-class lounge, pretending to read a magazine, he had watched Sylvester Greenwood talking at length with two of the Gurhkas aboard. All three men were so engrossed in their discussion that they did not even realize that Dillman was there. Eventually the meeting came to an end and both of the Gurkhas shook the Englishman's hand before leaving. When the M.P. tried to follow them, Dillman intercepted him.

"Good evening, Mr. Greenwood," he said.

The other man stiffened. "What do *you* want?"

"A little of your time, please."

"I've none to spare, Mr. Dillman. I need to dress for dinner." He tried to walk past but Dillman took a step sideways to block his path. "Will you please get out of my way, sir?"

"Not until we've had a talk about Dudley Nevin," said Dillman with firmness. "I've just come from speaking to him."

Greenwood glared at him. If he were the killer, then he would know that Dillman could not possibly have spoken to Nevin. The detective searched his eyes for signs of guilt but the other man's self-control did not waiver. Greenwood shrugged.

"Very well," he said reluctantly. "If you insist."

"I do. Shall we sit down for a moment?"

Dillman indicated two chairs in the corner of the lounge. Most of the passengers had gone off to prepare for dinner so the place was fairly deserted. They could converse in privacy.

"Before we start," said Greenwood, "perhaps you'll be kind enough to tell me why you have such an interest in Mr. Nevin."

"He's an acquaintance of mine."

"Is that enough to justify your obsession with him?"

"Mr. Nevin is unwell," said Dillman smoothly. "I feel sorry for him. He gave me the impression that you are partly to blame for his condition. I wanted to find out why you'd upset him so much."

"That's a personal matter."

"He tells me that you went to his cabin."

Greenwood needed a moment to compose his features. He ran his tongue over his lips before speaking. Dillman noted the way that the man's hands tightened on the arms of the chair.

"Do you deny it?" pressed Dillman.

"No," admitted the other. "We had a brief conversation."

"About what?"

"A matter of mutual interest."

"May I know what it was?"

"No, Mr. Dillman."

"When I first asked you about Mr. Nevin, you claimed that you hardly knew him. Now you confess that you actually went to his cabin for a private chat."

"So?"

"What else have you been holding back from me, Mr. Greenwood?"

"That's no concern of yours."

"Yes, it is."

"No, it isn't," retorted Greenwood, standing up. "I don't know who you are, Mr. Dillman, or why you're poking your nose into my affairs, but I'm not staying here to answer any more of your infernal questions."

"Perhaps you'd prefer to do so in the purser's office," suggested Dillman, remaining in his chair. "This may be the moment to tell you that I work for P and O as a detective, and that gives me the right to question any passengers I choose." Greenwood hesitated. "If you don't believe me, you can ask Mr. Cannadine. He'll vouch for me." Dillman pointed to chair opposite. "Why don't you sit down again?"

"What's going on?" asked Greenwood, resuming his seat.

"You tell me, sir."

"Why have you been checking up on me?"

"Let's just say that some of your behavior has been questionable."

"I resent that accusation."

"Then you have the opportunity to refute it. Let's go back to Dudley Nevin, shall we?" Dillman said calmly. "You went out of your way to arrange a confrontation with him."

"That's not true."

"So it was pure coincidence that you're both on this vessel?"

"Of course."

"I think that you're misleading me again, sir," said Dillman, trying to bluff him. "The purser keeps passenger records of every sailing between Bombay and Aden. When I studied those earlier,

I couldn't help noticing that you and your family had booked passage on the *Salsette,* then changed the date at the last moment. Was that not so?"

"We decided to stay in Bombay a little longer."

"Why was that?"

"My wife wanted to spend more time with her brother."

"So it was nothing to do with the fact that Mr. Nevin would be sailing on this ship at the later date?"

"How could I possibly know that?"

"There are ways of finding out these things," Dillman said levelly, "and you strike me as the sort of person who would know exactly where to look. You were a foreign correspondent for a newspaper, I hear. That means you'll have built up a network of contacts."

"What are all these questions in aid of, Mr. Dillman?"

"I told you. Mr. Nevin is unwell—extremely unwell."

"Don't ask me for sympathy."

"Are you still so incensed with him over what happened during that by-election?" said Dillman. "I would have thought that even your anger had cooled by now."

"Mr. Nevin did his utmost to rig that election," asserted Greenwood, smacking his knee with a palm. "When they learned what he'd done, his party had the grace to disown him. Left to me, he'd still be rotting in a British prison."

"You're a vengeful man, Mr. Greenwood."

"He tried to cheat me out of that seat in Parliament."

"Is that why you were so anxious to meet up with him again?"

"No—it was over something else." Realizing that he had given himself away, Greenwood winced.

"Ah," said Dillman with a smile. "So you *did* postpone your return in order to contrive a meeting with Mr. Nevin? We're getting somewhere at last. Have you been conducting a vendetta against him?"

"No, Mr. Dillman."

"But you have kept track of his movements in India."

"To some extent."

"Why—he's only a minor civil servant."

"Dudley Nevin is much more than that to me."

"In what way, Mr. Greenwood?"

"That's not something I'm prepared to discuss."

"You may be compelled to do so in time."

"By whom?" demanded the other. "I refuse to be treated as if I've done something wrong. As far as I'm concerned, my relationship with Dudley Nevin is finally over. I simply refuse to answer any more questions about him."

"Then answer a question about someone else," said Dillman, taking something from his pocket. "Do you recognize this young lady, sir?"

It was the photograph taken outside the large house. Dressed in a ball gown, the young woman was smiling joyously at the camera, as if she were on her way to a very special event. Greenwood's reaction was dramatic. Bringing a hand to his mouth, he let out a gasp of pain before thrusting the photograph back at Dillman. The detective was about to ask him to identify the person in the photograph when a worried Daphne Greenwood came into the lounge, searching for her husband.

"There you are, Sylvester," she said.

Greenwood got up. "I'm just coming, my dear."

"We don't want to be late for dinner."

"No, no, of course not."

Dillman rose to be introduced to his wife. They shook hands.

"I'm sorry to delay him, Mrs. Greenwood," he said before switching his gaze to her husband. "Perhaps we could continue this discussion after dinner, sir?"

"Yes," replied Greenwood apprehensively. "I suppose so."

"Thank you. I look forward to seeing you later on."

"As you wish."

"What's happened?" asked his wife, seeing his discomfort.

"Nothing, Daphne," Greenwood said briskly. "Nothing at all."

When she opened her wardrobe, Genevieve Masefield chose an evening gown of white silk with virtually no trimmings on it. She also wore very little jewelry. Since she would be engaged in searching cabins while their occupants were at dinner, she wanted nothing that would impede her or that might catch on a sharp edge. The gown was plain but it allowed her more freedom of movement than her other dresses. Satisfied with her appearance, she stepped out into the corridor as Tabitha Simcoe was locking her cabin door. The other woman sailed toward her, wearing a dress of cream taffeta and satin that made her look very stately.

"Hello, Genevieve," she said. "Are you dining with us this evening?"

"I can't, unfortunately," replied the other, forced to manufacture an excuse. "I have a friend in second class. Because she's unable to join me in first, I promised to go to her instead."

"That's very noble of you."

"The cuisine in second class is very palatable, I'm told."

"But inferior to what we'll be eating," said Tabitha. "Well, it's one of the things that we pay extra for, isn't it? Better food, better facilities, and a better class of person. Let's be honest, I'd never have met someone like you in second class, would I?"

"Perhaps not."

"I've learned so much from you just by watching."

"Have you?"

"It's been an education."

Tabitha was in a buoyant mood, not at all dismayed by the

fact that Genevieve would not be sitting beside her at dinner that evening. During her time at sea, she had obviously grown in confidence. Success at the card table had also contributed toward her self-possession.

"How did you get on this afternoon?" asked Genevieve.

"The Kingtons played well, but Mother and I came out on top. Two victories in one day," she noted. "Mother was thrilled."

"Where is she, by the way?"

"Our new steward wheeled her into the dining saloon some time ago so that she could settle in before everyone else arrived. She'll be disappointed that you've abandoned us, Genevieve."

"Not deliberately."

"Perhaps we'll see you in the lounge later on."

Genevieve was noncommittal. "Perhaps," she said.

"You must be there. Mother will expect it of you."

"I'll do my best, Tabby."

"I'm so sorry we haven't been able to lure you to the card table," said Tabitha. "I met the most interesting man today—tall, debonair, and very good-looking. He'd have been the ideal partner for you, Genevieve."

"Oh?"

"He's an American—a Mr. George Dillman. You must have seen him around in the last few days."

"No," said Genevieve, taking care to show no reaction to the name. "I don't believe that I have. And you say that he plays bridge?"

"Not at the moment," Tabitha said skittishly, "but it would be a pleasure to teach him the game. He really is so handsome."

"You've spoken to him, then?"

"Only briefly. I just wish that I'd discovered him sooner."

"Why?"

"Well, I've started to take your advice, Genevieve. There's no need for me to be tied to Mother all the time. In fact, she's encouraged me to make friends of my own." She gave a quiet smile. "Mr. Dillman is my notion of the perfect friend."

"I thought that you were interested in Herr Voigt," said Genevieve. "You seemed to be rather taken with him last night."

"I was—for a time."

"Did he bore you so quickly?"

"No. Siegfried was diverting company until I found out his secret."

"And what was that?"

"He's married, Genevieve."

"But traveling without his wife."

"Oh, she was there, in the metaphorical sense."

"How do you know that Mr. Dillman isn't married?"

"Instinct."

"You could be mistaken, Tabby."

"I'm never mistaken about things like that," said Tabitha proudly. "It's true that I only met him for a few moments, but they were enough for me. I could see at a glance that Mr. Dillman was one of them."

"Them?"

"A permanent bachelor. One of those dashing men who go through life breaking women's hearts without even knowing it. Take my word for it," she insisted, "George Dillman will never marry."

Genevieve had some difficulty retaining her composure.

Sukinder stood patiently beside the door as Matilda Kinnersley, in a dress of black taffeta and muslin, made the final adjustments to her hair in the mirror. The major handed the girl a clothes brush so that she could dust off the back, shoulders, and sleeves of his tailcoat. Sukinder brushed away assiduously.

"Thank you," he said when she finished.

His wife snapped her fingers and held out her hand. Putting the clothes brush aside, Sukinder collected the fan from the table and gave it to Mrs. Kinnersley, receiving no thanks.

"That will be all," decided Kinnersley.

"Yes, *sahib.*"

"Get off and have your own meal now."

"Thank you."

"And be sure to read the next chapter of that book before you go to bed," said Mrs. Kinnersley. "I'll expect to hear it tomorrow."

"Yes, *memsahib.*"

"Run along, then."

"Good night, Sukinder," said Kinnersley.

She gave him a smile of farewell and let herself out of the cabin.

"What's got into her, Romford?" asked his wife.

"I don't know what you mean."

"Sukinder seemed happy for once. Why was that?"

"I think that she's resolved to make the best of the situation."

"She ought to be down on her knees, thanking us," said Matilda Kinnersley, taking a last look at herself in the mirror. "It's a privilege to work for our family. It's about time that she understood that."

"I'm sure that she does, my dear."

"At one point, she had a kind of secret smile on her face. You don't suppose that she's been sneaking up on deck again, do you?"

"No, Matilda. She wouldn't dare to disobey us."

"How do you know that?"

"Because you put the fear of death into her," said Kinnersley. "In any case, she's had her exercise for the day. I took her for a walk around the deck earlier. It was chilly out there, even for Sukinder." She turned to face him and he managed a token smile. "You look wonderful this evening, my dear."

"One has to make the effort."

"It was well worth it."

"Thank you," she said, reaching for her purse. "By the way, we're dining with the Ackroyds tonight."

"Oh, dear!"

"Why do say that?"

"Gerald tells me that they're not really speaking to each other."

"I'm not surprised. He upset Phoebe by turning up to play bridge without the aid of his ear trumpet. She was furious with him."

"It's not a hanging offense, is it?"

"In Phoebe's eyes, it is. They lost heavily."

"We all take a beating at the card table occasionally."

"Yes," his wife said superciliously, "but not to someone like Mrs. Simcoe and her daughter. That is adding insult to injury. I mean, the Simcoes are such unbearable people. To lose to them is not merely an upset. It's a crushing humiliation."

"What exactly did you say to Tabitha Simcoe?" asked Genevieve.

"Very little," recalled Dillman. "We bumped into each other in the corridor and exchanged a few words, that's all. What did she tell you?"

"That you were not married." He laughed. "It's not funny, George."

"Would you rather that she'd told you I was?"

"Well, no."

"Then it proves that my disguise works," he said. "And so does yours, Genevieve. She may claim to have sharp instincts, but Tabitha clearly hasn't worked out that *you're* married, as well. Did she say anything nice about me?"

"Stop fishing for compliments."

"There were favorable comments, then?"

"Let's forget about Tabby," she said, bringing the discussion to a close. "She's beginning to annoy me."

Meeting outside the second-class lounge, they were waiting for Paulo Morelli to join them before the search began. The steward was punctual. He came bounding along the corridor with a broad grin on his face. It suggested that he had something to report. After being introduced to Dillman, he told his tale.

"I follow Madame Roussel, as you ask me."

"Where did she go?" asked Genevieve.

"Here, there, and everywhere. At four o'clock, she leave her cabin in a beautiful red dress and go up to the next deck. Madame Roussel looks for a number, finds it, and uses the key to let herself into a cabin. She is in there for almost half an hour," he went on, taking a piece of paper from his pocket. "I make the note of the time."

"Do you know the cabin number?" asked Dillman.

"Yes, sir." He handed the paper to Dillman. "Is on here."

"Good."

"What happened when she came out, Paulo?" said Genevieve.

"She is very cautious," replied the steward. "First, she put her head out of the cabin to make sure that nobody can see her, then she hurry off. Under her arm, she is carrying something that she did not take into the cabin. I could not see what it was, but it is valuable to her. Madame Roussel, she was hugging it to her."

"Then what?"

"She went back to her own cabin and stay there until it was time to leave for dinner. When I see her sit down in the saloon, I come here."

"Well done, Paulo!"

"This is good—no?"

"Very good."

"I can go back to first class?"

"Not yet," said Genevieve. "There's a lot more to do before that, and we need your help. George will explain."

Dillman told him about the search and what his role would be. He stressed the importance of an early warning if anyone should return to a cabin unexpectedly. Morelli tried to revise his plans.

"You keep the lookout," he said, "and I search the cabins."

"No," replied Dillman. "I know what we're after, Paulo."

"But I am in and out of cabins all day long. Is my job. I will be quicker than you. I know where people hide things."

"So do we," said Genevieve. "You just do as George tells you."

Dillman took control. "Let's get started, shall we?"

They were methodical. Since only certain cabins were being searched, Dillman had listed them so that he took those occupied by men or by married couples, while Genevieve concentrated on those with exclusively female passengers in them. Morelli was stationed at a strategic point in order to keep watch. Using a master key, Genevieve first let herself into the cabin of their prime suspect, Madame Roussel. She could smell the perfume in the air. Having been there before, she knew exactly where to look, but she found no clues to indicate that the Frenchwoman was the thief. Nothing of value was kept in the cabin. She abandoned the search.

It was the same with the next two cabins that she went into. While her search was extremely thorough, she came out empty-handed on both occasions. Morelli trotted along the corridor to whisper to her.

"What is it you look for?" he asked. "I will find it."

"You stay on guard, Paulo."

"But I have the skills, *signorina*. Let me use them."

"You're holding me up."

"I sorry," he said, retreating to his position.

Consulting her list, Genevieve checked the number of the next cabin that she was due to search, then noticed something. It was next door to the cabin occupied by Guljar Singh. Though that was not down to be searched, she had a sudden urge to go into it, to satisfy herself once and for all that the old man was not involved in the thefts. Knowing that Dillman would strongly disapprove, she waited until he vanished into a cabin himself before crossing to the one in question.

She let herself in and looked around. Guljar Singh had brought very little luggage with him. There was only one battered old case in his wardrobe. It contained a few items of clothing and some books. Tucked away on the shelf in the wardrobe was what looked like a bundle of washing. Genevieve took it down to find that it was a cotton sheet that had been tied into a ball. She could feel something jiggling around inside it. Setting it down on the bed, she was about to untie it when she heard the sound of a key in the lock. Genevieve's heart pounded. There was nowhere to hide. She would be caught red-handed by the very man to whom she'd been forced to give her abject apology earlier on. How could she explain herself?

But it was not Guljar Singh who entered. It was Dillman.

"What are you doing in here?" he demanded.

"I thought I'd check it out, just in case."

"This is Guljar Singh's cabin, Genevieve. It's not on the list."

"Yes, I know."

"Then why bother with it? I couldn't believe it when Paulo told me that you'd come in here. The man is *innocent,* Genevieve."

"Is he?" she countered, shaking the bundle. "Then what is Mr. Singh hiding in here?"

She undid the knot and opened the sheet. Expecting to find some personal items inside, Dillman was astonished to see instead three purses and a quantity of jewelry. From the description that Madame Roussel had given her of the stolen items, Genevieve recognized them as having come from the Frenchwoman's cabin. Controlling her own amazement, she looked at Dillman.

"What do you say now, George?" she asked.

TWELVE

*S*ylvester Greenwood was quiet over dinner that evening. An opinionated man by nature, he liked to be at the heart of any discussion but he was curiously reticent on this occasion. Seated beside him, his wife was worried about him, but their daughter, on the opposite side of the table, hardly noticed her father's comparative silence. Lois was ready to pronounce on any and every subject, talking happily to people close to her, as if celebrating her return to the dining saloon. It was during a lull in the conversation that Daphne Greenwood finally voiced her anxiety.

"Are you all right, Sylvester?" she asked.

"Yes, my dear," he replied. "I'm fine."

"You've eaten so sparingly."

"I don't seem to have much of an appetite this evening."

"Are you sickening for something?"

"No, Daphne."

"Has some of the food disagreed with you?"

He touched her arm. "Stop worrying about me, will you?"

"Or has something else upset you?" she wondered. "You haven't been the same since you spoke to that Mr. Dillman."

"Dillman?" said Lois, hearing the name. "Have you been talking to him again, Daddy?"

"Yes," he said.

"It wasn't about me, was it?"

"Not this time, Lois."

"That's a relief," she said. Leaning across the table, she lowered her voice. "Did you find out if he's a spy?"

"A spy?" echoed her mother. "What's this about spying?"

"A fanciful notion that Lois came up with," said Greenwood, eager to get off the subject. "Mr. Dillman is no spy."

"Then who is he?"

"He's the nice American that I met on deck, Mummy," said Lois. "That first night I went roller-skating. I liked him but Daddy warned me not to speak to him again."

"Why not?"

"It doesn't matter," said Greenwood.

"He seemed very courteous when I met him earlier."

"Oh, he is," confirmed Lois. "And he has such a lovely voice. I could listen to him all day." She glanced around. "For some reason, he doesn't seem to be here this evening."

"Can we please forget Mr. Dillman?" Greenwood said irritably.

"If you wish, Daddy."

"Let's talk about something else."

"But I thought you agreed to speak to him after dinner," noted his wife. "Why was that, Sylvester?"

"Never you mind, my dear."

"But I do mind."

"Daphne—"

"When someone disturbs you, I mind very much."

221

"It's not like that."

"Then what is it like?" she probed. "Is it to do with politics?"

"Indirectly."

"Is that what you and Mr. Dillman were talking about?"

"To some degree," he said.

"Everything seems to do with politics these days."

"It's my profession, Daphne."

"But it's taken over your whole life," she complained. "I thought that we went to India for a holiday, but even there you managed to get involved in political matters. It was very irksome. I was very proud of you at the time—I still am, of course—but I'm beginning to regret that you ever won that by-election."

Sylvester Greenwood felt more uncomfortable than ever.

Max Cannadine looked down at his desk with a mixture of delight and bewilderment. Arrayed in front of him was the stolen property that Genevieve and Dillman had recovered. A huge load was suddenly lifted from the purser's shoulders. He burst out laughing.

"That's incredible!" he exclaimed. "How did you do it?"

"I thought that the search would produce results," said Genevieve.

"It certainly did that. Congratulations!"

"Thank you, Mr. Cannadine."

"Where did you find all this?"

"In the last place we expected," she told him. "That cabin wasn't even on our list, but I felt impelled to check it out nevertheless."

"Thank heaven you did. Who was the occupant?"

"Guljar Singh."

He was flabbergasted. "But you assured me that he was innocent."

"That was a mistake."

"Mr. Dillman thought that *I* would be a more likely thief."

"He's been forced to revise that opinion," said Genevieve. "It came as a real shock to George—and to me, I must confess. The old man fooled me completely."

"Has he been arrested yet?"

"No, Mr. Cannadine. We thought we'd leave that until he'd eaten his dinner. After all, Guljar Singh is not going anywhere."

"He'll go straight to a cell for this," said the purser, indicating the haul on his desk. "I don't care how old or frail he is. A crime is a crime and it must be punished."

"Oh, I agree. Though I'm bound to feel sorry for him."

"Why?"

"I don't know," she confessed. "But having met him, I just don't believe that he's a bad man at heart. I think that Guljar Singh must have acted completely out of character."

"Maybe."

"The important fact is that we've recovered all the stolen items."

"Thanks to you and Mr. Dillman."

"You'll have the pleasure of returning them to their owners."

"I think that you should be here for that, Miss Masefield," he argued. "Credit where credit's due. You were the one who investigated the thefts so you should enjoy the gratitude of the victims."

"I'll certainly want to watch you returning the jewelry to Madame Roussel," said Genevieve. "She took rather a dim view of my detecting skills. I hope that she'll be more gracious towards me now. My advice is to see her on her own before the others."

"Oh, I will. When Madame Roussel is in here, there's no room for anyone apart from you and me. She has such a presence, especially when she's enraged."

"The sight of her jewelry will calm her down."

"It's certainly calmed me down. Well," he said reflectively, "that's four crimes solved. But the more serious one still remains, alas.

Given the choice, I'd much rather solve one murder than a dozen thefts."

"So would we, Mr. Cannadine."

"Has there been any progress?"

"George feels that there has," she reported. "And he may well be finding some new evidence as we speak."

"Why—what's he doing?"

"Searching the cabin of the chief suspect."

"Sylvester Greenwood?"

"Yes. George felt he had the man on the run earlier."

"That sounds promising."

"But Mrs. Greenwood interrupted them at the crucial moment."

"Damnation!"

"George arranged to have another interview with him later on."

"Meanwhile, he's rummaging through the man's cabin."

"With a lookout guarding his back," she said. "Paulo is definitely doing his share of the work this evening. We'll just have to keep our fingers crossed that George turns something up."

Sylvester Greenwood was not a person who believed in enjoying leisure. On his trip to India, he had brought an immense amount of work with him. While searching his cabin, Dillman was impressed by the man's diligence. In addition to sheaves of correspondence from his constituents, Greenwood was traveling with papers that related to various committees on which he sat, and with some hefty parliamentary reports. In India, he had acquired a number of books about its political activities. Dillman sifted through the documents as quickly as he could. Disappointingly, however, there was nothing there to connect Greenwood with Dudley Nevin.

Nor was there any bloodstained clothing in the wardrobe. That did not altogether surprise Dillman. Since he shared the cabin with his wife, Greenwood would probably dispose of anything that would catch her eye and provoke alarm. What did interest the detective was a leather-bound address book. Flicking to the correct page, he saw that Dudley Nevin was listed with no less than four different addresses, two in England and two in India. Each time the man moved, it seemed, his new location was carefully noted. Greenwood did not wish to lose track of him.

Many of the items in the cabin belonged to his wife, and Dillman merely glanced at them. Daphne Greenwood was not under suspicion in any way. Nevertheless, when he found a small case with her name on it, he felt obliged to search it. Hidden away in the corner of the wardrobe, it felt quite heavy when he pulled it out. Placing it on the floor, he opened the lid to find a collection of what looked like souvenirs. In the middle of them, wrapped up in a thick piece of cloth, was an object that attracted his attention. He unrolled the cloth and realized what he was holding.

It was a *kukri*, a knife that was identical to the murder weapon.

Before he could examine his find, there was an urgent tap on the door. It was the signal from the steward that someone was coming. Dillman moved swiftly. Wrapping the *kukri* in the cloth again, he put it back, closed the lid of the case, then replaced it in the exact spot where it had stood before. He left the cabin and gave a wave of thanks to Morelli, who then vanished around a corner. Seconds later, Greenwood appeared in the corridor. Dillman strode nonchalantly toward him.

"I was hoping that you'd come back here," he said. "It gets rather crowded in the lounge after dinner."

"We can talk in my cabin."

"That will suit me, Mr. Greenwood."

"I've told my wife not to disturb us."

"What about your daughter?"

"Lois will stay with her mother until I go back to them."

Dillman was about to say that there was a possibility he might not be rejoining his family, but he decided against it. Suspicion, however strong, was not the same as incontrovertible proof. Even at this stage, Sylvester Greenwood had to be presumed innocent until clear guilt was established. When he followed the man into the cabin, Dillman pretended that he was seeing it for the first time.

"P and O always puts an emphasis on comfort," he observed, looking around. "This is very well designed."

"You didn't come here to admire my cabin, Mr. Dillman."

"No, I didn't."

"Then let's not beat about the bush, shall we?" said Greenwood, sourly. "Take a seat and get on with it."

"I'd prefer to stand, if you don't mind."

"Please yourself."

Greenwood sat down in the chair beside the desk and crossed his legs. He looked calm but determined. There was no sign of the unease he had felt during dinner. He was ready to joust with Dillman.

"Perhaps we could start with the photograph," said the detective, producing it again from his pocket. "Who is this young lady?"

"I'm afraid that I can't tell you."

"Why not?"

"Because it's none of your damn business, sir," rejoined the other.

"It could be, Mr. Greenwood."

"What do you mean?"

"It's yet another link between you and Dudley Nevin—the man you denied knowing at one point. Look," said Dillman, deciding to put his cards on the table, "it's only fair that you should understand why I'm so interested in your relationship with him." He raised an eyebrow. "Unless, that is, you know already."

"I haven't a clue what you're talking about," said Greenwood, face expressionless. "Has Mr. Nevin accused me of something?"

"He's not in a position to accuse anybody, sir."

"Why not?"

"Mr. Nevin is dead."

The Englishman looked shocked. *"Dead?"*

"To be more exact," explained Dillman, "he was murdered. For obvious reasons, we haven't made this public, and I'm only telling you in strict confidence. At least you'll now understand why I must ask you certain questions. They're part of a murder investigation."

"When did it happen?"

"I don't wish to go into any details." He held up the photograph. "You obviously recognized the young lady. Who is she?"

"Eileen is nothing to do with this," insisted Greenwood.

"Is that her name—Eileen?"

"Yes. Miss Eileen Penfold."

"This photo was found in Mr. Nevin's possession. Why was that?"

Greenwood squirmed slightly in his seat. He was no longer as composed as he had been. Dillman sensed that the man was vulnerable.

"I think that she may be the link," he said.

"The link?"

"Between you and Mr. Nevin. That's what sent you to his cabin, wasn't it? Miss Penfold was a bone of contention between the two of you. Is that correct?" Greenwood was resolutely silent. "I intend to get an answer, no matter how long it takes. And if you won't give it to me, perhaps I should show this photograph to your wife."

"No, no," protested the other. "Daphne must be kept out of this."

"Why?"

"Because she knows nothing whatsoever about it."

"Is that because you're ashamed to tell her?"

"Of course not."

"Then why all this secrecy?"

"My wife is highly strung, Mr. Dillman," said Greenwood. "She's far too easily upset. That's why I've learned to suppress anything unpleasant in front of her. She was never even aware of Miss Penfold's existence. And before you misunderstand me," he went on, "let me assure you that nothing improper took place between me and the young lady."

"Why were you so shaken when you saw her photograph?"

"Because it brought back ugly memories."

"Of what?"

Greenwood bit his lip. Lapsing back into silence, he went off into a reverie. Judging by the pained expression on his face, he appeared to be wrestling with some kind of inner demons. Uncertain whether or not he was dissembling, Dillman adopted a more direct approach.

"Were you involved in the murder of Dudley Nevin?" he asked.

"Of course not!" exclaimed Greenwood.

"Do you deny that you had a motive to kill him?"

"That's irrelevant."

"I don't think so. Well, sir?"

"I've wished him dead a hundred times," he admitted.

"Is that why you've kept a careful note of his movements?"

"No, Mr. Dillman."

"Then what was the reason?"

"I wanted to tell him about Eileen," said Greenwood, snatching the photograph from him. "I needed to call him to account."

"Why?"

"Because nobody else was in a position to do so."

"Go on," encouraged Dillman.

There was a long pause. Greenwood gazed at the photograph as if trying to draw strength from it. When he finally spoke, there was wistful note in his voice.

"Eileen Penfold was a friend and colleague of mine," he explained. "She worked as a stenographer on my newspaper. She was young, hardworking, and eager to please. Unfortunately, she was also rather naive. That meant she was easy prey for him."

"For whom—Dudley Nevin?"

"Yes. He knew that he couldn't win that election by fair means, Mr. Dillman, so he resorted to foul ones. Nevin hit on the idea of discrediting me by finding some scandal in my past, and the only way he could do that was by befriending someone who'd worked with me."

"Miss Penfold."

"I'd left the paper at that point, so Eileen wasn't even aware of my political ambitions. It never occurred to her that Nevin had taken an interest in her to get at me. Frankly," he said with disgust, "I've no idea what attracted her to him. He did have an oily charm, I suppose, and he obviously knew how to flatter her."

"Was she able to tell him what he wanted?"

"No, Mr. Dillman. There was nothing to tell."

"How did Nevin respond to that?" asked Dillman.

"He didn't believe it. He thought that she was simply being loyal to me. If he wined and dined her enough, he reasoned, he'd win her confidence." He handed the photograph back to Dillman. "This was taken before they attended a ball in Chelsea. Eileen had never been to anything like that. It must have seemed like a fairy tale to her."

"What happened?"

"Dudley Nevin took cruel advantage of her," Greenwood said bitterly. "He told her that he loved her, naturally, but he was just using the girl. Eileen didn't realize that. She was enthralled by him, and would have told him everything that he wanted."

"But there were no skeletons."

"Not even a stray bone."

"So what did Nevin do?"

"Cast the girl aside," replied the other. "Since he couldn't find any real scandal in my life, he tried to invent some. But that, too, backfired. He lost the election and turned tail, forgetting all about the night he'd seduced that poor girl."

"Did she pine for him?"

"No, Mr. Dillman. By that time, Eileen had come to see the truth of the situation. It made her feel so foolish—and guilty. She even came to me to apologize, as if it were her fault." He ran a hand through his beard. "I felt so embarrassed."

"Why was that?"

"At a time when I was celebrating my victory in the election, Eileen was suffering so dreadfully. Her whole life had been ruined," he explained. "That night they spent together had consequences."

"She was pregnant?"

Greenwood nodded. "Have you any idea of the stigma that an unmarried mother carries in England?"

"Yes, I do," said Dillman. "We have more than our share of narrow minds on the other side of the Atlantic."

"Eileen faced a grim future. Girls like her are socially ostracized. What chance would she have of finding a husband when she had a bastard child in tow? She must have been at her wit's end."

"What about her family?"

"They supported her at first," said Greenwood. "Her father offered to pay for her to leave home before her condition became too obvious. She was to be hidden from view until it was all over. He took it for granted that Eileen would have the baby adopted."

"But she didn't."

"She was its mother. She wanted to bring it up."

"Is that what she's doing, Mr. Greenwood?"

"Unhappily, no," the other man said sadly. "Eileen Penfold died of complications that set in during childbirth. She'd brought a baby boy into the world. To their credit, her parents decided to care for it."

"Mr. Nevin should have taken some responsibility."

"That's what I told them, and Mr. Penfold wrote to him a number of times. He never even had the courtesy of a reply from India."

"I'm beginning to see why you disliked him so much."

"I detested him," said Greenwood, getting to his feet. "When I knew that we were coming to India, I was determined to get in touch with him somehow and put some pressure on him to accept his responsibilities. As it happened, my brother-in-law was able to save me the trouble of going all the way to Delhi. He found out that Nevin would be sailing to Aden on the *Salsette*."

"I know the rest, Mr. Greenwood." Dillman produced the other photograph. "Unless you can tell me who this is."

Greenwood looked at the picture of the woman in the automobile.

"I can tell you whom she was—Nevin's fiancée."

"How do you know?"

"Because he brought her to the count. He was so confident of winning that election that he turned up with a full complement of supporters." He gave a complacent chuckle. "I was able to send Dudley Nevin away with a red face. It was one more indignity for Eileen Penfold to endure, of course. In the very newspaper for which she worked, they printed a picture of the defeated Conservative candidate and his fiancée. Not that the engagement lasted very long," he continued. "When there were allegations of electoral misconduct against Nevin, this young lady had the good sense to get rid of him."

He returned the photograph and Dillman put both of them back into his pocket. Some of his assumptions about Greenwood had been wrong, and he chided himself for that, but he did not feel that the man had proved his innocence beyond doubt.

"Dudley Nevin was stabbed with a *kukri*," he said.

"So?"

"Do you know what that is?"

"It's a knife favored by Gurkhas."

"There are three of them aboard and they're friends of yours."

Greenwood stifled a laugh. "You think that I instructed one of them to act as my assassin?" he said. "That's preposterous."

"Is it?"

"Wait until you meet them, Mr. Dillman. They're the most peaceable characters, I assure you. On behalf of my party, I was asked to build up contacts with political groups while I was in Bombay. One of those men you saw with me is a member of the Indian National Congress."

"I see."

"As for the murder weapon, it's not only Gurkhas who carry a *kukri*. You can buy them as souvenirs in any market. As a matter of fact," he went on, crossing to the wardrobe, "I was given one myself by my brother-in-law. Would you like to see it?"

"That won't be necessary, sir," said Dillman, who had already examined the knife and now realized it had no sinister association. "I've taken up enough of your time."

"Have we cleared the air, Mr. Dillman?"

"Completely."

"I'm afraid that you'll have to look elsewhere for the killer."

"We will, sir."

"Though I would ask one favor."

"And what's that, Mr. Greenwood?"

"If and when you do catch the man, give me a call."

"Why is that?"

"Because I'd like to shake his hand."

"That's rather callous of you, sir," said Dillman. "I always have some compassion for a murder victim, whoever it might be."

"You didn't know him as well as I did."

"Perhaps not."

"And you didn't see the look on Eileen's face when she confessed to me how she'd got entangled with him."

"That's true."

"If you ask me," said Greenwood harshly, "Mr. Dudley Nevin got exactly what he deserved."

The purser had been very pleased to see the stolen property recovered, but Madame Roussel was positively delirious with joy. Emitting a cry of delight, she threw her arms around Cannadine's neck to plant a kiss on his cheek. There was only one thing that she felt was missing.

"Where is the other detective—*l'Américain*?"

"Mr. Dillman is busy, I'm afraid," explained Genevieve.

"But I ask him to return my jewelry in person."

"He might still do that, Madame Roussel," said the purser, looking at the items on his desk. "You can reclaim your property now, if you wish, but I'd urge you to leave it in my safe overnight."

"Yes, please. I will do that."

"Meanwhile, you might wish to thank Miss Masefield."

"Bien entendu."

"It was she who led the investigation into the thefts."

"Merci, mademoiselle," said the Frenchwoman, kissing Genevieve on both cheeks. *"Merci beaucoup."*

"We did promise to get it back for you," said Genevieve.

"And you keep the promise."

"That's official P and O policy," noted Cannadine. "We always honor our promises. Now, if you will, I'd like you to examine your property to make sure that all of it is there and that nothing has been damaged."

"Is what I would like to do."

Putting her purse down, Madame Roussel pored over the desk and inspected every item with care. She wore a two-piece dress that had been carefully shaped to fit her contours. Above the long, tight, embroidered black skirt was a white bodice with puffed sleeves and a draped lace corsage. She had on all the jewelry that had not been stolen. Cosmetics had been used artfully. In the limited space of the purser's office, her fragrance had more impact.

As she watched the other woman, Genevieve was reminded that she and Dillman had both considered Madame Roussel as a possible suspect. She was grateful that the Frenchwoman was unconscious of the fact, though she still wondered what the latter was doing when she let herself into a cabin that was clearly not her own. What had she been carrying when she emerged sometime later? There was still a veil of secrecy to be lifted from her.

"Is all there," said Madame Roussel, clapping her hands.

"Good," said the purser.

"Ask the other detective to bring it to my cabin in the morning."

"Mr. Dillman may have other commitments," warned Genevieve, slightly peeved at the preference shown to her partner. "But your property will be restored to you, have no fear."

"Then there is only one more thing I want."

"What's that, Madame Roussel?" asked Cannadine.

"The name of the thief."

"Why don't you let us worry about that?"

"Because this man," said the other, flushing with indignation, "he go into my cabin. He *invades* me. He makes me feel not safe. Is a terrible thing to do to me. I tell him so to his face." She swung round to stare at Genevieve. "Who is he, mademoiselle?"

"His name is Guljar Singh," said Genevieve.

"And where is this *voleur* now?"

"He is probably being arrested by my partner."

Guljar Singh was mystified. When he left the dining saloon, he was met by Dillman and asked to accompany him back to the cabin. The old man could not understand why. He padded along beside the American.

"Is something wrong, my friend?" he asked.

"I'm afraid so, Mr. Singh."

"There is trouble in my cabin?"

"Yes," said Dillman.

He was unhappy about being the one to accost the Sikh, especially as he was preoccupied with the murder investigation, but Dillman did not want Genevieve to make the arrest. She had already had two brushes with Guljar Singh. Besides, weak as he appeared, the old man might possibly be armed and therefore posed a danger. By the time they had reached the cabin, Guljar Singh had made a deduction.

"You are not only a passenger on this ship, I think."

"No, Mr. Singh."

"You work with the lady detective. Is it not so?"

"Yes," said Dillman. "I'm employed by P and O and I've been assisting Miss Masefield in her investigation into a series of thefts."

"But she has already spoken to me about those," protested Singh, "and she knows that I am innocent. She even gave me an apology."

"That may have been premature."

"I do not follow you."

"Mr. Singh," Dillman said quietly, "is there anything in your cabin that may have been taken from other passengers on this vessel?"

The Sikh was offended. "That is a horrible thing to ask me."

"Nevertheless, I have to put the question to you."

"Then I will give you your answer," said the other, unlocking the door and walking into the cabin. "There are no stolen goods here, Mr. Dillman. See for yourself. Go on—search high and low."

"We've already done that."

Guljar Singh gaped. "You came into my cabin without permission?" he said, appalled by the news. "You had no right to do that. None at all."

"Actually, it was my partner who first let herself in here."

"Miss Masefield? But she *knows* I am not a thief."

"She thought she knew," corrected Dillman. "That was before she discovered what you had hidden away in your wardrobe. I saw it for myself. Do you deny that you had a small bundle in there?"

"No, of course not."

"Then perhaps you'll explain why it contained the jewelry that had been stolen, along with the three purses taken from ladies on deck."

Guljar Singh was so stunned that he staggered back a few paces. Dillman rushed to grab him with a steadying hand and helped him to sit in the chair. The old man was saying something in Hindi that the detective could not understand. He began to sob quietly.

"I'm very disappointed in you," said Dillman. "I insisted that you could not possibly be the culprit, and you let me down. Why did you do it, Mr. Singh?"

"Do what?"

"Steal those things."

"But I did not, Mr. Dillman, I give you my sacred word."

"Then how did that property come to be in your cabin?"

Guljar Singh looked hunted. His eyes darted around the cabin. Wanting to proclaim his own innocence, he did not wish to incriminate anyone else, but there was no alternative.

"I did not know what was in that bundle," he asserted.

Dillman was skeptical. "Do you expect me to believe that?"

"Not from my lips, maybe. You will have to hear it from hers."

"Whose?"

"Suki's," explained the other. "She asked me to mind something for her as a favor. I was to carry that bundle off the ship for her so that Major and Mrs. Kinnersley did not see her with it. Suki told me that she would come for it later. Yes," he said sorrowfully, "I can see that I did wrong. I helped to conceal stolen goods—but only because I did not look inside the bundle."

Dillman knew that he was telling the truth. Having met Sukinder, and having seen how strictly Mrs. Kinnersley treated her, he could guess why the girl had taken the things in the first place.

"She wants to go back to India, doesn't she?"

"Yes, Mr. Dillman."

"She was going to run away in Aden somehow."

"I think that was on her mind."

"Then she'd use some of the money she'd stolen to pay her fare."

"Suki did not tell me that," said Singh. "All she talked about was going home to her mother in Simla. It is wrong to take her to a country where she will have no friends of her own color and creed."

"Her mother must have condoned the arrangement."

"Only because she was paid, Mr. Dillman."

"How do you know?"

"Because I have watched Suki every day being taken for a walk by Major Kinnersley. His wife is hard on the girl, but he is kind towards here when they are alone. It is easy to see why."

"Is it?" said Dillman.

"To my eyes, it is. Of course, Suki does not know it herself, and

Mrs. Kinnersley, the wife, is certainly not aware of it or she would not think of taking Suki to England with her." He gave a philosophical smile. "It is not the first time that this kind of thing has happened."

"What kind of thing, Mr. Singh?"

"A British soldier sleeping with one of his servants," said the other. "Major Kinnersley is the girl's father."

Paulo Morelli had enjoyed the experience of helping the detectives. The steward had developed a taste for it. Even when he was told that his work was over, Morelli was ready to keep on, determined to prove his worth and earn back his former place in first class. To that end, he decided to follow Madame Roussel again. When she came out of the purser's office, she was in a state of such high excitement that she would not have noticed if every steward on the ship were on her tail. The return of her jewelry had made her oblivious to all around her.

She surged along a corridor before going up a companionway. Morelli went after her. Without even looking over her shoulder, Madame Roussel walked along another corridor and rapped on a cabin door. When it opened, she gave a cry of delight and stepped inside. After waiting a few minutes, the steward strolled past the cabin and glanced at the door. In addition to a number, it had the name of its occupant printed on a card. Morelli goggled.

Being a detective was a job that was full of surprises.

The first-class smoking room was quite full that evening. Major Romford Kinnersley was enjoying a cigar and chatting to Wilbur Rollins. In spite of his prejudice against Americans, the major was intrigued to hear some of the stories that the man had unearthed in the course of his research.

"And you say this woman fought in the Siege of Pondicherry?"

"Apparently," said Rollins. "Hannah Snell always made mention of it when she appeared on stage."

"Nobody knew her gender at the time?"

"No, Major."

"Then the British marines have gone down in my estimation," said Kinnersley, before pulling on his cigar and exhaling the smoke. "In my regiment, we'd have sniffed out a woman in two minutes—whatever uniform she was wearing."

"Don't be too sure of that," warned Rollins, putting out his cigarette. "Still, I've talked far too much this evening. Thank you for listening, Major. I bid you good night."

Kinnersley waved him off. As one American vanished, however, another arrived to take his place, and he was far less welcome. When he saw George Dillman approaching him, the major scowled.

"What do you want?" he grunted.

"I need to speak to you as a matter of urgency," said Dillman.

"Really?"

"Could we find somewhere a little quieter?"

"I intend to finish my cigar."

"It's a rather delicate matter, I fear."

"We've got nothing to say to each other, Mr. Dillman."

"Oh, I think you'll find that we have."

"Can't it wait until morning, man?"

"No," said Dillman, looking him straight in the eye. "I'm afraid that it can't. If you're not prepared to discuss the crime, Major, I'll have to take the matter up with Mrs. Kinnersley."

"Crime? What are you gibbering about?"

"Sukinder."

"Something has happened to her?" said the other in alarm.

"It was she who committed the crime," explained Dillman. "Before I go into detail, I should explain that I'm working for P and O as a detective aboard this ship." Kinnersley was dumbfounded. "Given the nature of our discussion, perhaps you'll reconsider my suggestion that this may not be the ideal place to talk."

"Let's go," said Kinnersley, stubbing out his cigar in an ashtray.

Leaving the hubbub and the smell of tobacco smoke behind, they went out on deck and stood at the rail. It was a fine night and the ship was making good speed through the whitecapped waves. Dillman felt exhilarated by the keen air but his companion merely gave a shiver.

"What's this about Sukinder?" demanded the major.

"We've been put in rather an awkward position," replied Dillman. "In brief, the situation is this. A series of thefts has occurred on the *Salsette*. My colleague and I discovered that your servant was the thief."

"That's absurd! Suki is a good girl."

"We found all of the stolen property in her possession."

"I refuse to believe it."

"Then you must talk to Guljar Singh. He's an elderly Sikh who befriended Sukinder. It seems that she asked him to mind something for her until they left the ship in Aden. What Mr. Singh didn't realize," said Dillman, "was that the bundle she gave him contained three purses and a quantity of jewelry."

"Jewelry! How could she possibly have got hold of that?"

"By slipping into an unlocked cabin when it was empty."

"But she's not allowed to roam the ship on her own."

"You're in first class, Major, while she has a small cabin in second. You've no idea what she's doing when she's not on duty. Sukinder has no dining privileges, does she?"

"Of course not," said Kinnersley. "She takes all her meals in her cabin. I couldn't let a child of that age go into the dining saloon on her own—and my wife would never have accepted the notion of letting Suki eat with us. The girl is a servant."

"She was also one of the few people who was not in a dining saloon on the evening when the jewelry was taken. That gave her an opportunity to wander around the other cabins, and she found one that was unlocked."

"And you say there were other thefts?"

"Three purses were stolen from their owners on deck."

"But the only time she's allowed out here is with me."

"It seems that she disobeyed your orders, Major," said Dillman. "Sukinder was certainly on deck earlier today without you because she asked Guljar Singh if he would do her a favor."

Kinnersley was baffled. Having shown the girl what he considered to be kindness and generosity, he could not understand why she had, in effect, betrayed him. Yet he was responsible for her. If she was exposed as a thief, it was he who would have to answer for the girl. It was deeply embarrassing, all the more so because George Dillman was the man who had imparted the news.

"What's going to happen?" he growled.

"That's what you'll have to discuss with the purser."

"Is Suki with him now?"

"No, Major. She's not even aware that we're on to her."

"Why in God's name did she do it?" asked the major. "It's not as if she *needed* to steal. Dash it all, I provide everything for her."

"Not quite."

"What do you mean?"

"You've actually taken away the one thing that Sukinder really wants, Major," said Dillman. "She's desperate to stay in India with her family. That's why she stole those things. She was hoping to give you the slip in Aden, then use some of the money she'd taken to pay for the return journey."

Kinnersley was hurt. "Suki doesn't want to be with us?" he said, shaking his head in disbelief. "She'd have such a better life in England. Doesn't she understand that?"

241

There was a mingled bewilderment and affection in his voice. In spite of his dislike of the man, Dillman felt sympathy for him. The major was suffering the pain of rejection.

"Sukinder made her choice," the detective said softly. "Even though she probably didn't realize that she was choosing between her parents." Kinnersley glared at him. "It was Guljar Singh who told me, Major. He saw you and Sukinder together. She's your daughter, isn't she?"

"How dare you suggest such a thing!"

"Why else would you want to take the girl home with you?"

"As a domestic servant, of course."

"If there's to be a prosecution," warned Dillman, "then details of the girl's parentage will be needed. She may not know who her father is, but I'm sure that you do." Kinnersley's bluster slowly gave way to a sigh of anguish. "If it's any consolation to you, nobody else will hear about this from me—or from Mr. Singh, for that matter."

"Thank you, Mr. Dillman," said Kinnersley, chin falling to his chest. "It's not something that I'm proud of, I can tell you. It happened and I have no excuse to offer. I tried to make amends by taking the child to England, but I suppose that it would never have worked. I'd have had to go on deceiving my wife, and I've done that for far too long." He raised his head. "I just wanted to have Suki by me," he confessed with a nostalgic smile. "She reminds me so much of her mother."

"I understand, sir."

"Do you? I doubt it, Mr. Dillman."

"Perhaps we should speak to the purser, sir."

"Later."

"Mr. Cannadine is expecting you."

"Let him wait."

"The matter must be resolved tonight."

"It will be," promised Kinnersley, straightening his back and thrusting out his jaw. "But in the interest of decency, there's someone else I must speak to first—my wife."

Max Cannadine and Genevieve Masefield were in the office when he arrived. Surveying the stolen property on the desk, Guljar Singh gasped.

"Suki stole all this?" he said.

"Yes, Mr. Singh," replied the purser. "She has a nimble hand."

"I thought I was looking after her meager belongings."

"We don't blame you at all. That's why I asked to see you in my office. I want to make it clear that we'll be taking no action against you."

"Thank you, Mr. Cannadine."

"I was wrong about you for the second time, Mr. Singh," admitted Genevieve, stepping forward with a look of repentance. "I owe you another apology."

"Two apologies—that must be a record."

"I misjudged you badly."

"That, in a sense, was a blessing," said Cannadine. "If you hadn't harbored a lurking suspicion of Mr. Singh, you'd never have searched his cabin." He indicated the spoils. "And we'd still be looking for this lot."

"I still feel that I was unkind to Mr. Singh."

"The purser is correct," decided the old man, sagely. "You did something wrong yet it produced the right result. A very sad result for me, however," he said. "I am fond of Suki and do not like to see her in trouble. What will happen to her?"

"That's something I must discuss with Major Kinnersley," said the purser. "Mr. Dillman went off to apprise him of the situation."

"The major will be wounded by this."

"He's *in loco parentis,* Mr. Singh."

"Of course," said the other with a discreet smile. "Well, I may yet be right in my prediction. Suki asked me to foretell her future."

"What did you say?" asked Genevieve.

"That she would never reach England, but return home instead."

"It may well turn out to be the case."

"We shall see," said Cannadine. He looked at Singh. "How long have you had these strange powers?"

"All my life," returned the old man.

"And your predictions always come true?"

"Most of the time. But it's not only a question of foresight," he explained. "First, I read the character of the person who wants me to tell them their fortune. That guides me. I can see their hopes, understand their fears, gauge their ambitions. What I have to decide is whether or not they have the courage to fulfill those ambitions. In Suki's case," he went on, "I felt that she was determined to get what she wanted—though I didn't know the means that she would choose."

"How do you read someone's character?" wondered Genevieve.

"You look, you listen, you get vibrations from them. It was easy with Suki," he told them. "I watched her walking around the deck many times with the major. Her face was like an open book. That's my real secret, Miss Masefield," he revealed. "To understand someone's true character, you must study them when they do not know you are watching. People behave very differently when they are on view."

"We all wear masks, Mr. Singh."

"You did, and it was a very good one. I would never have guessed you were a detective. And those other English ladies— they wore masks, as well."

"Who do you mean?" asked Genevieve.

"The lady who is pushed around the deck by her daughter."

"That's Mrs. Simcoe. She's disabled."

"Then she has made a remarkable recovery on this ship."

"Why do you say that?"

Guljar Singh cackled. "If it is a clear night," he said, "I prefer to sleep on deck. Nobody ever notices me, curled up in a corner. That way, I am able to hear and see many peculiar things."

"Such as?" asked Cannadine.

"A young lady going around the deck on roller skates. A husband and wife exchanging blows. A man climbing into one of the lifeboats with a woman. And this person you know," he added, turning to Genevieve.

"Constance Simcoe?"

"By day, she is an invalid in her chair," said Singh. "At night, when she thinks nobody can see her, she walks around the deck without even needing a stick. That tells me a lot about *her* character."

Reclining in a chair, Constance Simcoe sipped a liqueur and gazed around the first-class lounge with interest. The first stage of their return home was nearing its end, but several of the people there would transfer to another P & O ship for the longer voyage to England. Among them, she hoped to find others who could be drawn to play bridge against Tabitha and her. She turned to her daughter.

"Do you think that the Ackroyds could be tempted again?"

"Not after this morning," said Tabitha.

"She got so cross with that long-suffering husband of hers."

"Recriminations are still going on."

Tabitha glanced in the direction of the Ackroyds, who were seated not far away. Phoebe Ackroyd was stern and implacable. Judging by his apologetic gestures, her husband was still seeking her forgiveness for his lapses at the card table, but she ignored him. At length, Gerald Ackroyd gave a weary smile and sought solace in his glass of brandy.

"We seem to have caused a rift between them," said Constance. "Does that worry you?"

"No, Tabby. It delights me."

"Mrs. Ackroyd was overconfident, that was her trouble."

"One needs a cool head for bridge. As soon as she began to lose her temper with him, I felt that we were bound to win."

"They trounced us the day before," Tabitha reminded her.

Constance smirked. "There's nothing quite so sweet as revenge, is there?" she said.

"No, Mother."

"I'll be sorry to leave the *Salsette*."

"I won't," said Tabitha.

"But it's been such a lucky ship for us." She saw Phoebe Ackroyd getting up from her chair. "Watch out—I think she's coming over to us."

"That must be a relief for her husband."

Summoning up a cold smile, Mrs. Ackroyd walked toward them. She was wearing a frock of black taffeta that set off the pallor of her face and gave her an almost funereal air. When she stopped beside them, she tapped her thigh repeatedly with her fan.

"Good night, ladies," she said.

"Must you leave?" asked Constance. "Can't we persuade you to join us for one last drink?"

"No, thank you. My digestion is not what it should be this evening."

"Did your husband find his ear trumpet?" said Tabitha.

"Not yet."

"Where did he lose it, Mrs. Ackroyd?"

"He thinks that it may have been in here, or perhaps in the smoking room. Gerald's mind gets rather hazy after a few brandies."

"Somebody will find it, I'm sure."

"Yes," said Constance, "we hadn't realized how much he depends on it. That's why we've been feeling so guilty about what happened this morning."

"Guilty?" said Mrs. Ackroyd.

"For having an unfair advantage over you. I've talked it over with Tabby, and she agrees with me. In the circumstances," she offered, "we feel that we should reimburse you."

"I wouldn't hear of it, Mrs. Simcoe."

"But you lost because your husband was distracted."

"We lost because we played badly," the other woman said sharply. "We have no quibble about that. Money lost at the card table is money better forgotten. We wouldn't take a penny of it back."

"You could always try to win it back," suggested Constance. "We'll be sailing to England from Aden together."

"I think that we need a rest from bridge, Mrs. Simcoe."

"We'll play with your cards, if you prefer—and in your cabin."

"No," said Mrs. Ackroyd. "Thank you for the invitation, but my husband and I will be far too busy with other commitments to indulge you. Once again, good night."

"Good night," said the others in unison.

Beating her thigh with the fan, Mrs. Ackroyd moved quickly away.

"I told you that she'd refuse the money," said Constance. "But it was a good idea of yours to offer it to her, Tabby. It helped to rub salt into the wound."

Warming to his role as an auxiliary detective, Paulo Morelli waited, concealed in a recess, until Madame Roussel finally came out of the door. He watched her blow a kiss to the occupant of the cabin, then set off down the corridor. Keeping well back, he followed her all the way to her own cabin. Morelli then went off in search of the detectives, hoping that his discovery would improve his chances of a return to first class. He found Dillman on his way to the purser's office, and gave his report.

"The second officer?" said the American.

"I see his name on the cabin door," explained Morelli. "That is why the lady go to and fro across the sea. Madame Roussel is in love."

"She must be, Paulo."

"Is wrong, mind you. The crew should not get involved with any of the passengers. Is the rule for me—and for the second officer."

"That's probably why he arranged to meet her in another cabin—the one that you saw her go into earlier. It would have been dangerous for Madame Roussel to go to him all the time."

"Why did he not visit *her*? That's what I would have done."

"You're a steward," said Dillman. "You have license to enter a passenger's cabin. The second officer does not and his uniform would make him very conspicuous."

Morelli laughed. "But when he is with the lady, he will not wear the uniform." He beamed at the detective. "Did I do well?"

"Extremely well, Paulo."

"You will speak to the chief steward for me?"

"That's a job for Mr. Cannadine, but I'll put in a good word for you with the purser. So will Miss Masefield."

"*Grazie.*"

"We thought we'd finished with you," said Dillman, "but you stuck to your task, and solved another mystery for us."

"Next time you sail on the *Salsette,* please use me again."

"We will, Paulo."

"Because I go into cabins, I see things that most people do not see. I know what people have in their wardrobes. I know how they behave when they are not in the public. On every voyage, I find strange things."

"Such as?"

"Well," said Morelli, tapping the side of his nose, "take the two ladies who get me put in second class."

"Mrs. Simcoe and her daughter?"

"They are not what they seem, Mr. Dillman. That is why they get rid me, I think—because I see too much. I begin to wonder."

"What do you mean?"

"Well," he said. "Mrs. Simcoe, she is supposed to be unwell, so she has to be pushed around in the chair with wheels. On the first day I meet her, I find her lying on the floor of her cabin."

"Go on."

"She want to convince me that she is a weak old lady. Then I look in the wardrobe and what do I see in there? Mrs. Simcoe is traveling with ten pairs of shoes. Why does she need so many when she is not able to walk?"

Dillman was interested. "Are you certain of this, Paulo?"

"Why should I tell the lie?"

"How do you know that the shoes were not her daughter's?"

"The *signorina* has almost as many pairs herself. And that is not all," he added, putting a hand to the side of his mouth as if about to impart a secret. "She has the beautiful dress that she cannot wear."

"Why not?"

"It is covered with blood, and will have to be cleaned first."

"*Blood?*"

"I see it with my own eyes. Now," Morelli said darkly, "how did it get there? That is what I ask myself. Why all those shoes, and why all that blood?"

They were questions with which Dillman was still grappling.

Having first checked that Constance and Tabitha Simcoe were still in the first-class lounge, Genevieve went swiftly to their cabin and let herself in with a master key borrowed from the purser. There was a faint smell of lavender in the air. She began first with the cupboard, opening each of its drawers in turn to inspect the contents. Evidently, the Simcoes had money to spend on themselves. Everything she found—costume jewelry, undergarments, even the souvenirs—was quite expensive.

Several packs of cards were stacked in the bottom drawer, along with a small account book that showed how much they had earned from their games of bridge. Genevieve was amazed to see the amount of winnings they had accumulated on their voyage to India. All the names of the losers were carefully listed. Some had lost up to a hundred pounds. The Ackroyds, she saw, had parted with over fifty pounds in that cabin. With their success at the card table, the Simcoes could have funded their trip many times over.

There was also a cream-colored purse in the bottom drawer, and Genevieve recalled having seen it in Constance's possession on the night when the latter wore a dress of the same hue. Opening the purse, she took out a comb, a small mirror, a few coins and—the object that really interested her—a photograph of Constance with an elderly man, who, from the way they had posed, looked as if he might have been her husband. What startled Genevieve was that the man was sitting in the Bath chair while Constance, standing beside it, seemed in good health.

Genevieve put everything carefully away. Covered with shame when she realized that she had wrongly accused a man of theft for the second time, she was now reaping the benefit of that mistake. Guljar Singh's comment about Constance had been a revelation. The woman was a fraud. Why did she use the Bath chair when it appeared she could walk perfectly well? And why were she and her daughter so punctilious about listing their winnings from various passengers?

Turning her attention to the wardrobe, Genevieve first noted the number of pairs of shoes that each woman had. They were of the highest quality. Constance Simcoe's mask had been torn away. Genevieve went through the clothing, moving the hangers one by one so that she could give each dress a cursory glance. Some of them she had seen before, worn by either of the two women, but there were several that were new to her.

Once again, expense was the watchword. Every frock there was extremely costly, so much so that Tabitha was not prepared to throw one away even though it was badly sullied. At first, Genevieve could not make out what the dark stains were, until she recalled that the dress in her hands was the one that Tabitha had been wearing on the day that she met and befriended Dudley Nevin. Genevieve shuddered when she realized that the marks over the front and arms were dried blood. Wanting to throw the dress aside immediately, she somehow could not let go of it.

She was still holding it when Tabitha let herself into the cabin.

"Genevieve!" she exclaimed. "What are *you* doing here?"

"More to the point," said Genevieve, holding up the dress, "what is *this* doing in here? It's covered in blood."

"That's sauce. I spilled it over myself by mistake days ago."

"Why—was there a sauce bottle in Mr. Nevin's cabin?"

"What on earth are you talking about?"

"Don't try to bluff your way out of this, Tabby," warned Genevieve. "I've seen far too much—all those packs of cards, all those shoes of your mother's. The charade is over."

"Who *are* you?" challenged the other.

"I work for P and O as a detective. You know my partner, Mr. Dillman, I believe. It's was no accident that you met him as he was coming out of Mr. Nevin's cabin, was it?" she went on. "Ever since the murder, you must have been keeping an eye on it." She pointed to the bottom drawer. "When you weren't cheating passengers at cards, that is."

Genevieve was too clever. Realizing that she had been caught,

Tabitha sought ways to limit the damage. Genevieve's face was hard and her manner determined, but she was still a woman and Tabitha knew that she had a softer side to her. She tried an appeal for sympathy. Taking the bloodstained dress from Genevieve, she fingered it ruefully.

"It was an accident," she said. "A terrible accident."

"So you admit that you killed Mr. Nevin?"

"I had no choice, Genevieve. As you know, I met him over breakfast that day, and he seemed amenable to a game of bridge. Mrs. Ackroyd agreed to be his partner, but he was hopelessly distracted and played without any conviction."

"How did you come to be in his cabin?"

"He left his cigarette case behind," said Tabitha, "so I went to return it to him. I suppose that it was naive of me to go into his cabin, but he said that he had a souvenir he wanted to show me. It was a *kukri*, a curved knife with a blade that widened towards the end."

"The murder weapon."

"It was self-defense, Genevieve. I swear it."

"Then why didn't you report it at once?"

"I was too confused. Heavens!" she said. "I only went there to return his cigarette case, and Mr. Nevin suddenly jumped on me. Don't you understand—he tried to rape me. I just grabbed the knife and lashed out wildly. I didn't *mean* to kill him. I just wanted to get away. When I saw what I'd done, I was absolutely horrified. I threw the knife away and ran straight back here."

"Didn't you do something else before you left?" asked Genevieve.

"No—I was in a complete panic."

"So you didn't take any money from his billfold?"

"Of course not."

"His watch was also missing," remembered Genevieve. "If you're innocent of any theft, I'm sure you won't mind us searching for the watch." Tabitha spread an arm to show that she could look anywhere in the cabin. "That means it's not here or you wouldn't be so confident. In that case," Genevieve decided, working it out as she talked, "there's only one place it can be, isn't there?"

"And where's that?"

"Concealed in your mother's Bath chair. Yes, I daresay that we may find Mr. Ackroyd's ear trumpet and all your other trophies in there, as well. No wonder it felt so heavy when I pushed it."

Tabitha's manner changed. She grabbed Genevieve's arm.

"Nobody needs to know about this," she insisted.

"Yes, they do."

"Mr. Nevin was a silly man. Who cares if he's dead?"

"I do, Tabby."

"How much do they pay you to do your job?"

"Don't try to offer me a bribe."

"It's a friendly gift," said the other with a persuasive smile. "After all, we like each other. We get on so well. Think of it, Genevieve," she purred. "I'll give you more than you can earn in a year if you forget that you've seen this dress."

"No, Tabby."

"Two years—three, if you like. We can afford it."

"I'm not for sale," said Genevieve with disgust.

Tabitha gave in. She shrugged her shoulders and walked toward the wardrobe, as if about to hang up the dress again. Instead, however, she suddenly wheeled round and flung it in the other woman's face. By the time that Genevieve had disentangled herself, she felt a sharp blow at the base of her skull and sank to her knees. Holding her mother's walking stick, Tabitha stood over her. Dazed and in pain, Genevieve put both hands to her head, furious with herself for being caught off guard.

There was a tap on the door. Tabitha grabbed her by the hair.

"Say one word," she whispered, "and I'll knock your brains out."

It was no idle threat. Tabitha had nothing to lose. Having committed one murder, she would have no compunction about killing someone else if it helped to save her.

The second tap on the door was accompanied by a voice.

"I know that you're in there, Miss Simcoe," said Dillman. "I've just spoken to your mother. She sent you to fetch some cards so that you could play bridge in the lounge." The door was banged. "Miss Simcoe!"

Genevieve felt that she had to do something. Her head was still pounding but at least she had gathered her wits. As Tabitha stood over her with the walking stick, Genevieve launched herself upward as hard as she could and struck the other woman in the stomach. Tabitha let out a cry of anger. Hauling herself to her feet, Genevieve managed to dodge a blow from the stick and grab Tabitha's wrist. It was only a temporary solution. Genevieve was in a weakened state. Enraged by the resistance, Tabitha was by far the stronger of the two.

Flinging Genevieve to the floor again, she was about to move in for the kill when the door burst open and Dillman came charging in. He took in the situation instantly. Tabitha tried to strike at him, but he caught the stick in midair and twisted it out of her hand by sheer force. She backed away from him.

Genevieve was not finished. Wanting to make her contribution to the arrest, she thrust out a foot and tripped Tabitha up. Dillman overpowered the woman at once. He had brought reinforcements with him. On his instructions, two members of the crew hauled Tabitha unceremoniously out of the cabin.

Dillman bent over Genevieve, cradling her in his arms.

"Why didn't you wait for me?" he asked.

"I thought that I could do it on my own, George."

"And now?"

"I should have remembered what Mr. Rollins told us."

"And what was that?"

"That women can be every bit as ruthless as men."

Max Cannadine could not stop thanking them. At a time when he was beginning to wonder if the crimes would ever be solved, George Dillman and Genevieve Masefield had found the thief and apprehended the killer. They had even exposed Constance Simcoe as the confidence trickster and cardsharp that she was. With the mother and daughter now behind bars, the *Salsette* felt a much cleaner and safer vessel.

"The captain sends his compliments," said the purser.

"What about the second officer?" asked Dillman with amusement.

"I'll need to have a quiet word with him. We'd all like to have the arrangement with Madame Roussel that he has, but it's not permitted. I'll remind him of that and point out that he still has a wife back in England." He pulled a face. "I do so hate to be a figure of moral authority, but someone has to draw the line."

"What about Madame Roussel?" said Genevieve.

"I don't think she'll lack company for long somehow."

"At least you won't have her traveling to and fro with you."

"Love on the Arabian Sea—a tempting prospect, isn't it?"

"Not when you have work to do, Mr. Cannadine."

"No, Miss Masefield," he said. "I have to agree. By the way, how's that head of yours now?"

"Just about staying on my shoulders."

"You must have taken a fearful crack."

"Oh, I did," agreed Genevieve, feeling the bump at the base of her skull. "Fortunately, it didn't break the skin. I'll just have to endure having this egg on the back of my head."

"Tabitha Simcoe was a powerful woman," said Dillman.

"Yes, George. If I pushed that Bath chair around as much as she did, I'd have muscles like that, as well. It's really heavy."

"Only because it was packed with all those things they'd won, stolen, or tricked out of people. Dudley Nevin's watch was one of three in the collection. When I opened up the box underneath that chair, it was like looking into Aladdin's cave."

"Everything but a magic lamp," said the purser.

"It was a profitable ruse," Dillman pointed it. "Mrs. Simcoe's husband was the real invalid, and she used to be jealous at the amount of sympathy and attention he used to get. So she decided to trade on a fake disability herself. It worked well. Who would suspect an invalid of being ready to fleece you at cards?"

"Yet the Ackroyds beat them on one occasion," observed Genevieve.

"That's why they had to be reeled in for another game. On that occasion, of course," he said, "Mr. Ackroyd was handicapped because they'd stolen his ear trumpet. That was under the Bath chair, as well."

"Why did she do it?" wondered the purser.

"Mrs. Simcoe?"

"No, Mr. Dillman—the daughter. I mean, why did she go to Nevin's cabin in the first place?"

"Well, it wasn't to return a cigarette case," said Dillman, "I can tell you that. Apart from the fact that we never found it in their treasure trove, I know for a fact that Dudley Nevin didn't smoke. That's why the major and I had a brandy with him in the lounge on the first night, not in the smoking room."

"Tabby was after his money," explained Genevieve. "She admitted as much when the master-at-arms locked her up. Mr. Nevin was carrying a substantial amount, as she saw when he opened his billfold during the game of bridge."

Cannadine was puzzled. "She went to his cabin to steal it?"

"There are other ways a woman can charm money out of a man."

"Other than by marriage, you mean?" said the purser, smiling.

"After realizing that Sylvester Greenwood was onboard, Mr. Nevin was frightened and depressed. Tabby could see how vulnerable he was. She went there to offer a show of sympathy, and perhaps something more." Genevieve sighed. "She's certainly not the plaster saint that she pretended to be. George discovered that."

"Yes," said Dillman. "She gave me the sort of knowing look that I wouldn't get in a convent. Tabitha Simcoe is a woman of the world in every sense. I fancy that Dudley Nevin wouldn't have been the first man to pay for the pleasure of her company."

"But things got out of hand," continued Genevieve. "That much of her story, I do believe. I think that she led him on too far. Nevin started to molest her and she resisted. The *kukri* was on the table with various other presents he was taking to his cousin in Aden."

"In other words," added Dillman, "it wasn't premeditated. That, at least, will count in her favor. She'll face a charge of manslaughter. Of course, she'll still have to explain why she stole his money and his watch, and failed to report the incident."

"It's so unsettling, isn't it?" mused Cannadine.

"What is?"

"All these crimes have been committed by females. You're supposed to be the fairer sex, Miss Masefield. What's happening to you?"

"Don't condemn the many for the faults of the few," she said.

"Well, it does make me worry."

"The irony is," said Dillman, "that the one woman whom we did suspect of a crime turned out to be innocent."

"Innocence is not a word I'd associate with Madame Roussel."

"You'll have to take that up with the second officer. Well," he added, rising from his chair, "I think that we're finished for the night."

"Yes, time for me to turn in, as well—now that I've had the satisfaction of returning the three purses to their owners, and locking the jewelry away in my safe. What a day!"

"It has been rather eventful, hasn't it?" agreed Genevieve.

"Yes, Miss Masefield. We started off with a daunting crime sheet, yet you've wiped it clean." He shook hands with each of them in turn. "My heartiest congratulations—and thanks."

"While you're in a thankful mood," said Dillman, remembering his promise to Morelli, "may I draw your attention to the work that a certain Italian in second class did for us?"

"I'll speak to the chief steward tomorrow," said Cannadine. "After what you've told me, Paulo belongs in first class."

"Thank you. He was only demoted because he did what nobody else had done. He dared to look at Tabitha Simcoe as a flesh and blood woman, while she was presenting a very different face to the rest of us."

"She took me in completely," admitted Genevieve.

Dillman grinned. "I think it's fair to say that you did the same to her," he remarked. "What must she have thought when she found you searching her cabin?"

"I don't think she mistook me for a new stewardess."

"It must have been a terrible shock for her."

"It was a terrible shock for *me*, George," she said. "I thought she was safely out of the way in the lounge. When she came in through that door, my heart missed a beat."

"You recovered very well," said Cannadine. "It's been a pleasure to watch you both at work. I do hope our paths cross again sometime."

"So do we."

"But next time," suggested Dillman, "we'd be grateful if you could persuade your female passengers to behave themselves a little better."

In the course of her voyage, the *Salsette* had passed a number of other ships, but when she reached the Gulf of Aden she joined a procession of vessels that were heading for the port. The sight of land brought most of the passengers up on deck. Lois Greenwood was one of them. She was chatting to Guljar Singh when George Dillman strolled over to them.

"Whatever did you say to Daddy last night?" she asked.

"Very little," replied Dillman.

"You must have said something because he's changed his opinion of you completely. He told me that you were a good man, and that he was wrong to forbid me to talk to you."

"That's nice to hear."

"So I struck while the iron was hot."

"In what way, Miss Greenwood?"

"It's not often that Daddy is in such a pleasant mood," she said, "so I decided to speak my mind for once. I told him that it was unfair of him to confiscate my roller skates and to treat me like a child, when I'm old enough to have a child myself." She giggled. "That really made him listen. He thought for a moment that I was going to tell him that he was about to be a grandfather."

"I can see why he'd be upset," observed Guljar Singh.

"All that I wanted was my rights," said Lois, "and I spelled them out. Daddy is not the only person in the family who can make speeches, you know. The amazing thing is that it *worked.* He was so surprised that I'd answered him back for once that he admitted he'd been too harsh on me and promised to give me more leeway in the future." She giggled again. "I felt so proud of myself for standing up to him."

"There you are," said Singh, chuckling quietly. "I told you that you would do something on this ship that would make you proud."

"And I did—thanks to Mr. Dillman."

"I only chatted to your father for a while," said Dillman.

"You softened him up for me. He's almost human this morning."

On impulse, she reached up to put her hands around Dillman's neck before kissing him on the cheek. Surprised at her own boldness, she blushed slightly, gave a nervous laugh, and skipped off along the deck. Guljar Singh was amused.

"You are very popular this morning, Mr. Dillman."

"Not with all the passengers," he said, thinking of the two women who were locked up in the cells. "And I don't think that I'm Sukinder's favorite person since I put her under arrest."

"What will happen to Suki?"

"That's for the magistrate to decide, Mr. Singh. In fairness to him, Major Kinnersley is taking full responsibility. As soon as the mail is unloaded in Aden, he's sailing back to Bombay on the *Salsette* with her, so that his daughter can face justice in her own country. Given her age," he said, "I suspect that she'll be treated very leniently."

"Suki is not a criminal. She was forced to do what she did."

"I think that the major appreciates that."

"Does he accept that she belongs with her family in India?"

"Yes, Mr. Singh."

"That is good."

He looked over Dillman's shoulder and smiled serenely when he saw Genevieve Masefield approaching them. They exchanged greetings. Genevieve looked contrite.

"You will be glad to see the back of me, Mr. Singh."

"Not at all," he said. "You only did what you thought was right."

"I misjudged you cruelly," she confessed, "and I'm terribly sorry for that. I feel so guilty about it. Please forgive me."

"You hear that, Mr. Dillman?" asked Singh, beaming. "This is the third apology I have had from this beautiful lady detective. Do you remember what I said to you the other day?"

"Oh, yes," recalled the other. "I remember it very well. You told me that the English never apologize."

"However did you make your partner do it *three* times in a row?"

"That's easy," said Dillman, winking at Genevieve. "I married her."

POSTSCRIPT

When war broke out in September 1914, the *Salsette* continued her normal routine between Bombay and Aden. In November 1915, she made her first sailing from London to Bombay, taking her place on the Indian or Australian mail routes. In July 1917, sailing from London to Sydney via Bombay, and carrying onboard a large amount of money to pay the British garrison in Egypt, she was hit by a German torpedo some fifteen miles southwest of Portland Bill. Fifty minutes later, she sank. Fifteen members of the crew lost their lives.